"The locals call it a flamingo moon,"

Kerry explained. "After the color of the bird. The moon turns pink sometimes when the weather's right. Seminoles believe a flamingo moon means a successful night of romance."

"I'd enjoy teaching you about romance, Kerry," Jace said. "Who stole the romance from your heart? Your ex-husband?"

"The money you pay me as your guide doesn't buy you my life story."

Jace stared down at her, and desire, quick and hot, rippled through him. He sensed he was perilously close to slipping the boundaries of his self-control. He wanted to take Kerry into his arms and taste her warm, sweet lips under that flamingo moon.

"As a paying customer, Kerry, I believe I'm entitled to certain privileges."

"Such as?" she asked softly.

Jace grinned—wickedly.

Dear Reader,

When two people fall in love, the world is suddenly new and exciting, and it's that same excitement we bring to you in Silhouette Intimate Moments. These are stories with scope and grandeur. The characters lead lives we all dream of, and everything they do reflects the wonder of being in love.

Longer and more sensuous than most romances, Silhouette Intimate Moments novels take you away from everyday life and let you share the magic of love. Adventure, glamour, drama, even suspense— these are the passwords that let you into a world where love has a power beyond the ordinary, where the best authors in the field today create stories of love and commitment that will stay with you always.

In coming months, look for novels by your favorite authors: Kathleen Eagle, Marilyn Pappano, Emilie Richards, Judith Duncan and Justine Davis, to name only a few. And whenever—and wherever—you buy books, look for all the Silhouette Intimate Moments, love stories with that extra something, books written especially for you by today's top authors.

Leslie J. Wainger
Senior Editor and Editorial Coordinator

ANN EVANS

Flamingo Moon

SILHOUETTE·INTIMATE·MOMENTS®

Published by Silhouette Books New York

America's Publisher of Contemporary Romance

SILHOUETTE BOOKS
300 East 42nd St., New York, N.Y. 10017

FLAMINGO MOON

ISBN: 0-373-07415-8

First Silhouette Books printing January 1992

Printed in the U.S.A.

ANN EVANS,

a lifelong procrastinator, finally sent a manuscript to an editor after four years of encouragement from friends and family. A year later, *Flamingo Moon* won a coveted Golden Heart Award from the Romance Writers of America. A native Floridian who now juggles a writing career with her work as an investment banker, Ann hopes her readers will discover the magic and mystery of the Florida Everglades through her work.

For my dear friends and mother hens:
Lyn, Terri, Gwen, Jacki and Lori—
my experts on Seminole villages.

Chapter 1

At his side the blood flowed freely again, charting a fiery path down his hip. He'd thought he could make it across the clinic waiting room without doing anything embarrassingly stupid and weak, but his body had other ideas. The pain had become a raw, insatiable hunger, a treacherous reminder of just how foolish he'd been to underestimate his prey.

Jace blinked hard, trying to still the clawing panic within. *Doc Sanders will be here. Not much farther now.*

The reception room telescoped away, a wavering gauntlet of vinyl furniture, filing cabinets and one ancient-looking wheelchair. The young woman behind the cheap metal desk hurried to reach him, her features drawn in concern. He was dimly aware that she was tall and darkly exotic, and his hand stretched in her direction, a silent communication of need. She responded by offering her own, but even as their fingertips touched, he knew she couldn't reach him in time.

Spots danced before his eyes and the roaring in his ears took on the volume of a runaway train. "Damn, I feel stupid,'' he muttered. His voice was a harsh whisper that quickly disappeared down a long, wintery tunnel of pain. He released a wobbly sigh, and his lips thinned in disgust. *The Duke would never have reacted this way.*

As the last remnants of self-control gave way, his knees sagged, and terrazzo, cold and unyielding, came up to meet him.

It took Kerry Culhane three attempts to get the man off the floor and onto the clinic's stretcher. The guy was limp, yet seemed to be made of solid granite. None of the body lifts she'd been taught during three years of training seemed to work. Kerry hefted her patient, her legs staggering under his weight. His arms dangled uselessly at his side and his head lolled to crack hard against her cheek. She felt the heat emanating from his body, and her nose crinkled under an odd mixture of scents—flannel and swamp humus, shampoo, male sweat, the iron unpleasantness of blood.

By the time she'd gotten his body flopped across the gurney, Kerry found herself panting for breath while her heartbeat galloped. She took a moment to collect her thoughts, debating what her next course of action should be.

Doc wouldn't be back from the seminar in Miami until late tonight. Until then she was the only experienced medical help in Flamingo Junction. But with hunting season over and the tourists yet to come, it had been weeks since she'd treated anything more serious than a bad sunburn. The few days a week she helped out in the clinic weren't exactly taxing her ability as a nurse practitioner.

She cast a worried glance at her new arrival when a breathless moan slipped from him. His arm fell away from his side, revealing an ugly smear of blood, fresh and bright against the fabric of his clothes, and way too much to Kerry's way of thinking. She stared at it in frozen concentration, fixing her thoughts on practical matters. *Stop the*

*bleeding first. Then clean the wound. So, you're a little
rusty. You're still qualified. You know what to do.*

Wheeling the stretcher into Doc Sanders's tiny examining room, Kerry decided to forego the pulse-temperature-
blood pressure routine. She reached for a sterile pressure
bandage, frowning down at her hand when she saw that it
trembled. The reaction worried her. Her nerves were normally steady as a rock and she didn't rattle easily.

She pulled at the waistband of the man's jeans, which
were tight and confining and offered only a small peek at the
damage. Her face sagged with relief. What she saw didn't
look too bad. Not pretty, but not fatal, either. A bullet had
sliced a ragged piece high out of her patient's side, an angry red slash that still seeped blood. The slug had been
obliging enough to keep on going, exiting out the fleshy
curve beneath the man's ribs.

Unfortunately, she couldn't tend the wound with his pants
in the way. It would require superhuman strength on her
part to move him, and probably result in further loss of
blood.

"Sorry, fella. The pants will have to go." Quickly she began unbuckling his belt to slide it out through the loops,
stealing a glance at her patient's face for the first time.

Loss of blood had reduced his skin tone to an unhealthy
pallor, but beneath a week-old growth of beard his features
were strong and well-defined. She didn't recognize him as
one of Flamingo Junction's locals. A stranger, in trouble,
in a part of South Florida that wasn't particularly kind to
newcomers.

The man groaned as she wedged a pressure bandage over
the wound. With quick, decisive movements, Kerry lifted
scissors from Doc's instrument tray. They made short work
of her patient's grubby jeans and bloodstained shirt.

His clothing might be plain and insignificant, but the
body beneath was anything but that. Tall and well propor-

tioned, this was a man who took good care of himself. No wonder he'd been so heavy. His arms and legs were corded by powerful muscles that could only have been cultivated by a strict regimen of diet and exercise. Broad, straight shoulders supported a deep, tantalizingly masculine chest pelted with fine dark satin in the same shade as his beard, and in startling contrast to hair the color of newly minted gold.

The man exuded virility, and a cynical smile twisted Kerry's lips. She could imagine this fellow working out vigorously in a gym back home, pumping iron to impress wide-eyed women who would ooh and aah over such a profusion of well-planned muscles. She wondered what they'd think to see him now, so weak and vulnerable.

She had him down to his briefs in no time, and Kerry's mouth curved at the sight before her. Nothing conservative about his underwear. Bright red, tight and expensive. Probably designer stuff, she thought derisively, and her smile broadened. When this guy got back on his feet he wasn't going to appreciate her having made paper dolls out of the briefs. The problem was, they had to come off, and modesty couldn't be a consideration. Taking a deep breath, Kerry slid the tips of her scissors under the elastic band.

"Honey, whatever you do," a soft male voice intruded, stilling her hand, "please be careful with those things."

Kerry's head swung around. Her patient was awake, his chin tucked into his chest to watch her movements. His lips stretched into a weak smile, and as their gazes connected, Kerry realized the man had beautiful eyes, the soft hazel of autumn leaves.

"I can't save your underwear," she replied firmly.

The look he gave her was curiously intimate. "I wasn't talking about my underwear."

Hectic color stained Kerry's cheeks. A tendril of warmth curled around her belly, too, and the combined reaction to this man's words brought instant resistance. She never allowed men, especially outsiders, to affect her one way or the other. That this man had so easily breached her defenses grated on her nerves.

She flashed him a deliberately wild-eyed look. "Don't get nervous. I can skin a squirrel without nicking the meat."

She could tell he wasn't expecting that. He blinked in surprise, paled a little more and muttered, "Lord, help me."

Kerry turned her head to hide a grin. *Take that, Romeo.*

With more flourish than was needed, she divested the man of his briefs. She was amused to note her patient seemed to be holding his breath, and though Kerry felt his eyes on her, he was silent. Perhaps he'd decided it was a mistake to antagonize a woman with a pair of sharp scissors poised over his groin. Smart fellow.

Jace Warfield couldn't take his eyes off the woman's face. Who would have guessed a backwater, hole-in-the-wall town like Flamingo Junction would have someone so lovely in its midst? Her profile was delicately carved, yet strong. High, exotic cheekbones gave her an arresting beauty. Her hair, a satiny midnight color, was yanked into a no-nonsense braid falling nearly to her waist. Jace liked the way she carried herself—confident and proud, with the slim strength of a dancer and the unconscious grace of someone completely comfortable within her own skin.

Flamingo Junction's proximity to the reservation and his own lifelong fascination with Indian cultures told him Seminole blood flowed through this woman's veins. Close, too. Not diluted by years of mixed marriages. Yet she seemed unaware of her own beauty and had chosen to downplay her looks. Everything about her was understated, and Jace wondered why she tried so hard to be something she was not—unattractive. Used to the sleek sophistication of some of the women in Denver, he was intrigued.

"Where's Dr. Sanders?"

She tossed him a surprised look. He knew Doc by name? "On his way back from Miami."

"Who are you?"

"I'm minding the place until he gets here."

"Great," Jace mumbled. "I'm being treated by a Girl Scout trying to get one more merit badge."

"Relax. I'm a nurse practitioner."

"I don't want a practicing anything," he said, an odd note of desperate insistence in his voice. "I need the doctor."

She turned her head and favored him with an annihilating glance. Jace found himself breathless. Thick, sooty lashes sheltered eyes the color of a robin's egg. The contrast between light eyes and dark hair was particularly vivid, and though her brow had gathered like an angry storm, Jace's blood warmed.

"I don't think you can afford to be too choosy right now," she commented in an even tone.

She had a point there. His side felt as though ground glass had been thrust into it, and the room was beginning to spin. He sent her a strained little smile of acknowledgment and apology.

Kerry covered her patient with a clean sheet, leaving exposed a small area of flesh around the wound. With brisk efficiency, she began cleaning the blood away. "This may hurt."

Jace inhaled sharply as fire spread to encompass more flesh. "No kidding," he ground out through clenched teeth.

"Try to lie still and relax. Trust me, I know what I'm doing."

"Is it bad?"

"You'll live. And the bullet's not in, so I won't have to root around for it."

He couldn't help a sigh of relief. No matter how capable and confident this woman seemed, he wasn't anxious to have her poke around his innards for stray bullets.

He wished Sanders were here. He knew he could trust the old man. But this woman was an unknown entity. "Have you seen gunshot wounds before?"

She nodded. "Every hunting season we get a few nitwits who don't know the business end of a gun."

The quiet mockery of her words fanned his sense of helplessness. "I'm not a nitwit," he said. The words came on the sharp edge of anger.

The dark, silky wing of one eyebrow shot up as she treated him to a superior smile. "Didn't say you were." She tossed blood-stained gauze into a steel basin. "Do you know who took a shot at you?"

Jace hesitated, realizing too late his answer would make her previous assessment of him seem embarrassingly accurate. Briefly he considered telling this woman the truth, but he quickly rejected the idea as far too dangerous. He couldn't afford to trust anyone. Bad enough Sanders knew. "I shot myself," he said. Even to his own ears the lie stumbled lamely from his tongue.

The woman's head snapped around. Her features turned glacial, the high planes of her cheek bones tightening subtly. The eyes that a moment ago had been as soft and clear as a summer sky darkened. There was an odd flicker in their jeweled depths, and with cold, hollow dread Jace waited for her anger to erupt. *She's not buying it. Not one word. She's going to accuse me of lying, and then she's going to call the police.* Fear teased along his spine.

"You were a little low for suicide," she said in a voice that had taken on a peculiar, flat emphasis.

"It was an accident. I was cleaning the gun and it went off." Amazing, Jace thought. Lies were beginning to fall so freely from his lips.

"I see." Her slim fingers began to pack the wound with sterile gauze, her movements short and jerky.

Jace watched her as she worked, noting her tightly clenched jaw.

"What kind of gun do you own?" she asked.

There was a note in her voice Jace distrusted, but he'd come too far to turn back now. "A thirty-ought-six." *Brilliant, Jace. This woman's probably seen enough bullet wounds to know the difference between a deer rifle and a handgun.* And he'd been ninety-five percent certain Burkhardt's men had carried .45s.

He sensed her stiffening. Her gaze raked him with exacting slowness. It occurred to Jace that she looked almost disappointed in him, yet she said nothing further. With quiet, confident movements she continued to cleanse and bind the wound. Meekly, he accepted the pain pill she offered, swallowing it down with a small cup of water she held to his lips.

She didn't give him another glance, but his own gaze drifted over her again and again. He decided he liked the way her chin tilted as she turned her head, the innocent, sultry curve of her mouth. His eyes were mesmerized by the slow, sliding movement of her braided hair.

The knife in his side began to disintegrate, no longer slashing at his vitals, disarmed by modern medicine. Jace blinked a few times, finding it difficult to focus his eyes. His body felt disconnected. His beautiful savior seemed to be fading from sight like a desert mirage.

From somewhere deep inside himself Jace found his voice. "Don't...go...."

The sweet mouth that gave him such pleasure to look at lifted encouragingly. "I'm right here. We're almost finished," she said softly.

"What's... your name?" It seemed suddenly important to Jace to be able to put a name to someone who could so easily tangle his emotions.

"Kerry Culhane."

"Irish."

"My father was born and bred in County Cork."

Jace frowned. At least he thought he did. He was having a little trouble controlling body movements. And when had his words started to slur? "Then your mother... has to be... Seminole."

"One hundred percent."

He wet his lips. "Impressed by... my perception?"

She laughed. It was a nice laugh, but it had a curious echoing quality. "Not really. The reservation's ten minutes away. You'll see a lot of Seminole features on the folks in Flamingo Junction."

"Not... like yours...." he said meaningfully, and even in his drugged state Jace could see she was uncomfortable with that comment as color came up in her cheeks. Vaguely, he wondered if she was unused to compliments from men. "More than a... good guess. I'm very familiar with Indian cultures." He fixed her with a hard stare. "Do you have a Seminole name?"

She slanted him a glance to say that that was none of his business, but Jace was undaunted. "Tell me," he commanded with a smile designed to melt honey from the comb.

"Night Dove."

Jace's smile widened. "Fits you. Different... special." He reached out, somehow managing to capture the long braid that had fallen over her shoulder. In his hand the ebony rope seemed a living thing, curling around his fingers with a crisp life of its own. He used it to pull her closer. She seemed surprised and amused by his action, as though she hadn't expected him to have that much control. His tongue felt thick and useless, but Jace swallowed around it, his senses reeling in foggy delight. "Kiss me, Night Dove. If...I'm going to die...one last kiss from a beautiful woman."

There was a second of suspended time, an exquisite blend of torment and pleasure as Kerry Culhane sent him a quick, encompassing glance from under dark lashes. Her smile stretched. "You're not going to die."

"Kiss me...anyway...."

"I'd say the medicine I gave you is starting to kick in."

"Mmm...powerful magic. Ancient Indian herbs and potions?"

"Sorry, white eyes. Plain old painkiller. I can try to dredge up a Seminole chant if you like." Her hand plucked at his fingers holding her hair. "Let go and I'll give it a whirl."

He shook his head. "Never mind. Present's never as good...as good as the past, is it?" There was a certain sadness to his tone.

"Right now, let's worry about the future. Yours. You need to rest."

"Stay...with me...."

"I'll be right here."

Her hand caressed his, seductively gentle. He issued a soft growl of regret, realizing his mind was shutting down in spite of his wishes.

"Just relax," Kerry coaxed softly. "What's your name?"

"John...Wayne. You can call me...Duke."

"Try again, cowboy. I don't believe you."

He looked mortally wounded by her skepticism. "Because he's...dead?"

"No. Because John Wayne would never shoot himself."

"No...guess he wouldn't. Sorry...." The words slid out in a slow whisper, but a moment later Jace's eyes flew wide.

She was so beautiful. It really would be a shame if he did die and never had the chance to touch her. He wished she would come closer. Just a little. He realized suddenly he still held her captive by her hair, and with the last of his ebbing strength he pulled Kerry to him. Before she could react, his lips brushed hers briefly. Cool and pleasant and too quickly gone.

Her blue eyes were suddenly very watchful, as though she wasn't quite certain how to deal with him. "Why did you do that?"

"The Duke always...gets the girl. Such...good care, Kerry Night Dove. Thank you...and for not asking questions...can't...can't answer."

Jace was proud to be able to get the words out of his mouth. At least he thought he'd gotten them out. He really had to rest now. Do what she said. Forget the unexpected passion blurring his brain. Forget the mess he'd made of his plans.

He wobbled a smile at Kerry Night Dove Culhane. "My name's Jace...Warfield. Please. I need—" his eyelids shuttered down as he expelled a heavy sigh "—help." Unconsciously his grip on Kerry's hair loosened and he felt the length of its satiny thickness slide up and out of his palm. He made a last fretful attempt to recapture it, but it was gone.

Through a dark, enveloping fog he heard her voice, soft and comforting as a downy blanket on a winter night. "Rest, Duke. I'll be right here."

According to his wallet, Jace Warfield was thirty-one, a registered Republican, and had a season lift pass for a Denver area ski resort. Thankfully, there were no medic alert cards, something Kerry chastised herself for not looking for earlier. Except for the Colorado driver's license, there was little personal identification, not even a next-of-kin notification card.

There were, however, several pictures of people who bore a distinct likeness to her patient.

A mature, attractive couple who had to be his parents smiled up at her from one photograph. They glowed with vibrant good health, the man especially resembling Jace Warfield. The same unusual blond hair and tawny eyes. The woman was more handsome than pretty, her features strong, yet refined. His parents' love for one another was evident in the way they had positioned themselves for the camera. Close, as though they did a lot of touching.

One picture particularly caught Kerry's attention. Jace with another young man and woman in jeans and cowboy hats tipped back on their heads. Behind them, glorious snow-capped mountains formed an idyllic backdrop. The trio laughed into the camera, the girl between the two men, their arms linked behind their backs. They were teenagers, beaming with exuberance only the young enjoy, as though none of them had a single care in the world. The resemblance between all three was startling. Evidently the Duke had a brother and sister near his own age.

An only child, Kerry felt a pang of envy for Jace Warfield and his close, golden family out in Colorado. Her own mother had died in childbirth when Kerry was five, taking her weak newborn brother with her to the grave. Her father had never remarried, and for years it had been just the two of them.

It occurred to Kerry that there were no recent pictures of small children or any female who might be a wife. She concluded he didn't have one, then immediately wondered why the idea should please her so.

Her gaze traveled to the nearby bed where her patient now lay. Her mouth puckered in bemusement. *Who are you really, Jace? And why don't you want the police to know someone took a shot at you?*

The gunman picked up the rustle of sound amid the tall grass to his left and he swung his .45 quickly in that direction. A raccoon hopped out of the weeds, gave him an unperturbed glance, then disappeared into the shadowed undergrowth of the swamp. The man's heartbeat settled. "Jeez, I hate this place," he said, and meant it. He'd been in the Everglades less than two weeks, but already he missed the dark, familiar streets of Detroit. The dank alleyways and smoke-filled bars. The women. Hell, he even missed the smog.

Beside him, Dawson, a thin-lipped blonde with raw-boned features, laughed and scratched a mosquito bite along his jaw with the butt of his gun. "What's the matter, Collins? You afraid of a little coon?"

"I don't like swamps. I never have." As he spoke, Collins's left foot skidded into a soggy patch of humus. Mud slid into his shoe with cold, repugnant fingers of decay. The man swore, pulled his foot out of the muck with a slow, sucking pop, then scraped his shoe against a nearby cypress tree. "Why the boss would pick a place like this to deal..." he muttered in disgust.

"Take a look around you, man. Two hundred feet in any direction and the swamp will swallow you up."

"Yeah. That's what worries me." They'd been searching the area for the past three hours, following the trail of blood and trampled grasses of the marsh until they'd run out of land. Now a weedy lagoon stretched out before them. Dark and mysterious with low fingers of vines hanging from every tree, and the slow-moving water hiding unknown inhabitants, it didn't invite exploration. "So what do you think? Where is he?"

Dawson had wandered off the deer path to crouch in front of a churned up patch of ground at the water's edge. "Take a look at this," he said, flicking a finger across grass matted with blood. Lots of it.

"I knew I'd hit him good," Collins said with a grin.

"Sure you did," Dawson agreed, but his sarcastic tone denied the words. He was ninety-nine percent certain the man they were after had taken a slug from *his* gun.

"From the looks of all that blood, I'd say our nosy friend can't last much longer. He's as good as dead."

"We have to make sure."

"Uh-uh. I've had it."

"Burkhardt won't like it if—"

"You want to lead the way through that?" Collins asked, pointing out into the water. He scraped the last of the mud from his shoe, anxious to get back to camp where he could scrub the stench of the swamp from his skin.

"No."

"I say, if the bullet we put in him doesn't do the trick, the gators will. Next big hunt the state sponsors, what do you want to bet they'll open up some bull gator's stomach and find pieces of the guy? One more tourist who didn't pay attention to the warning signs." He shrugged. "Who cares? We'll be long gone."

Dawson frowned. "I don't know..."

For the first time in hours, Collins reholstered his gun. Impatience simmered to the surface. "You want to go back and tell the boss we couldn't find some jackass tourist who didn't know enough to mind his own business?"

"No."

"Then it's settled. We managed to hit him with a couple of slugs each, he fell in the water and we saw a big gator drag the body under." He snapped his fingers and his eyes dared Dawson to deny his words. "No more witness. The guy's dead. Got it?"

Dawson nodded reluctantly. Collins was probably right. The guy didn't stand a chance out here with one of their bullets in him and nothing but snakes, gators and who knew what else lurking in the tall grass.

He didn't like lying to Burkhardt, though. They'd better rehearse their story a couple of times before they showed up back at camp. If the boss ever found out they weren't playing square with him, they'd be better off fighting a gator.

Doc Sanders arrived back at the clinic around midnight, looking rumpled and travel-weary. He was a tall, thin man in his early sixties, who'd come to Flamingo Junction shortly before the Vietnam War. He'd established a two-bed clinic at the rear of his home to offer the area its only link with modern medicine. A dedicated physician, he had brought most of the town's population into the world. Ushered some of them out of it, too. He was a man who could be trusted, one of the few men Kerry liked and respected in The Junction; she was delighted to see him back.

A moment after he dropped his suitcase by the front door, he began examining his latest patient. Kerry stood on the other side of the bed, explaining the steps she had taken to treat Jace Warfield's injury. "I started him on antibiotics, but he's already spiking a temp," she said as she watched him lift the sterile dressing she'd placed over the wound.

"That's to be expected."

Gently he patted the adhesive tape back in place. He sagged back in the chair Kerry had pulled beside the bed, sitting there so long in quiet contemplation that she began to worry she'd missed something important in her treatment. "Did I forget something, Doc?"

"No, of course not," he reassured her quickly. "The wound looks good." Then, more slowly, he asked, "Did you notify the police?"

"No, not yet. It's late and I figured he wasn't going anywhere for a while. First thing in the morning I'll call Crant's office." She moved to the stainless-steel sink to fill an aluminum basin with water. "I was just getting a witch hazel bath ready when you got here. I know you must be beat.

Why don't I take the first shift cooling him down and you get some rest?''

He was suddenly beside her, taking the basin from her hands and setting it on the counter. "No, you've done more than enough. A splendid job, as usual. I'll handle everything from here on out, including the report. Now go home, Kerry, and get some rest yourself."

"But, Doc—"

Shocked by such an obvious attempt to get rid of her, her gaze flew to his. She could read nothing in his face. The pale, blue eyes stared back at her as though she were a stranger. That in itself was alarming.

He hustled her out the door, barely giving her time to grab up her car keys. In the cool late-night air, Kerry stood frowning at the front steps of the clinic. What was going on? What had she done?

For what remained of the night, those two questions turned themselves over and over again in her mind. By the time morning came, Kerry awoke from a fretful sleep determined to get some answers.

She drove back into town, rammed the clinic's key into the lock and entered the small ward like a ship under full sail. She crossed the room in determined strides, not surprised to find Doc slumped in the chair beside the sick bed. Jace Warfield was still unconscious.

"All right, Doc," she said, in soft, yet resolute tones. "What's going on?"

"What do you mean?"

Morning light streamed in from the windows of the outer office, soft and lovely, yet even in its pale diffusion Doc looked every one of his sixty-two years. All thought of interrogating the man fled Kerry's mind with the reminder of how tired he must be. "My God, you look horrible. When's the last time you ate?"

"Yesterday. At lunch, I think."

"Honestly, I'll be lucky if I don't end up with *two* sick men on my hands." She left him to search the clinic kitchen, which consisted of a hot plate, microwave and a small refrigerator. Doc considered food an annoying necessity, and she wasn't surprised when her search turned up only a box of crackers and half a carton of milk. Returning to the sickroom, she planted her hands on her hips. "Do you have any food in your house?"

He shook his head absently, totally absorbed in checking his patient's pupil response.

"How's he doing?"

"Fever's still up."

"I'm going over to the diner to get you breakfast. You need to eat something and then get some rest. I'll take over for the rest of the day."

"No."

"Doc, I've done this a dozen times before. This one's no different from the rest." She paused, favoring him with a sharp look as suspicion began to take hold in her brain. "Is he?"

"No," he said abruptly, evading her gaze. "No, of course not."

But he was, and right then and there Kerry knew it. Her glance bounced back and forth between Jace Warfield and Doc. Something wasn't right here. At first, she'd thought the doctor was just overtaxed. But the longer she watched the old man's movements, the more she noticed his agitation, the intensity in every look he tossed his patient's way. There was more at stake here than Doc's ability to heal another human being. She just didn't know what it was.

"Doc..."

As though he sensed Kerry's renewed interest, the doctor suddenly smiled at her. "You know, I believe you're right. Breakfast sounds wonderful. Do you suppose Maya's made her cinnamon buns yet this morning?"

She actually felt sorry for him. Doc Sanders was one of the few truly honest men in Flamingo Junction, and subterfuge didn't come easily for him. He pretended to search his pockets for his wallet so he could avoid meeting her eyes. Frowning, Kerry cast a glance at their patient. *Who are you, Jace Warfield, that you can rattle Doc this way?*

Kerry slipped across the street to the town's only restaurant, a small, but tidy establishment cleverly named The Flamingo Junction Diner.

Maya Nichols was behind the counter, aimlessly paging through the latest issue of a grocery tabloid. As Kerry entered, she looked up and smiled. "Hi, Kerr. What are you doing in town so early?"

"Lots of paperwork to catch up on at the clinic," Kerry explained, wondering why she felt the need to forego mentioning the fact they had a patient. Doc's evasiveness must be catching.

She ordered breakfast to go, chatting while Maya tossed bacon onto the sizzling grill.

"Doc's cupboard bare as usual?" Maya asked with an exasperated shake of her head.

"You know Doc. He'd never eat at all if his stomach didn't remind him."

"Not like some people we know," Maya said with a meaningful glance to the opposite corner of the diner where Bobby Michaels forked scrambled eggs into his mouth at an alarming rate. As always, his baseball cap was perched precariously at the back of his head, his pants had settled low on his hips and he made no effort to stifle a low belch of relief.

Kerry grimaced, wishing the man weren't so typical of the eligible bachelors in Flamingo Junction. "I see he hasn't given up on you," Kerry said softly.

"No, and I guess I shouldn't mind as long as he keeps eating three meals a day here." Maya grunted in disgust as she watched Bobby's teeth tear into a slice of toast and poke it into his mouth. Using the end of the greasy spatula to stress her point, she added, "He's some piece of work, isn't he?"

Kerry grinned. "Oh, I don't know. You could do worse."

"How?"

"In Flamingo Junction? Are you kidding? At least raising sugarcane is an honest enterprise."

Maya gave Kerry a skeptical look. "Who says Bobby's on the up-and-up? I'll bet half his crew came into the state illegally. You know the men in this town are never what they seem. They all have something else going on the side."

Unfortunately, that was only too true, and one of the biggest reasons Kerry seldom dated.

As though aware his gender was being secretly maligned, Bobby Michaels hollered across the room in a gruff voice, "Maya! How 'bout some service? Coffee's cold."

"I'm coming," Maya called back. Under her breath she added, "Ain't he a charmer?"

When her order was slipped into a paper bag and paid for, Kerry offered Maya a thumbs-up sign of encouragement and trooped across the dirt road to the clinic.

Rednecks, criminals and tourists. Those seemed to be the only kinds of men who ever came through Flamingo Junction. She wondered which one of those categories Jace Warfield fit into—and was bitterly afraid she already knew the answer.

Chapter 2

Curiosity became secondary as Jace Warfield's temperature climbed in spite of the antibiotics. Kerry and Doc concentrated their efforts on cooling the patient down as quickly as possible. Over and over again they sponged his fevered body with cold witch hazel until his limbs no longer twitched and the demons he fought seemed to recede.

Kerry knew there were demons because they tormented his sleep relentlessly. He called out to them, begging them to stop, begging them to listen, his voice cracked with anguish and despair. Sometimes his jumbled speech was soft and frustrated, at other times bright-edged with anger, a ringing, masculine command demanding obedience. Kerry listened, unable to piece together much of what he babbled.

Once her gaze met Doc's across the sickbed while Warfield tossed and turned to get away from the heat. Her eyes questioned him. *Who is he? A friend? Relative?*

Doc shook his head, spreading his hands over his eyes as though they pained him. He looked so exhausted, she didn't have the heart to pursue it. She trusted the old man's judgment. When, and if, he wanted to reveal his involvement with Jace Warfield he would. Regardless, she would help him make sure this man survived.

She *wanted* him to survive. Even with blood streaming unchecked down his side, he'd had a disarming warmth, a devilish wit she grudgingly admired and that irresistible smile that brought a quick, strong pull of attraction and made her heart give a queer jump against her ribs.

Face it. He fascinates you. You haven't met a man like him in a long, long time.

And look where that last one got you, she brutally reminded herself.

She sat beside Jace Warfield, hoping she could somehow summon up a healthy dose of dislike. Doc seemed to want to protect him, but this man could be a criminal. Lord knew, Flamingo Junction had harbored more than its share.

Perched on the edge of the Florida Everglades it was a perfect hideout. Sooner or later, every kind of criminal element came through the sleepy little town. Law enforcement was too far away, too understaffed, or simply too disinterested to make much of a difference. Flamingo Junction was a throwback to the rough-and-tumble days of the Old West. Out of touch with the rest of the world, closemouthed and suspicious of strangers. Residents were proud of their independent reputation, and did little to encourage progress. It was a tough town to live in, and an even tougher place to make a living.

Amazingly, Kerry had done just that after inheriting her father's business. She'd made a go of it in spite of the skeptics who insisted she was biting off more than she could chew.

Kerry sent a sharp scowl in Warfield's direction as the man moaned and mumbled in his sleep.

So why are you acting like such a dolt over this guy? A
man who thinks he's John Wayne, but doesn't know the
difference between a .45 and a deer rifle.

No hero. A liar, plain and simple. Maybe running from
the law, too.

A splash of dull, red color flushed his cheeks, evidence
that his fever still raged. She drew a cooling washcloth
across his brow, down the bearded planes of his face and
neck, across one rock-hard shoulder. Beneath her fingertips Kerry felt the contoured strength of muscle.

She smiled in spite of her best efforts not to. No matter
what this fellow was or wasn't, he sure had one hell of a
great body.

*Maya's right, Kerry girl. You've been in the swamp too
long.*

Around midmorning, Jace Warfield opened his eyes.
They were no longer bright with fever, merely tired and unfocused. He had been sweating profusely for the past half
hour and Kerry knew the worst was over. She was tempted
to wake Doc, but didn't. Dead on his feet, he'd allowed
Kerry to push him into bed the moment their patient's temperature had broken.

She leaned closer so Jace wouldn't have to work to see
her. He gazed up at her in woozy confusion, a frown puck-
ering his brow.

"Welcome back, Duke," she greeted softly. "Do you
know who I am?"

"Nurse...Dove."

"Close enough. How do you feel?"

"Like I've been trampled by a herd of wild mustangs."
His mouth curled. "Am I gonna live?"

"That's a fair assumption. With a few days' rest. Is there
someone you'd like me to call? Someone who should know
you're here?"

His mouth flattened. "No. No one. My family's...far away. There's no reason to upset them."

"All right. You'll rest here for a few days and be good as new in no time."

"I can't stay here."

"You have to."

He made a tentative, restless movement. "Can't. I need my clothes."

"I could see to it you're *forced* to stay here," she said with vinegary sweetness.

Momentarily, his eyes darkened with temper. Jace was alert enough to sense the implied threat in her words and it surprised him. There was steel behind that Southern drawl. "You'd stoop to blackmail to have your way?"

She met him look for look. "Would you play on my sympathies to have yours?"

Jace pretended to object to the question, but his indignation only made her laugh. Uncertain how to deal with her, he swore and let his head fall back against the pillow. He was in a vulnerable, risky position here, but at the moment he couldn't summon the strength to change it.

He was still trying to think of a solution when he fell asleep.

In the years since her father's death, Kerry had come to rely on the wisdom and guidance of three men. Her grandfather, her uncle and Doc Sanders. She sat at the clinic's reception desk, staring down at the telephone and wishing the first two men in her life were here to tell her what to do about the odd behavior of the third.

Doc had not filled out the necessary paperwork to report Jace Warfield's gunshot wound. No one from Sheriff Crant's office had come to the clinic to question the man. Yet with the immediate danger over, and their patient once more coherent and conscious, it was the next logical step.

Doc knew that. She knew that. So why hadn't he made that call?

She wondered if Doc's decision had anything to do with the conversation he and Jace had shared a few hours ago. With the laughable excuse that he needed certain supplies from the local pharmacy, the old man had sent her out of the clinic. Kerry went, simply because she couldn't bear to accuse such a dear friend of lying.

When she returned, Kerry half expected to find Jace gone. He wasn't. She didn't know whether to be happy or sad about that.

She fingered the phone receiver. She should make the call. If for no other reason than to protect Doc's license. But she couldn't. She'd never questioned Doc's judgment before, and she didn't believe he'd ever knowingly break the law.

Still, the law in The Junction could hardly be considered a model of police enforcement. Sheriff Crant was a bully, a backwoods cretin who'd once been called up on charges of brutalizing a prisoner in his care. His methods of interrogation were calculated to intimidate. If Doc was trying to protect Jace Warfield, Kerry had to hope there was a good reason for it. Until she had some kind of proof that she should do otherwise, she'd continue to let him call the shots.

For the next twenty-four hours, Jace was an exemplary patient, amiable and cooperative. Though mystery shrouded his presence here, he proved to be an easy man to like. Meekly, he allowed Kerry to spoon Maya's homemade stew into his mouth. Without a word he swallowed the liquids she forced on him. And although Kerry could see he was uncomfortable with this sudden dependency, the man even accepted her steadying hand as he eased back against the pillows she piled behind him.

He balked at only one of Kerry's dictates.

"I'm not wearing that," Jace said with an adamant shake of his head.

"You'll have to," Kerry replied mildly. She dangled a blue-and-white flowered hospital gown toward him on one finger. He pulled back from the shapeless creation as though she offered him a hissing snake.

"Nope."

Kerry's eyes narrowed. Patience was a virtue she seldom practiced. "You can't walk around naked."

"Why not? I do it all the time at home. I sleep in the nude. It gives you a great feeling of freedom. You ought to try it."

She resisted the temptation to tell him she already knew what that feeling was like. Wonderful. She slept that way all the time. It suddenly seemed like dangerous ground to be discussing with a man like Jace Warfield. "Be that as it may," Kerry said succinctly, "this is a small town and people talk. If you're trotting around nude and someone walks in, they aren't going to put much stock in the fact I'm a nurse and you're a patient."

Jace looked disappointed in her. "Do you care what a bunch of nosy busybodies say?"

"No. But Doc might catch some flak over it."

"Okay. Get my clothes and I'll put them on every time I have to get up."

Kerry shook her head. "I had to cut up your clothes to get them off you."

"What!" Jace's voice rose. "Those jeans cost me fifty bucks."

"I don't think you'll be able to get that much for them now," Kerry said sweetly. With an annoyed sigh she added, "Look, in a couple of days you can worry about clothes. Until then, this is the easiest solution. What are you so afraid of—damaging your macho image? Haven't you

heard? Real men aren't afraid to look a little...
vulnerable.''

He mulled her words over for a moment. His hand
reached out and fingered the garment disgustedly. ''It's got
no back.''

''I promise I won't look,'' Kerry vowed quickly.

With a disgruntled glare, he snatched the gown from her
hand.

Later, Kerry was tidying the clinic waiting room when she
heard him get out of bed. Thinking he might need help, she
entered the infirmary, stopping just outside the door when
she saw that he seemed to be managing just fine without her
assistance.

Her lips lifted in an appreciative smile at the sight of him.
In spite of his protests, she thought there was never a man
more ideally suited to wear a hospital gown than Jace Warfield, flowers and all.

By the morning of the third day their patient was a
changed man. He had amazing recuperative powers, perhaps because he'd been in excellent shape before his injury.
Kerry came into the clinic to find Jace awake and fully alert,
sitting up in bed as he talked with Doc Sanders. He looked
vitally alive, his eyes sparkling devilishly. The incandescent
smile he offered her set her pulses skittering.

He crossed his arms. Above the loose neckline of that ridiculous gown Kerry caught a tantalizing glimpse of the
dark hair curled upon his chest. She remembered it well.
Crisp, yet satiny soft to the touch. She swallowed hard and
tried to keep her eyes from straying to that delightful exposure.

''Where have you been?'' he demanded to know. ''I'm
hungry and Doc says he can't cook.''

She declined to rise to that gentle baiting. ''You're looking well this morning.''

"I feel great." He glanced at Doc. "I want to get out of here."

The old man shook his head.

"I demand a second opinion."

"No problem," Doc said. He inclined his head and shifted his gaze to Kerry. "Miss Culhane?"

"I'd say another two days."

Jace arched a sullen look their way. "You're both petty tyrants."

"And you're an ungrateful wretch," Kerry added. "Now, what would you like for breakfast?"

"An eight-ounce steak and three eggs. Fried."

Kerry rose, executing a genie's bow of obedience. "Your wish is my command, Master."

She had left her hair unbound, and it tumbled forth in wavy splendor around her shoulders. As always, she wore jeans and a T-shirt, exquisitely filling out the most unusual nurse's uniform Jace had ever encountered. He felt a jolt of pure desire plunge along his senses. "Oh, if only that were true," he said recklessly. He didn't bother to hide the husky promise in his voice.

His words startled a laugh from Kerry and made her grateful for Doc's presence. Before she could move away, Jace caught her hand. "I really am feeling better," he said softly. "Thank you."

Kerry felt the headiness of their touching, but refused to acknowledge it. Jace's eyes had shaded to a deep bronze. She decided she liked it better when he was teasing and lighthearted. "Thank us later. After your steak and eggs. Which, by the way, will look and taste suspiciously like dry toast and oatmeal."

He pulled a face and Kerry and Doc laughed. When she tugged her hand from his, she was relieved that Jace let it go without further comment.

* * *

The morning passed pleasantly. After breakfast, Kerry changed Jace's bandage while Doc drove out to visit a patient who'd been treated the previous week for bronchitis.

They played cards and checkers. Jace was embarrassingly inept at both. He swore Kerry cheated.

After a particularly one-sided game of checkers, in which Kerry's tough surviving platoon of red kings were lined up in a solid wall on Jace's side of the board, he threw up his hands in defeat. "I give up. How did you get to be such a champ?"

"You may have noticed that Flamingo Junction lacks considerably in the entertainment department."

"It's not exactly a metropolis."

"It suits my needs."

"You must have very few needs. Have you always lived here?"

"Almost always."

"Why?"

Kerry looked slightly offended by the question. "Well, for one thing, I have a business here that I couldn't have just anyplace else."

Jace looked surprised. "I thought you worked for the doctor?"

"Three days a week during this time of year. I go out to the reservation with him to help with anyone who's sick. Doc's been here a long time, but he's still considered an outsider to my people. My being there gets him in the door."

"Why?"

"My grandfather used to be a tribal councilman. He's a direct descendent of Aripeka. Aripeka was—"

"Wild Cat."

Her brows lifted in surprise. Few people outside South Florida knew of Wild Cat, a renegade Seminole who'd died never having sworn allegiance to the United States. He was a hero to the Seminoles. "How did you know?"

He shrugged. "Indian cultures are a hobby of mine." When Kerry continued to regard him curiously, he asked, "So what's your business?"

"I run a guide service called Paradise Found. There are four or five of us locals who've contracted with the Parks Department to take hunters and shutterbugs through the Glades."

"You take them through the swamp—by yourself?" He sounded amazed.

"My uncle helps out, and I have a couple of Seminoles who hire out to me as needed. The tourists love to be air-boated around by 'Native Americans.'"

"It doesn't seem like the sort of thing a woman should be doing." He realized he risked Kerry's wrath with such a remark, but the words were out before he had a chance to recall them.

She chose to be amused rather than angry. His reaction was no more or less than what she expected. Many a client had gawked in surprise to find a woman in charge of their excursion into the wilderness. A few had even refused to accept her guidance. "Spoken like a true chauvinist," she said with a militant sparkle in her eyes. "You really *are* John Wayne. Actually, it wasn't something I ever intended to do. My father suffered a stroke and I came home to take care of him. He had commitments for tours, and I kept them. After his death, it just...evolved."

"Where were you living before?"

"Washington, D.C."

He gave her an incredulous look, unable to imagine anyone leaving the excitement of living in the capital to return to a hick town like Flamingo Junction. "You left Washington for this?"

"I hated Washington." Her tone was flat, leaving no room for disagreement.

"Then why were you there?"

"Because that's where my husband was."

Jace sat up straighter in bed, his eyes piercing hers. Her words came as a chilling shock of disappointment. "You're married?"

"I was. I came home, and shortly afterward, my husband, Edward, and I had a parting of the ways."

He looked relieved. "Why?"

Kerry didn't want to be drawn into a conversation about the reasons for her failed marriage. Edward was past history. The anger and humiliation of their breakup had been diluted by two years of immersion in her business.

She took refuge in evasion. "You ask an awful lot of questions."

"I like to get a lot of answers."

"How about answering a few of mine?" Kerry challenged.

His shoulders lifted to display indifference and he winced when the movement pulled at his wound. "Go ahead. Ask me anything. I have no secrets." His eyes widened with deliberate innocence.

Too knowing to be so easily deceived, Kerry threw him a skeptical glance. *Okay, Jace. Tell me the truth. Tell me why someone took a shot at you. Have I proved I can be trusted? Have I, Jace?* She had an agonizingly clear image of herself asking the questions that had teased the back of her mind since the moment he told her that ridiculous story about having shot himself. But just as clearly, she could see more lies being offered up as gospel, layer upon layer of untruths that in the end would do nothing but turn her away from him.

Kerry hated lies and the people who told them. Her own father had woven a tapestry of intricate stories about himself, constructing a life in America with no basis in truth. She had listened to those embroidered tales all her life. Roon Culhane was a sweet, gentle soul, a shrewd businessman, and a loving father. He was also a compulsive liar who would not have recognized the truth if he'd fallen over it. And Edward. Handsome, charming Edward, who had taken her to Washington and tried to teach her how to be the perfect political wife, even if it meant pretending to be someone she wasn't. Oh, no. She wasn't brave enough to hear lies from Jace Warfield. Not when she'd discovered just how much she could like him.

Feeling an undeniable edge of sadness, Kerry thrust aside her frustration. She gave Jace an intense look, realizing the man had gone curiously still. *He's waiting for me to ask. He knows I want to. But I can't.* Did he know that, too? she wondered.

With a bitter curve to her lips, Kerry settled for safer ground. "So why do you fancy yourself to be John Wayne?"

It seemed to Kerry that his square, chiseled features imperceptibly sagged with relief. "Who said I did?"

"You did. While I was patching you up."

"Oh. I must have been pretty out of it."

"You were. But you were rather insistent."

The cat-and-mouse games over, Jace laughed heartily. "Actually, I've always admired the man. He followed a strict code of right and wrong in the movies he made. You were either a good guy or a bad guy. Very simplistic logic, but I like it."

Which one are you, Jace? Good guy or bad? "Very unrealistic logic if you ask me."

He threw her a menacing look. "Them's fightin' words, pardner. When I was a kid, I worshiped him. For a while I thought we might be related. We have the same initials and the same birthday."

Kerry had to laugh at the absurdity of that idea. "Twins! Separated at birth."

"Don't laugh. When I was nine I believed it. My parents had to convince me otherwise, and for a long time they were afraid I'd never get an identity of my own."

"I imagine all little boys want to be a hero."

Jace frowned in remembrance. "I suppose so. Although my brother never wanted to be anyone but Tonto. Joel liked taking orders and I liked giving them. I tried to convince him Tonto was the Lone Ranger's friend, not the Duke's, but he didn't listen. I have a sister, and all she ever did was boss both of us around. She never believed me when I told her the Duke didn't take orders from a woman."

"Good for her!" Kerry said with a fluid laugh. She began removing red checkers from the board, stacking them in her hand. "There's such affection in your voice when you speak of your family. Do you see them often?"

There followed a silence that lasted a little too long, and Kerry lifted her lashes in time to see a strange thing happen.

Jace Warfield's face shut down. Suddenly and completely. One moment his features were soft and dreamy with reminiscences of boyhood years. The next his eyes took on a flinty hardness and his pliant smile had become brittle and forced.

"No. Not often," Jace said softly with dull finality. For a moment he frowned down at the black-and-red checkerboard that lay across the bed tray. He fingered a black disk distractedly.

The thought snapped into Kerry's brain that here was a wound that had yet to heal. Perhaps a family argument still unresolved. Remembering the pictures she had seen in Jace's wallet, it didn't seem possible. But one look at his face and Kerry knew this was a subject even less approachable with the man than the mystery surrounding his injury. *Leave it alone, Kerry.*

"What do you say to a rematch?" he asked at last. "This game can't be that hard to master."

"It's not difficult. Once you know the right moves."

He looked up at her suddenly, his brow harshly furrowed. His eyes seemed to have splintered into a hundred small chips of mahogany. "Have you always known the right moves, Kerry Culhane? God knows, I haven't."

She sensed frustration in the soft timbre of Jace's voice and remembered this was a complex man who was in trouble, possibly serious trouble. He seemed determined to handle it on his own. After all, the Duke had never needed anyone's help.

She shrugged. "I know enough moves to get by in life. That's all that matters. And stop trying to sidetrack me. It was my turn to ask questions."

Jace's noncommittal mask was back in place. "Ask."

"What are you doing out here in the middle of nowhere?"

"Taking pictures. I'm a free-lance journalist. Right now there's a national magazine willing to pay me big bucks to do a story on Florida's vanishing wetlands."

"Are you any good?"

"At what? Taking pictures or writing?"

"Both."

"I'm no Ansel Adams, but I get by. My brother Joel got the talent in that department. First and foremost, I'm a writer."

"Do you usually write about nature?"

"No. Six months ago I won a Pulitzer for an exposé I did on a neo-Nazi group that had sprung up in Washington, D.C."

Kerry's brow lifted in respect. "I'm impressed."

"Yeah. So was I," Jace replied with studied indifference. "Maybe a little too much."

"What does that mean?"

He sighed heavily. "Nothing really. Just that for a while I got pretty high on myself. I forgot the things that are really important."

His comment puzzled her. "Such as..."

He offered her a sudden smile of dazzling whiteness. "Such as figuring out how to beat someone at a simple game of checkers. Are you going to put your men down on the board or keep asking questions?"

She felt the ache of disappointment. There were so many questions she wanted answers to. Answers that could warrant her helping Doc in this. Answers that would justify this disturbing tendency to want to trust Jace. But he wouldn't be drawn into further discussion about his personal life, and irritated by her willingness to believe him anyway, Kerry plunged into an unexpected attack. "Just one more question. If you're just here to take pictures, why did you find it necessary to bring a gun?"

Chapter 3

Good question, Ms. Culhane. You should be the journalist.

He couldn't tell her the truth, so he dug himself in a little deeper, rattling off a ridiculous lie about his fear of meeting some primeval swamp creature face-to-face. Judging from the way her dark brows tugged up toward her hairline, she either thought he was a damned fool or a liar. He wasn't sure which was better.

Lately, it seemed as though everything was a delicate balancing act. He had come to Flamingo Junction to accomplish one goal, then leave. If he had to tell a few lies along the way, so be it. He couldn't afford to be sidetracked by anything. Any ends justified the means. It was that simple.

What wasn't so simple was the way his gut rolled every time he lied to Kerry Culhane. He felt the uncomfortable sting of conscience. Hell, she'd probably saved his life! Kerry deserved the truth, didn't she?

Every time he rattled off one more untruth, he felt the heat of the woman's gaze on him, the disbelief in her eyes. He liked her too much to continue insulting her intelligence this way. Doc had told him she was a woman who could be trusted, a realist who understood that sometimes fate dealt a complicated hand. It would be easy to enlist her help, but he couldn't afford the luxury of involving another person. It was too dangerous. He should have ignored Doc's orders to rest. He should have been gone from here by now.

Ruthlessly Kerry swept two of his black kings off the board, shaking him out of his reverie. She looked up, offering him a smile of superiority.

She was such a beautiful woman. Involuntary images of the two of them, together, rose constantly in his mind. Kerry Culhane woke an emotion that had been slumbering deep inside him for a very long time.

But that still didn't mean he could share the truth.

Kerry beat him at every game of checkers and gin rummy. They switched to a trivia game where they were more evenly matched. He excelled in the literature categories, but she slaughtered him in the sciences.

He managed to squeak past her and capture the last game piece necessary to win. With a triumphant flourish he snatched the pieces from the board. "Finally! A game you're only *good* at. I can die happy now that I've reestablished man's superiority over woman."

"The Duke would be so proud of you." Amusement crinkled around her eyes.

She packed the pieces back into the box, then carried it to the bookcase on the far side of the room.

Jace watched as she stretched to place it on the highest shelf. Kerry's hair streamed behind her like a midnight curtain, but Jace was more deeply appreciative of the way her jeans slid up her legs to hug her buttocks. She had great legs, but an even greater rear end. Tight, small and just right to fit a man's hands, he thought. He observed Kerry with a darkening veil of passion, his rapidly warming perusal creating a hungry need within.

When Kerry returned to his bedside, she was immediately aware of a change. Jace had birthed an absurd smile and the way he looked at her threatened to unravel her control. "What's so funny?" she asked.

"Nothing." Yet his smile became wicked.

Her brows knit together. "Tell me."

"You won't like it," he warned.

She tossed her head and ebony tresses sifted over her shoulder. "Try me."

"Watching you just now, I was thinking you have a terrific . . . legs," he amended quickly. "Great legs."

"Thank you. So do you."

"How do you know? Have you had firsthand experience with my legs?"

Kerry shrugged. "Of course. I'm the one who sponged you down during your fever. Remember?"

"No. But I sure wish I did."

She laughed. "My interest was strictly professional," she assured him.

"Well, that's a damned shame," Jace grumbled. "A little unprofessional interest wouldn't hurt."

Kerry pinned him with a withering look. "I'm trying to remember you're a sick man."

Jace grinned wolfishly and one eyebrow quirked. "Getting better all the time. Want to play Doctor? I'll let you examine me." He patted the spot closest to him on the bed.

Kerry ignored him. "I'm going to start supper. You rest."

Without a backward glance she headed toward Doc's quarters. Jace felt his pulse crawl to a standstill. "Come on, Kerry," he called coaxingly. "I'll let you win the next game."

"No deal," she tossed back over her shoulder. "I let you win the last one."

She reappeared thirty minutes later, supper tray in hand, followed closely by Doc Sanders, who insisted on taking vital signs before the patient ate. While the old man took his pulse, Jace watched Kerry set the tray aside, then bend to deal with the tangled bedcovers. He found himself enjoying her movements. Her hands were quick, every turn executed with maximum efficiency. His heart began to pick up speed and he wondered if Doc could feel it in his wrist.

She placed the tray over his lap, and Jace looked down at the plate in disappointment. He must be irritating her too much. She'd decided to starve him. A meat-and-potatoes man all his life, he couldn't drum up much enthusiasm for a huge bowl of chicken-and-rice soup, one small roll—dry, no butter—and a symmetrical square of gelatin.

Jace hated gelatin, and lime flavor most of all. It was on the tip of his tongue to reject the meal, beg for anything else, but one look in those wildflower-blue eyes and he was sure he could eat every bite.

He looked up at her. What was this woman doing to his good sense?

Kerry caught the question in his glance. "Something wrong?"

"No."

"Would you like me to feed you?"

He waved the spoon at her like a weapon. "Not a chance. I can manage." He poked his finger at the gelatin and it quivered disgustingly. "Lime, huh?"

"Good guess. I've made a huge pan of it, so feel free to ask for more."

"Great." She made a move to leave him and he asked quickly, "Have you eaten? Why don't you join me?" Doc glanced up from scribbling notes on a progress chart, and with an afterthought Jace added, "You, too, Doc."

Before either could respond to that invitation, they heard the clinic's front door open, then bang shut. A deep, booming voice called, "Doc? Anybody here?"

"Yes, I'm coming." The edge of tension in Doc's tone made Jace look at him closely. The old man recognized the newcomer's voice, and this was definitely someone he did not want to see.

Doc Sanders crossed the room in hurried strides. The glance he darted at Kerry over his shoulder did little to assuage Jace's sudden apprehension.

In the next moment, Jace understood their constraint.

Before the doctor reached the outer office, the doorway was filled by the biggest man Jace had ever seen. He easily topped six feet, every inch of him solid muscle. Sandy hair buzzed into a crewcut accentuated a bull-like neck and torso originally intended for a tree trunk. He resembled the Denver Broncos's best hopes for the ultimate linebacker, and although his face was pleasant enough and he was probably somewhere near Jace's own age, there wasn't the remotest chance of the two men forming any kind of friendship.

The guy wore the crisp, brown uniform of a Florida state trooper.

Doc had pulled up short. "Hello, Mac."

The cop's eyes flickered to Jace, then he smiled broadly. "Hi, Doc. Kerry."

Doc Sanders stood stiffly silent, obviously ill at ease, and it surprised Jace to hear Kerry fill the void. With deceptive casualness she asked, "What are you doing out our way? I thought you were assigned to Alligator Alley."

"Still am. I got pulled off for a couple of days on special duty." He unbuttoned his cuff and rolled up one sleeve to expose his forearm to the doctor. "I think I got into some poison sumac out in the Glades. It itches like crazy. You gave me some salve once before. Do you think you can find a little of it?"

"Of course," Doc said. "Kerry, I think there's some in that cabinet against the wall." Kerry nodded and began opening drawers along the built-in counter.

The officer waited patiently, one hand planted lazily on top of his gun handle. The leather holster creaked under the weight. The man's pale eyes drifted back to Jace. He offered a short nod of acknowledgment. "How you doin', sir?"

"Fine, thank you."

"Doc takin' good care of you?"

"Very good care."

He had a cop's natural inquisitiveness. "That your rental car out front?"

"Yes."

"Where you from?"

"Denver."

"Long way from home."

"Yes."

Jace kept a friendly smile plastered on his face, though his answers were deliberately brief. He knew cops were often suspicious of people who blathered on and on or who offered detailed explanations.

"What brought you to Doc's place?"

"A bad cut," Doc interjected. "He was chopping firewood at his campsite and the ax slipped."

Mac made a face. "Ouch. Bet that hurt. Not much of a pioneer, are you?"

"No, I'm afraid not," Jace replied smoothly. "My vacation's nearly over and I've spent most of it right here in bed."

"He's been here almost a week," the old man added quickly. "Recuperating."

"Darn shame," Mac replied. "Not much to share with the folks back home."

Absently, Jace nodded agreement. His gaze was fixed on Kerry. She had stopped rummaging through the drawers, though it didn't appear she'd found what she'd been looking for. He knew she hadn't missed the lies he and Doc had offered, and he wondered if they'd made a mistake in thinking she'd go along with them.

The trooper was watching Kerry, too, the light of curiosity beginning to glow in his pale gaze. To distract him Jace asked, "What's Alligator Alley?"

The man's eyes swiveled back to Jace. "Just a lonely stretch of nothing that runs from coast to coast. I spend most of my time pulling tourist vehicles out of the canals on either side of the road. Tramping through the Glades is a nice change." He waggled his arm in the air. "Even with the poison sumac."

"What's happening in the Glades?" Kerry inquired nonchalantly.

"Every available man is combing the area. They found a body in the National Park."

There was a thoughtful, deadly silence. Doc asked quickly, "A tourist?"

"Not likely. Somebody took a .45 and used the guy for target practice. Looks like there was quite a tussle. Probably a fight over drug money. But since it happened in the Park, the heat's on. Can't have the tourist season ruined, even if the guy obviously wasn't there to bird-watch."

Kerry had found the cream at last. Wordlessly she turned and came to stand in front of the officer. Jace shot her a speculative glance as she passed and was not surprised to see dark hostility in her eyes. She captured the trooper's hand, and rubbed salve along the reddened area of his inner arm. Her head was dipped low, intent upon her work.

Jace didn't have to guess what her thoughts were. Kerry's profile was a stony mask, the only movement a sudden tensing of her jaw. Apprehension skittered along his spine. Exposure seemed imminent. A few evasions were one thing, but she didn't know him well enough to be willing to harbor a murderer. And Jace would have taken bets that that was exactly the conclusion Kerry had drawn. Only concern for Doc's involvement kept her silent.

"Feels better already," the trooper said with a huge sigh.

"When did you find the body?" Kerry asked. Her voice was soft and distant.

"Three days ago."

I'm sunk, Jace thought. This guy's going to be reading me my rights in no time. He sent a silent message across the room, his senses flaring with the first real fear. *Don't do it, Kerry. Trust me.*

The quiet in the room seemed deafening. Jace could think of nothing to say that wouldn't make a bad situation worse. Doc seemed turned to stone. The cop gazed down at the top of Kerry's head in pleasurable content. No fool, he wasn't about to interrupt Kerry's stimulating touch with talk of murdered bodies. Kerry seemed to be entranced, her fingers gliding over Mac's arm again and again until the cream had disappeared. Her movements were dangerously precise, mechanical.

Eventually, and much to Jace's relief, Kerry dropped Mac's hand. She offered him the tube of salve and he slipped it into his breast pocket. Gingerly he rebuttoned his cuff. "How much do I owe you?"

"It's a free sample," Doc replied. "Keep it."

"Great. Thanks." He hitched up his belt, and the gun at his hip wobbled a moment. "Well, I got to get back out there and catch bad guys." He tipped his head in their direction. "Kerry, Doc, I'll see you soon."

They nodded.

He was almost out of the room when Kerry called his name. Jace's nerves screamed as the big man turned back around.

"Mac," Kerry said slowly, "do you have any idea who killed that man?"

"Nope. But we'll know more as soon as the evidence reports come back from Tallahassee. Don't worry. Keep your doors locked at night and you'll be fine."

The trooper departed, leaving behind a raw, uncomfortable silence. Kerry hadn't moved. The color had washed out of Doc Sanders's face. He looked old and tired. Somewhere Jace could hear a clock ticking, a slow, meticulous sound that seemed too loud in the stillness.

"Kerry..."

Her mind barely registered the fact Jace had called her name. It was too busy skimming through Mac's words, trying to grasp a reason, trying to sort through conflicting emotions that had kept her silent when she should have done what was right. What was sensible. Why had she played along and said nothing?

She told herself it was because of Doc. He was like family. You couldn't betray someone you cared about, could you? No. Of course not.

"Kerry..."

She turned suddenly as though startled from a sound sleep. Her eyes were glitteringly bright. "I have to clean up the waiting room. I'll be back later to pick up your supper tray."

Before he could protest, she was gone.

She cornered Doc Sanders in the waiting room the moment MacGruder's patrol car backed out of the clinic parking lot. "Enough, Doc. I want to know, and I want to know now. Who is Jace Warfield, and why are you protecting him?"

"Kerry, I can't discuss it."

She expelled a long, unsteady breath, forcing her voice to remain even. "Doc, I want some answers."

He shook his head. "I'd tell you if I could, but it's not my decision."

"You lied to MacGruder. And you haven't reported the gunshot wound." Impatient with him, her fingers balled into fists at her sides. Doc could be as stoic and stubborn as her Seminole uncle and grandfather. "Have you lost your mind? This could mean your license to practice."

"I'll report it—soon."

Doc looked miserable. It was infuriating to know he was as distressed as she by the lies he'd told. A sudden thought chilled her blood, and her voice lowered. "Has he threatened you in some way?"

"No, of course not. You've been around him enough in the past few days to know he's not that type."

"I don't know any such thing."

"Kerry, trust me. Trust *him.*"

"That was a murder in the Park, Doc. Not petty theft. You can't harbor a criminal without suffering the consequences."

He sent her a long, direct look, the first real honesty she'd seen in his face since they'd begun this conversation. "He's not a murderer, Kerry. And you know it."

"I don't know what to think anymore."

He issued a tired sigh, and after a moment, asked, "What are you going to do?"

She took a glimpse around the small, tidy room, as though the answer to that question was somehow written on the walls. This clinic was Doc's life. He loved Flamingo Junction and the odd assortment of people who lived here. Surely he'd never do anything to jeopardize it. So why was he determined to protect this stranger?

"I don't know," she replied wearily.

* * *

The evening crawled by. Bored without Kerry's company, Jace tried to interest himself in an old Louis L'Amour novel he'd found, but his thoughts kept returning to the state trooper's visit and its unfortunate results.

He summoned the vision of Kerry standing in front of the cop, listening to words that painted a pretty damaging picture. He could tell from the cold, set look of her profile that she believed him to be involved, if not outright responsible, for the murdered man in the Everglades. Not very flattering to have someone think you were a murderer, but hardly an unexpected conclusion considering the tap dance he'd been doing for her benefit. Again he entertained the idea of telling her the truth, and yet again he rejected it as foolish and unnecessary.

She had not, after all, turned him in.

Why? he wondered. Calm reason told him that Kerry's concern for Doc had kept her quiet, but he couldn't help hoping there was a small part of her that believed in him. Just a little.

Throughout the evening he occasionally heard Kerry in other rooms. Running water, the soft "whump" of cupboards being closed. He knew she was deliberately avoiding him, and although he wanted to clear the air between them, as much as he could, he made no effort to confront her.

Jace told himself there was a good reason for his reluctance to seek her out. How could you convince anyone of anything while barefoot and clothed in only a silly hospital gown? He'd look weak and vulnerable, and he had a feeling in a clash with Kerry Culhane he'd need every bit of armor he could scrounge.

But it was nearly midnight and still Kerry hadn't returned. The untouched meal sat on the floor beside the bed, the soup now cold and unappetizing. Jace had turned on the bedside lamp as darkness fell. Its soft, warm glow touched eerily upon the various pieces of medical equipment positioned about the room. Even Doc Sanders seemed to have deserted him. Feeling forlorn and forgotten, Jace remained propped against the headboard, his arms crossed over his chest.

His anger simmered. All right. So she wasn't going to turn him over to the police. Did she intend to ignore him completely? Leave him to Doc's care? Even prisoners on death row got to see their jailers once in a while.

Jace had just about decided to yell his head off or fake a relapse, anything to bring the stubborn woman to his side, when she appeared in the doorway.

She hesitated there for a long moment. In the subdued lighting, her hair gleamed with blue-black highlights. Her features were shadowed and he couldn't read her eyes, but her body language told Jace everything he needed to know.

Kerry had hoped he would be asleep when she returned to the infirmary. Finding him wide-awake and obviously determined to confront her did little to ease her troubled mind. She squared her shoulders and strode into the room.

"I was beginning to think you were never coming back," he scolded mildly.

He was so insufferably cool, as though she were somehow the guilty party. Kerry's anger rose. She bit back the scathing words that crowded her throat, trying to remain impervious to anything the man said.

Her gaze fell on the discarded bedtray. "You didn't eat your supper."

"I lost my appetite."

She bent to retrieve the tray, and Jace's hand captured her wrist. She jerked back. Dishes clattered as they settled back on the floor. "Let go." She enunciated each word with slow care.

"Kerry, we need to talk."

"I don't think so."

"I do."

She pulled against Jace's hold, but it was unbreakable. "Talk? Don't you mean, tell more lies?"

"You're not giving me a chance to explain."

"On the contrary. There have been plenty of chances to explain. Instead, you choose to stay here and endanger Doc's career."

"Doc made his own decision."

"You're hiding from the police."

Jace's features hardened. "So you've already convicted me."

"You convicted yourself. You lied to MacGruder."

"That doesn't make me a murderer. Kerry, stop and think a moment...."

Determined not to be swayed by his seductively coaxing tone, Kerry renewed her struggles against his grip. "Let go! I'm warning you."

Jace tugged hard on her wrist and, off balance, she fell across his lap in a tangled heap. He winced as the movement pulled at his healing wound, but desperate to make Kerry listen, he ignored the pain that dug into his side.

With her free hand she swiped midnight hair out of her eyes, glaring up at him in livid silence.

Seeing her face, Jace gentled his grasp. He didn't want her furious. He wanted her calm and reasonable, and willing to take a chance on him. "Kerry, these past three days... they're important to me."

"Trust and respect is what's important to me," she countered. "We don't share either one."

"There are reasons—good reasons. I'm not the monster you're ready to think I am. Look at me, Kerry." He shook her shoulders slightly when he realized her gaze had settled somewhere along the region of his collarbone. "Damn it, look at me!"

Reluctantly, she lifted her eyes. They were dark with turmoil.

"Do I look like a murderer to you?" he asked softly.

Her lips curled in a sneer. "There are plenty of presentable-looking young men on death row. My father used to say the Devil can quote Scripture if it suits his purpose."

"I don't care what your father used to say. I only care what *you* say. Put aside your anger for a minute and look into my eyes. Tell me what you see." With one hand Jace made an abrupt, careless gesture. "Not with your mind." His hand became a fist, and he pulled it against his upper abdomen. "In here. Tell me what your gut feels. What does it say, Kerry?"

Solemnly she studied his features and her composure slipped a little. He looked heartsore, as though her accusations had hurt him. There was weary resignation in his expression, and his normally strong, invincible facade was nowhere to be found. She tried to remember this was a man she barely knew, a man who had lied to her. Jace Warfield might be capable of anything.

He must have sensed her confusion, because he pulled her closer until their gazes locked. His hands drifted up to her shoulders to entwine at her nape. "Trust me," he whispered in a tender, frustrated tone. "Believe in me...."

Something odd fused between them. With Jace's mouth hovering just above hers, Kerry's senses were swimming. His nearness disturbed her, dissolved the tight knot of anger within. She tried to resurrect the feelings of mistrust, but there was only Jace, his deep voice mesmerizing, the soft warmth of his hazel eyes stealing her resistance.

His mouth touched hers briefly. She felt the prickle of beard and mustache, then his soft breath fluttered against her cheek. "Come here, Kerry. Give me your trust...." he murmured. His voice, cracked with exhaustion, seemed to vibrate through her.

His lips found hers again, ghosting over them for a moment before claiming them. Kerry closed her eyes because the earth seemed to be shifting.

Uncertainty was gone. There was only a dizzying anticipation as Jace pressed to explore the dark cavern of her mouth. Responding to his blatantly sensuous touch with blind instinct, Kerry's lips parted. His kiss was hungrily explicit. Teasing, stroking, Jace's mouth blended with hers.

When it ended, she felt bereft and shaken. He pulled away, his eyes still on her. The look in them was hot and commanding and self-assured. As though she had already capitulated to his side. Murderer he might not be. But the damned man was too cocky for his own good. With an effort, Kerry tore her gaze away.

"What's the matter?" he asked. "Didn't you like that?"

Of course she liked that. What was there *not* to like? But did he think kissing her was the answer to everything? Resentment warred with pride. She met the audacious twinkle in his eyes and treated him to a cold, inimical smile. "Oh, I liked it well enough. How much silence do you think you just bought, Jace?"

His brow clouded as astonishment threw him off stride. It was clear he hadn't expected that kind of reaction. Eyes that had been heavy-lidded with passion burned savagely bright for a moment, then he sighed. "I deserved that." He offered her an engaging half smile. "But for what it's worth, I didn't kiss you with any ulterior motive in mind. I kissed you because I've wanted to from the moment I saw you. I'm sorry if I pushed too hard. I just didn't want to lose these past few days." His fingers slid along her jawline. "I'm not a murderer, Kerry. What do I have to say to make you believe me? I want you to understand—"

She placed her fingers against his lips. "No, don't. I don't want to know any more. I'm already more involved than I want to be." The look in her eyes was clear and intent. "I hate that you've involved Doc."

"I would change that if I could. But I can't."

Resigned, she shot him a level look. "Don't hurt him, Jace."

"Nothing's going to happen to him. I won't let it."

She shook her head. "You see everything in terms of black or white, and forget there can also be shades of gray. You're out of your element here. You should go home. Now. Before a better shot comes along and sends you home in a box."

It was obvious he didn't care for her assessment. Jace's lips thinned, and when he spoke, his tone was barely controlled. "I can't say that I agree. And I've come too far to turn back now."

"It's never too late. Just stop what you're doing. Go home," Kerry repeated.

He shook his head slowly. "No."

Frustrated, she lashed out at him. "This isn't the movies. When people get killed they stay dead. You don't just get up and dust yourself off. Don't you realize how close you came to being killed?"

She witnessed the flash of anger in his eyes. "You don't need to lecture me about death. I know only too well how permanent it can be."

Kerry stared at him in defeat. In a moment of vivid clarity, she saw he was absolutely committed to a course of action, and nothing she could say would make any difference. She wondered what could be so important. Money? Power? She wished she could make him realize nothing could be worth forfeiting his life.

Exasperated beyond measure, her eyes desolate, Kerry said, "I just don't want anything to happen to you."

Wry amusement tinged Jace's laugh. He tilted her chin upward with one finger. "Why, Ms. Culhane, you almost sound as if you care about me."

She fended him off, twisting away from his touch and off the bed in one fluid movement. "I just don't want all my hard work undone. Do as you please. I won't stop you."

Chapter 4

Kerry stepped back, surveying her handiwork with a critical eye. The fresh coat of paint had transformed the decrepit rowboat into a fairly passable conveyance, and when Charlie replaced the leaky flooring, it would be watertight.

"What do you think, Uncle?"

Charlie Longtooth straightened from the bottom of the boat, removing nails from his mouth. His dark, Seminole features, so like those of Kerry's mother, eyed the new paint job. "I think it is a sad waste of good paint. Replacing the rotted boards would have been enough."

Kerry tossed him a disapproving glance. "I don't want our guests thinking we can't afford to keep up the equipment."

It was Charlie's turn to look displeased. "In four years I have never seen a guest take out this boat."

"There's always a first time," Kerry replied, tossing a paint-spattered rag into the empty paint can. "When you're finished here, I want to get started on the roof of Cottage

Two. After the last rain there was a wet spot on the bedroom ceiling.''

"We don't have a booking for at least another month."

"Still, I don't want water damage to the unit in the meantime."

"There will be no rain for many days."

Kerry narrowed her eyes, pointing at the older man with the end of her paintbrush. "One more objection and you're fired."

Charlie grunted, disregarding the threat. Nearly every week Kerry dismissed him or he threw up his hands in rebellion and quit. It had become their private joke. Since her father's death, her uncle had overseen the property, tackling the manual labor required to keep Paradise Found a functioning enterprise. And the guests loved his tales of Seminole folklore.

No matter how she argued, Charlie had never accepted one cent in salary, and Kerry had given up offering him money. Instead, she often cooked special Seminole dishes for him, mended his clothes and tried to keep his favorite pipe tobacco on hand. Seminoles were a maternally-driven tribe, and without a wife, Charlie had been at a loss on the reservation. Next to her grandfather, he was her closest relative, and Kerry was delighted when he'd moved into the abandoned cabin a half mile from Paradise Found. She suspected her grandfather had had a hand in that decision, that the old man was kept apprised of her every move. She didn't mind. Although she seldom saw her grandfather, Kerry liked the idea that she was never completely alone.

"You mad at me about something?" Charlie asked.

"No. Why?"

"'Cause ever since you got back from the clinic three days ago it's been nothing but sweat and blisters. We been going from sunup to sundown."

Kerry sighed. "I just want the place to look good." She gestured toward the lodge, across the immaculately groomed carpet of grass that sloped down to the water. At the dock, two airboats bobbed placidly at their moorings, their metalwork shiny in the sun. "And it does, doesn't it? The place is spotless."

"Too bad there is no one to appreciate all this hard work," Charlie grumped.

Unfortunately, that was all too true. The four guest cottages made of hand-hewn cypress were polished and aired, waiting for the next deluge of visitors. But they were empty, and likely to stay that way for at least another month when the season began in earnest.

"Do you want to talk about what is bothering you?" he coaxed.

Kerry's mouth formed a tight line and she shook her head. "No. I want to fix the roof on number two."

Her uncle shrugged. He knew better than to push. "When you are ready," he said simply, and began nailing boards again.

She squeezed his arm in wordless thanks and left him to his work. A short time later she watched him saunter off toward Cottage Two, toolbox in hand. She busied herself with hosing down the bare planks of the dock, wishing she'd found the courage to confide in him, wondering why she couldn't seem to find the right words.

It should have been easy. Kerry knew she had deliberately pushed herself hard these past few days, hoping to find some sense of inner peace, hoping the dull monotony of hard physical labor would get her mind off that impossible man back in Doc Sanders's infirmary.

At least she had escaped, returning home without saying goodbye to Jace Warfield. Cowardly, maybe, but it was the only thing she could do under the circumstances. She couldn't get involved with a man who chose to work outside the law, no matter how much Doc trusted him. Kerry didn't know his reason for being here in Flamingo Junction, and she didn't want to be around when it was over. She was honest enough to admit she liked Jace, maybe a little too much. The man did unexpected, frightening things to her heartbeat. Uncomfortable with the idea that Jace Warfield might have the ability to wield some sort of control over her emotions, Kerry had abandoned him the day after MacGruder's visit.

Barney, her German shepherd-Labrador mix, set up a fierce barking, startling Kerry out of her reverie. She swung around in time to see a familiar blue Camaro crunch to a halt on the crushed oystershell drive.

Her stomach churned with dread. She had hoped never to see Jace Warfield again. She should have guessed it wouldn't be that easy.

She watched him walk toward her. He moved with easy grace and was clean-shaven now, dressed in jeans and a cotton shirt with the sleeves rolled back. The sun glinted off his bright, golden hair.

Without the beard and mustache, his facial features were strongly evident. She hadn't realized how finely cut his jaw was, how sensually full his upper lip. Her gaze reached his eyes. The murky brown depths were dark and unreadable.

She stood her ground, waiting for him to reach her, willing composure. She tried to take comfort from the fact that Charlie was within calling distance, the pounding racket of his hammer vying with Barney's barking to destroy the peace of the morning. She whistled softly to the dog. With a disappointed snuffling sound, he subsided and trotted back to the front porch of the lodge.

Jace stopped a few feet from her, hooking his thumbs into the pockets of his jeans. He held her gaze for a long, uncomfortable moment. "You didn't say goodbye," he said simply.

"I needed to get back here. I have a business to run."

His eyes traveled around the deserted compound. "Yes. I can see business is booming."

His penetrating gaze made her shift uneasily. She tried to remind herself that she owed him no explanations. "I didn't say goodbye because I didn't think we had anything further to say to one another."

"I thought we had reached an understanding of sorts. I thought our relationship—"

"There is no relationship," she cut in. "I don't want to get involved with you, Jace."

"I thought you trusted me."

"No. I believe you're not a murderer, but that's a long way from trusting you."

He offered a challenging smile. "Are you sure it's me you don't trust, Kerry? Or yourself? When I kissed you the other day, you didn't give a damn about trust. You opened up to me. That's what has you so scared, isn't it? What are you running from, Kerry—"

"I don't have to listen to this." Kerry made a move toward the lodge, but Jace's hand came down on her wrist with bruising strength. She flashed him a fulminating look. "One whistle from me and that dog on the porch will have you for dinner," she said in a low tone.

He shrugged. "Go ahead. I'm the man who doesn't understand the finality of death, remember?"

She glared at him. "What do you want from me, Jace?"

"Two things. I want you to sit down and listen to me, let me explain. Then," his voice became serious, "I want your help."

They sat side by side on the end of the dock, watching water beetles stitch erratic patterns across the surface of the slow-moving water. A shy slider turtle broke the surface to investigate their dangling feet, then slid quickly beneath the water again. Far out, amidst the river of grass, something big flopped and splashed. The sun was high overhead, glaringly bright and warm on the tops of their heads.

Feigning a bravado she didn't feel, Kerry manufactured an expression of indifference. Having Jace seated so close set her heart to thudding wildly.

"I came to Flamingo Junction to find a man named Eric Burkhardt." Jace's voice broke the stillness.

Kerry didn't recognize the name. "Is he the man who shot you?"

"No." His expression took on an icy hardness. "He doesn't get blood on his own hands. He and the fellow killed in the park had a meeting that afternoon. There was an argument, and Burkhardt had the man shot. He believes in quick justice. When he realized I'd witnessed the murder, he set his men on me. They got off a lucky shot. I had to wade through waist high water to throw them off my tracks."

"You're lucky a gator didn't find you."

"You don't know Burkhardt. My chances would have been better with a gator." The words were bitter, deadly serious. "I came to the clinic for help because Doc was a man I could trust."

"How did you know Doc wouldn't report what had happened?"

"He and my father were interns together. They've been friends a long time, keeping in touch over the years. We've actually only met a few times, but when I came to Flamingo Junction I contacted him. Doc was the one who put my informant on to Burkhardt's activities."

"Why?"

"The Everglades is too big an area to be policed well, and you know law enforcement often turns a blind eye to what goes on in the swamp. Doc thinks the local cops can't be trusted. He cares about the people here. He's tired of patching up good men who just can't say no to easy money."

Kerry gave him a close look. "Are you a cop?"

His mouth lifted in a small smile. "I'm who I said I was. A journalist. The things I told you about my personal life were true."

"Are you working for the police?"

"In a roundabout way," he said.

That answer didn't satisfy her. "If that's true, why did you lie to Mac? He'd be on your side, too."

"Maybe. I'm not willing to trust any of the locals at this point. And even if your friend MacGruder is clean, I don't want some hick traffic cop poking around my investigation." Am I making a mistake telling Kerry these things? he thought. Too many people have died. Almost to himself, Jace added, "The fewer people involved, the better."

"Does this man Burkhardt know who you are?"

"No."

"Is he still after you?"

"I don't think so. Doc's done some discreet checking around town. No one's asking questions."

"Why are you after this man?"

"Gun smuggling."

Two white egrets lifted off from a nearby cypress tree. They swept low across the sky and Kerry's gaze followed their path. "So why are you telling me all this now?"

"To clear the air and make it right between us. To give our... friendship a chance."

She swiveled back to face him. "I'm not looking for a relationship, Jace."

He chose to be amused rather than angered by her rejection. "That's not the impression I got the other day."

"You place too much importance on a kiss. I won't pretend I didn't find it enjoyable, but that doesn't mean I'm looking for anything more. Haven't you ever made overtures to a woman and been rejected?"

He paused a moment to give the idea some thought, then shrugged. "Actually, no."

"That's part of your problem," Kerry declared. "You're much too sure of yourself."

His touch was suddenly on the back of her hand, light and disturbing. He ran a finger slowly up her bare forearm, and Kerry wondered why he should assume this familiarity was acceptable to her, and why she made no move to pull away.

"With you, I'm never sure of anything," he said, his voice softly lilting.

His fingers encountered a heavy lock of midnight hair that curled around her shoulder. Jace lifted the soft, sun-warmed tresses, letting them sift through his hand and re-settle in charming disarray. "You have such beautiful hair," he said, and the look in his eyes was warm and deeply appreciative. "Like a velvet curtain."

Tantalizing shivers raced through her body. Anxious to break the contact, Kerry tossed her hair over her shoulder, pulled her knees up to her chin and wrapped both arms around her long legs. "You said something about needing help," Kerry prompted, hoping to divert Jace's attention to less dangerous ground.

"Doc says you know the Everglades better than anyone else in Flamingo Junction. Is that true?"

"Yes."

"Do you know a fellow named Gator James?"

She turned her head sharply. "Gator? He's just a harmless old man."

"I want you to take me to him. Doc says he's a crazy old coot who roams the swamp planting flowers."

"Not exactly," Kerry said. "Gator was a botanist with a university up north. He had some pretty unconventional ideas and eventually he was fired. That was thirty years ago. Since then he's devoted his life to developing new strains of orchids. He's got four or five small greenhouses throughout the swamp. It's illegal, but he's not harming anyone."

"When's the last time you saw him?"

"Maybe six months ago. He and Uncle Charlie barter occasionally. He's a loner. I'll admit he can be a little strange, but he's a character, not a criminal."

"According to my informant, he's had contact with Burkhardt."

She didn't want to believe that. Not Gator, who'd never had much use for people, but could rhapsodize for hours over his latest hybrid. "He won't talk to you, and even if he does, what help could he be?"

"He might tell me where to find Burkhardt. For the right price—" the glint of a shrewd smile crossed his eyes "—and an introduction from you. Someone he trusts."

"I'm not interested in fighting your war, Jace," Kerry said coldly.

"That's the last thing I want," he replied. "If there was anyone else I could go to, I would. I know Burkhardt's headquarters are somewhere in this area. If James can point me in the right direction, I'll take it from there."

She shook her head.

"You said yourself this guy is harmless. I would never let you be placed in any danger."

She made a swift, dismissing gesture. "That's not the reason I won't help you. I won't lead you to your own execution. If Burkhardt is the cold-blooded killer you say he is, that's what I would be doing."

"I'm not asking for a free ride. I'll pay you twice your standard fee."

Her eyes took on a frigid expression that would have given a less determined man pause. "Money has nothing to do with my decision."

He released a breathy little sigh of weariness. "All right." Jace got to his feet.

He was nearly off the dock before Kerry leaped to her feet and called after him. "Jace!"

He turned. She was surprised by the lack of anger in his eyes. His features were bland and accepting.

"What will you do now?" she asked, afraid she already knew the answer.

"Find Gator James," he answered with a slight shrug.

"How?"

"With a rented boat and the best maps I can find."

"Ridiculous." Kerry's tone was sharp. "The terrain in the swamp is constantly changing. He moves around a lot. You could search for years and never find him."

Jace smiled. "Right now it's the only lead I have."

"You'll get lost out there. Maneuvering through the Glades isn't like a stroll through Central Park. There are other dangers just as deadly as Eric Burkhardt."

"So what are you trying to say, Kerry?" he asked with the edge of exasperation in his voice.

What was she trying to say? She wasn't sure. She didn't like to think of him exploring the swamp on his own, plunging into the dark, shifting marshes of the Glades, blundering into a gator's wallow. He was a civilized man, intent upon traversing an uncivilized world. Jace Warfield might fail to find Gator or Eric Burkhardt, but he would surely find death. Kerry told herself she shouldn't care what happened to this impossibly stubborn man—she told herself—but her heart wasn't listening. It slammed against her ribs with bone-jarring fear.

"I'm saying, don't go." Lost in her own bitter battle with her heart, she added, "Please."

He didn't try to comfort her with meaningless words. "I have to finish what I came here to do, Kerry."

She pinned him with a look that bordered on accusation. "Just what *did* you come here to do, Jace? When you find Burkhardt, what then?"

"Burkhardt has to be brought to justice. He's hurt a lot of people, Kerry."

"You're not John Wayne. You can't bring a man like that in single-handedly."

His gaze touched her, then danced away. "I don't intend to. The local cops may be corrupt, but they're not completely stupid. There are people in Washington who want Burkhardt. If I can find him, they'll put pressure on law enforcement down here to round him up."

"If Washington wants this man, why don't they come down here and get him? Why does it have to be you?"

Because I'm the one J.D. came to for help. And I'm the one who let him down. He couldn't tell her that, of course. Hell, he still had a hard time admitting it to himself. Instead, he let his mouth drift into a smile of mysterious regret. "I've already told you more than I should. Maybe I'll see you around when all this is over. Goodbye, Kerry."

Without being cognizant of her movement, she closed the distance between them. "Jace, wait!" He turned, his eyes roving over her. "I'll help you." The words were out before she could recall them. Once spoken, Kerry realized this was the decision she had come to from the moment he'd asked her to guide him through the Everglades. Foolish to deny it. She couldn't send him out into the swamp alone. She must be mad to entangle herself in Jace's quest for this man Burkhardt. But as much as she wanted to tell him he was on his own, she simply could not do it.

Concern darkened Jace's eyes. He longed to read something vital and revealing in her words. "Why?" he asked at last.

She couldn't tell him that the thought of his coming to harm created a deep ache within her. She couldn't. Instead, she latched on to the first plausible reason she could think of. "I've changed my mind. I can use the money."

She could see too clearly that he found her explanation suspect. He didn't close the distance between them, but nothing escaped his notice. Her confidence bruised, she blushed scarlet.

"Of course..." Jace smiled. "For the money. I'll be back in one hour. Try to be ready."

He turned and crossed the spongy grass in long, quick strides. Kerry watched him drive away, wondering if her peaceful, boring little existence in Flamingo Junction would ever be the same.

That afternoon Kerry took up the controls of the airboat while Jace settled himself into the shallow bow. Under one arm he carried a sheaf of well-worn maps, and Kerry had to smile at that. Gator James's whereabouts weren't likely to be on any of them. She glanced down at the camera case Jace stowed with great care in the driest corner of the boat. Expensive, with the commanding scroll of his initials, JDW, stitched in the center of the leather handle.

His gaze took in the sight of a careworn shotgun wedged against the high rear seat of the airboat, and he gave Kerry a questioning look. "I thought you said this Gator James wasn't dangerous."

"He isn't. I never travel the Glades without a gun."

He acknowledged the wisdom of her words with a short nod, and made no mention of the fact his own fully loaded .38 rode under his belt, its cool hardness comforting against the small of his back.

They traversed the calm, protected waters of the Everglades, cutting through aggressive water hyacinth that competed for space with the tall sawgrass, their first stop Gator James's tar-paper shack. Poised atop stilts in a quiet, hidden lagoon, the old man's home was surprisingly clean and tidy, but vacant. No one had been around in at least a week. Kerry suggested they begin a methodical search of the hermit's temporary camps where he nurtured his beloved orchids.

Jace followed in Kerry's wake as she wove a path through the high grass back to the boat. He wished she would talk to him. The roar of the airboat's engine made it difficult, but in the quiet moments as they tromped through the undergrowth, a little conversation would have been welcome. It might even keep his mind off the fact that the Everglades, with their mysterious coves and wild, shifting landscape, had proven to be far more vast than he'd first thought.

He watched the twist of her shapely hips as she moved around a palmetto blocking the path, and realized he'd never gotten anywhere by keeping silent.

"Are you always this uncommunicative with people who pay for your services?" he ventured.

She looked back at him, her features impassive except for the quick lift of an eyebrow. "People pay me to be their guide, not their friend."

"It might make the time go faster."

She shrugged her shoulders as though it didn't matter one way or the other. "So talk. I've learned to be a good listener."

Her lack of interest bothered him. He discovered the sudden desire to rattle her somehow. "Was your ex-husband one of your clients?"

She flashed him an indecipherable look, then shook her head and favored him with a tight smile. "Not hardly. Edward thinks this part of Florida should be given back to the Seminoles."

"Then where did you two meet?"

"In Miami. I was in nursing school. I went to hear one of our state senators give a speech about the lack of adequate health care in Florida. Edward was his aide at the time, fighting his way up the political ladder."

"And he got off the ladder long enough to marry you."

Her pace slowed, but only for a moment. When she spoke, her voice was matter-of-fact. "He needed a wife. Someone to give his image stability."

"That doesn't sound like a very romantic beginning."

"I suppose it was at first. Edward loves control. I suppose he liked the idea of molding me into someone he could flaunt as totally his creation."

"You make him sound very cold. Calculating."

"Some men are," she stated in a cool, deliberate tone.

He wanted to know more about Kerry's feelings on the subject of men, but he didn't miss the hint she gave him, the way her stride lengthened as she put distance between them. *End of conversation, Warfield.*

Back on the airboat, she took him to every remote stretch of wilderness she could think of, into the deep woods and sandy hammocks where Gator James had created a tropical paradise of aromatic plantings. At each of the makeshift nurseries they saw signs of recent occupation, but nothing to suggest Gator intended to return soon. The Everglades might as well have swallowed the old man.

The sun began to go down on their second day of fruitless exploration, tinting the rippling waterways a brilliant gold and silver. With darkness imminent, Jace reluctantly allowed Kerry to turn the airboat back to Paradise Found.

He thrust aside his disappointment and gave his mind freedom to roam, finding his attention caught once again by his skillful, if somewhat unenthusiastic, guide.

A simple leather thong held her hair away from her face. The thick, shining mass of it teased along her back in playful chaos, catching the last of the fading light like a dark cloud infused with lightning. As always, she wore no makeup, and glaring sunlight on the water had tinted her flesh an even deeper honey-gold. For two days Jace had been fascinated by the sight of her slim strength, the competent glide of smooth muscles as she moved.

She had not encouraged conversation between them again, and he hadn't pushed. She was the only female he had ever met who so easily resisted his attentions. But as unaccustomed as he was to having his advances rebuffed, Jace found it intriguing instead of annoying.

Kerry cut the motor and they scraped against the dock at Paradise Found. She jumped to the planks, tying off the boat with an economy of motion. Jace followed, taking a moment to savor the quiet peace. The surrounding landscape was still, tinged an unearthly rose shade. He looked toward the rising moon, surprised to see that its fullness was a gentle pink. He'd never seen a moon that color before, not even in the deserts of Arizona, where the canyons and mesas could paint the scenery a palette of vivid hues.

Seeing his glance, Kerry said softly, "The locals call it a flamingo moon, after the color of the bird. It happens sometimes when weather conditions are right."

"It's beautiful." Jace slung his Nikon forward and took a few quick pictures. "No camera filter can recreate what nature provides on its own."

Kerry scoffed lightly. "What romanticism from a guy who thinks John Wayne was the ultimate ladies' man."

Jace's moonlit gaze touched Kerry. "Such a skeptic. Don't you believe in romantic atmosphere?"

Kerry's mouth curled in derision. "No. Seminoles believe a flamingo moon means a successful night of romance. The only thing I've noticed is that my animals are unaccountably cranky the next day."

Laughing deep in his throat, Jace's eyes settled on Kerry with a bright, calculating gleam. He lifted his fingertips to her face, stroking lightly across the plane of one high cheekbone and causing a tingle of anticipation to leap along

Kerry's nerves. "You ought to listen to your Seminole ancestors. They might be on to something."

Kerry remained unmoving, struggling to appear poised and unaffected by Jace's touch. "There are scientific reasons for a flamingo moon."

His fingers paused to memorize each hardness and curve along the side of her face, cool and feather-light. Kerry inhaled sharply, unable to manage even one small croak of objection. She was flirting with disaster. She should make him stop. She must make him stop!

"Your skin is so soft and smooth," he murmured, his voice filled with husky longing. "Like pink pearls." His hand slid along the satiny rose-tinged column of her throat. "I'd enjoy teaching you what romance is all about."

She tilted her head back out of his reach and favored him with a dubious look. "I don't need lessons. I know exactly what romantic notions can make a person do."

Jace's features clouded over with regret and a quiet anger. "You sound so cynical. Who stole the romance from your heart, Kerry Culhane? Your ex-husband?"

The flash in her eyes should have warned him. She brought her hand up quickly to capture his, forestalling further exploration. Her vulnerability was painfully obvious, and Jace wished he had not reminded her of the past, and memories better left alone.

"Your money doesn't buy you my life story, Jace," Kerry said sternly. "It's late. Can I assume we're through for the night?"

He stared down at her, watching the glowing luster of her proud features. Desire, quick and hot, rippled through him, and Jace sensed he was perilously close to slipping the boundaries of his own self-control. He wanted to give those sensations free rein, to take Kerry in his arms and taste the warm, sweet femininity of her against his lips.

And Jace knew, as surely as he knew his own name, that to do so would be disastrous.

In a voice barely controlled, he said, "As a paying client, I believe I'm entitled to certain privileges."

"Such as?" she asked with soft venom. Just what did this man think he was entitled to?

He grinned. Her words were frosted with such shards of icy danger that Jace knew her thoughts instinctively. "Dinner."

Chapter 5

While Kerry rattled dinner together in the lodge's kitchen, Jace studied the maps he'd brought from the boat. Every square mile they'd traveled had been crossed off, vivid reminders of how elusive one old hermit could be. After thirty minutes, he shoved them aside in disgust. Burkhardt might die of old age before they found him.

He poked at the fire Kerry had built. He'd been surprised to see such a huge stone fireplace this far south, but she'd told him her father had insisted the lodge have one, if only to keep away the pervasive damp in winter. The flames snapped, spreading comforting fingers of orange warmth across the walls of rough-hewn cypress logs. It was a pleasant room, open and conducive to long conversations or companionable silence.

Photographs taken in the Everglades lined one wall, a near professional quality that reminded him a little of his brother's early works.

The furnishings were heavy, masculine, but there were touches of femininity to be found—fresh flowers in a terra-cotta vase, colorful rugs woven in unique Seminole patterns, a collection of sculpted birds, each of them inhabitants of the swamp. It was easy to imagine guests gathering here in the evening, sharing adventures of the day, before strolling off to their individual cottages.

In front of the fire, Barney lay stretched on the rug. When Jace placed his hand on the dog's head for a friendly scratch, the mutt lifted one eyelid and growled deep in its throat.

Jace smiled. "As prickly as your owner, aren't you, pal?" He let the beast sniff his hand, and the dog offered a tentative wag of its tail.

Lowering himself to the floor beside the animal, Jace braced his back against the couch. With slow, decisive movements he stroked the dog's ears. It continued to watch him warily, but made no move to bite or move away.

Just like Kerry, he thought. Cautious, but curious. Ready to run if need be, but willing to be swayed.

She had said little since he'd invited himself to dinner. Perhaps she'd decided to poison his food. He grinned at that idea, almost hoping he could stir her to such anger. Better that, than to think his presence made little difference to her at all. He hated to admit it, but in Kerry Culhane he might have finally met his match. The idea was damned irritating. And very, very exciting.

With a sigh, Jace closed his eyes, letting his head fall back against the couch cushion. He wished he could give the pursuit of Kerry Culhane his full attention, instead of trying to track down an old geezer who seemed as evasive as swamp mists.

I could sure use your help, J.D. Any suggestions? In his mind's eye he could see J.D.'s easygoing shrug, hear the echo of his chiding laughter. They'd made good partners, so close they often knew each other's thoughts instinctively, so compatible there had been only one argument in twenty years.

Wearily, Jace ran the pads of his fingertips along his eyelids. One argument. Coming on the heels of his Pulitzer, when he was being wined and dined and lauded as the foremost journalist in the nation. He wasn't ready to give up all that glory for J.D.'s sudden interest in an unknown like Eric Burkhardt. So they had argued.

And J.D. had lost.

Drifting into the memory of that last confrontation, Jace willed himself to relax. Lord, he was tired. Along his side the healing wound twinged and nagged like a pestering child, reminding him not to overestimate his recuperative powers. His lips lifted briefly, thinking how Kerry *would* probably finish him off if he undid all her hard work.

Entering the living room to announce dinner, Kerry was brought up short by the sight before her. Jace, relaxing on the floor in front of the fire, his legs crossed at the ankles, his hand flexing rhythmically along Barney's ear. The fire turned his features to sculpted lava, deepening golden highlights in his hair. His chest rose and fell in long breaths; he looked bone weary, despair evident in the slump of his shoulders.

She could guess his thoughts, and in a moment of intense wanting, Kerry wished she could go to him, place her lips along the hollow of his throat, the slight indention where the fire had created a shadowy pool. His flesh would be warm and pulsing and she would make him forget Eric Burkhardt and this foolish pursuit.

She searched for her earlier resentment, but it eluded her. All that remained was a potent desire that made the nerves under her skin flutter. Her heart skidded along at breakneck speed.

Jace's lashes lifted and he looked at her. Their eyes locked. He made no attempt to veil his emotions. Hungry longing burned in his gaze, and Kerry refused to flinch from the sight of it.

Somehow she managed to announce that dinner was ready. Jace uncoiled from the floor, and the moment was lost.

Dinner wasn't going exactly the way Jace hoped. Kerry seemed absorbed in her own thoughts. At first he was content to simply enjoy the sight of her sitting across the table from him, her hair shining blue-black in the dancing candlelight. But watching her, his heart beating in thick, heavy strokes, it occurred to him that he hadn't engineered this invitation just to sit quietly and allow this woman to occasionally toss him that infuriatingly indifferent smile.

"Who took the pictures over the bookshelves?" he ventured.

"I did."

"I like them. Especially the one of the sun burning through the swamp mists."

"Thank you."

"You've got a good eye for detail." Among other things, he added mentally.

She thanked him again, then returned her attention to her plate. That wasn't the reaction he had hoped for—not at all—but he was nothing if not persistent.

"This is delicious," Jace said into the tense silence. "Some mysterious Seminole dish?"

Kerry glanced up. Her mouth softened, losing the stubborn line. "Very mysterious. Veal from the meat counter at the market and frozen spinach."

"Oh."

"Disappointed?"

"A little. I'd like to sample a few native recipes while I'm down here."

She shrugged. "Sorry. I was fresh out of swamp cabbage and gator tail."

"Do you usually provide three meals a day for your clients?"

"Most of the time. Flamingo Junction isn't exactly overrun with a selection of fine restaurants."

"So guests eat and sleep here. You cater to them twenty-four hours a day."

Kerry slipped a bite of veal into her mouth, chewing slowly. What was the man getting at? She didn't trust him for a moment. "That's usually the way it works."

"I'm a paying client."

"I'm taking that on faith. What's your point?"

Jace shrugged. "Seems to me I'd be entitled to bed and board just like anyone else. I noticed a few empty cottages. A real bed would certainly be an improvement over a sleeping bag and a tent."

Her fingers tightened around her fork. So that's what he had in mind. Oh, no. She wasn't stupid enough to have Jace Warfield sleeping within ten miles of her. Because she'd just bet sleeping wasn't what he had in mind at all.

He watched her, an insufferable grin plastered on his face. Kerry smiled back. "My uncle and I are working on the cottages, trying to get them ready for the season. I'm afraid they're not habitable yet."

"Bound to be better than the hard ground," he persisted.

Jace had maneuvered her enough for one day. "Probably not. Mildew gets into everything down here." He looked disgruntled. She asked quickly, "Where are you camped?"

"Just to be on the safe side, I've moved my campsite farther off the beaten track. Near as I can tell from the map, it's a spot called Shark Tooth Hammock. Do you know it?"

Kerry lifted her iced tea glass to her lips to keep from laughing aloud. Did she know it! It was off the beaten track, all right. Everyone in Flamingo Junction knew Shark Tooth was a low-lying sandspit—a soggy marsh during the rainy season and a mosquito nursery in the summer. Great choice, John Wayne!

She tried to summon a look of vague delight. "Yes, I know it. If you'd really like to experience the true Everglades, you should stay right where you are. Explore Shark Tooth a little. I believe there have even been reports of panther sightings in that area. The panther's very rare here, you know."

"Yeah. Kinda like native hospitality," Jace mumbled under his breath.

"I beg your pardon?"

"I said, I haven't seen much of anything out there."

No kidding! Kerry feigned wide-eyed encouragement. "Keep looking."

After that, the tension eased a bit.

With dinner behind them, Kerry began setting the kitchen to rights. Jace cleared the dirty dishes and offered to dry while she washed. She refused his help, and she actually seemed uncomfortable to have him invade this familiar territory. Every time he came close, he could sense Kerry's wariness. Finally, he gave up and drifted into the living room. He settled into the comfortable leather sofa and prepared to wait. If she thought he was going to go away peacefully, she had a surprise coming. He hadn't been able to engineer an invitation to stay in one of the cottages, but he wasn't down for the count yet.

Eventually she joined him, and when he suggested an after-dinner drink, Kerry made no objection. He chose wine, wondering how long he could make one bottle last. Kerry produced a corkscrew, two glasses and bottle of California's finest.

She settled on the couch in that loose-limbed way she had of moving that never failed to arouse him. Firelight sharply defined the planes of her Seminole features. Jace came to his feet to get leverage on the wine cork and it gave up the fight easily. He poured a generous helping into each glass, passed one to Kerry, then offered his own in a clinking salute.

"To my beautiful hostess and guide," he said, his gaze lingering fondly.

Her eyes carried mild rebuke, but Kerry smiled and lifted her glass to meet his. "To my generous, *paying* client," she returned. Her voice held a defiant edge.

Their eyes met in perfect understanding. Jace's mouth tilted upward. Did she really think he could be put in his place that easily?

He turned toward the fire, his senses heightened by a new awareness. His gaze drifted over the mantel to the gun rack. It held three expensive, well-cared-for rifles. He fingered the stock of the piece nearest him. It was engraved with delicately curling initials: KC. It occurred to Jace that this was the first time he'd ever tried to get intimate with a woman who actually owned her own guns. Maybe he ought to rethink his plans for this evening.

He arched an inquisitive look in Kerry's direction. "Yours?"

She nodded. "It was a high school graduation present from my father."

He couldn't suppress a grin at that answer.

"What's so amusing?" she asked.

"My sister got a gold bracelet for her graduation."

"Your sister doesn't live on the edge of a swamp."

Jace didn't miss the offended tone. "True. And that wasn't meant to be a criticism. Actually, I suspect you and Joan are a lot alike."

"How so?"

"You're both stubborn and independent. Very career-minded. Joanie's the third violinist with the Denver Symphony. She won't rest until she's in the first chair."

"Nothing wrong with having a goal."

Jace nodded and took a sip of his wine, then reached out to refill Kerry's glass. "Nothing at all."

"So your sister's a musician, and you're a writer," Kerry mused. "And I think you said your brother is an excellent photographer. That's a lot of talent in one family."

"Good genes."

"Very good genes, I'd say. When you first came to the clinic I went through your wallet for identification. I hope you don't mind, but I looked at the pictures of your family. They look like nice people. Very attractive. Very...blond."

Jace's eyes pierced her with a sudden, sharp look, holding her gaze a shade too long for comfort. Was he offended that she had invaded his privacy? She smiled with a boldness that betrayed none of her inner wariness, unwilling to marshal excuses for her behavior.

After a long pause Jace remarked simply, "They are nice people." Not liking this trend in the conversation, he changed the subject. "I take it you don't have any brothers or sisters."

"No."

"Is your mother still alive?"

"No. She died when I was a child."

"It must have been a strange childhood for you. Just you and your father here in the wilderness."

Kerry stiffened. As much as Jace disliked discussing his family, she found dissecting her own just as uncomfortable. "It didn't seem so at the time."

"Still," he continued, "raising a child alone out here—After your mother died, why didn't your father move to a larger city?"

"He had a business to run." Kerry frowned into the bottom of her wineglass. She didn't want to talk about her father. With a slight feeling of resentment, she realized Jace was very adept at getting her to open up.

"He had a daughter who needed more than alligators for friends and neighbors," Jace said. "What about your education? Interaction with your peers?"

"I wasn't aware that I was lacking in those areas." Frost tinged her voice. "I'm not a savage."

Jace watched a subtle play of emotions cross Kerry's features. He knew he'd inadvertently hurt her with his line of questions, and his heart twisted. He'd only wanted to turn the conversation away from his own home life. But in doing so, he'd trounced on some raw, unforgotten pain of Kerry's own.

"I'm sorry," he apologized. "I didn't mean to sound like I was faulting you or your father's judgment. It's the writer in me. I guess I'm curious why a man wouldn't look for a better life for himself and his daughter. You have to admit, Flamingo Junction has little to offer."

Kerry stared into the hypnotic swirl of her wine. The fire popped as it ate into a pine knot. Barney snuffled in his dog dreams, the only sounds in the tomb-quiet room.

At last she sighed heavily. "Roon Culhanc was an Irish hell-raiser who believed passionately in home rule, and got involved with the wrong people. He was forced to leave Ireland with a fake passport because he was wanted for questioning by the police. When he got to America, my father took a new identity. So you see, he wasn't anxious to draw attention to himself." She chewed her bottom lip. "Like most people who settle in Flamingo Junction. He met my mother and made a life for himself here, but I imagine he worried until the day he died that someone would find out he came here illegally, that he would be deported."

"What did the police in Ireland want to question him about?" Jace asked quietly.

Her eyes found his. "Murder."

Surprised, he asked softly, "Did he do it?"

She shrugged. "I'll never know for sure. But I suspect he did."

"Why?"

"Love. He met a young Irishwoman, and after a whirlwind courtship of two weeks he proposed. She accepted on the condition he'd quit his involvement with the political gang he ran with. By that time, several of the more radical members had committed serious crimes." Kerry downed the last of the wine from her glass. "Supposedly, an argument ensued between my father and the head of the group. There was concern my father's fiancée would give information to the police that would lead to arrests. My father swore that wouldn't happen. All he wanted to do was immigrate to America and start a new life. But a few days later, two members were picked up for questioning in a car bombing. The ringleader was convinced someone had tipped off the police. Less than a week later, my father's fiancée was killed by a hit-and-run driver under suspicious circumstances."

"My God."

Silently Kerry extended her empty glass and Jace refilled it. She took several small sips before continuing. "My father was certain he knew who was responsible. Two days after he buried her, the police put out a warrant for my father's arrest. The ringleader's body had been found, shot to death at close range. My father was the logical suspect."

A long moment passed. Kerry downed the last of her wine, and watching her, noticing the brightness in her eyes, Jace suspected she waited for him to be shocked. Waited for him to be disgusted, almost daring him to find fault with her father.

He wasn't going to condemn the man. He couldn't.

Not when he was as committed to an act of revenge as Roon Culhane had been.

"Your father..." Jace thought for a moment, trying to settle on the right words. "In spite of his past, you still loved him."

She rose in agitation. Leaving the empty wineglass on the cypress knee coffee table, Kerry moved toward the shelf that held the collection of clay animals Jace had noticed earlier. Her features were thrown into shadow. He strained to see her expression. By moving away from him, was she somehow distancing herself from the past, as well?

Absently, she fingered one of the figurines, a snowy egret caught in midflight. In the subdued lighting the bird glowed with a creamy warmth. "My father sculpted these. One a year until my eighteenth birthday. He loved the intricacy of this piece." Kerry suddenly looked at Jace. "Do you think it's possible for a man to love delicate art, to create such beauty and still be a murderer?"

"You don't know all the circumstances. And he was your father—not a saint. Obviously he loved you very much," he replied softly. "That's what you should remember, isn't it?"

"I suppose so," Kerry conceded. "But it makes his whole life a lie, you see. That's the part I hate. Never to have been trusted enough to be told the truth."

She gestured toward the figurines. "He was a gifted sculptor. We had a guest here once, an owner of a large art gallery. He offered to display some of Roon's pieces for sale in New York." She smiled faintly with poignant remembrance. "That was the first time I ever saw my father panicked. He refused so adamantly that the guest left the next morning. It was very embarrassing and I was furious with Father. At the time I didn't understand, but now it makes perfect sense. Before the trouble in Ireland he was an up-and-coming artist, a man with a brilliant future ahead of him. But ultimately revenge was more important to him."

Suddenly uneasy, Jace's features clouded. *You don't understand how powerful hate can be,* he wanted to tell her. He wanted to explain how it could burn inside a person, consuming every thought, every action. Until there was nothing left.

There was so much he wanted to say.

And so much that couldn't be said.

"Sometimes," Jace said at last, in a voice so grimly quiet Kerry's head turned sharply in his direction, "thoughts of revenge are all that keep a man sane after a loss like that."

He witnessed a momentary puzzlement in her eyes, and wasn't surprised when she rejected his words with a look of pure scorn.

"It wasn't worth it. I saw what it did to him. One foolish moment of retribution shattered his entire life."

The conversation was tilting dangerously into territory better left unexplored. "Whether your father committed the crime or not, would you have loved him any less?"

She offered him a tight smile. "No."

"Then that's what you should remember. Nothing else matters now." He frowned, trying to put the pieces of Kerry's past together with the present. "Kerry, how did you find out about your father?"

"After Dad's stroke, my husband happened on the truth and flew down here to tell me." There was a catch in her voice. Embarrassed by emotion, Kerry lowered her gaze back to the clay animals.

"Nice guy," Jace murmured.

"Edward works for the government. He has...ambitions. Skeletons like that in your closet can bring a career in Washington to a screeching halt. Our marriage was already shaky, so Dad's past just put an end to it once and for all."

Her voice was choked with barely suppressed pain. Desperately wanting to ease this hurt, Jace set his wineglass next to hers and crossed the room. Her back was turned toward him, its slim strength bowed in defeat. Too full of emotion to say a word, Jace allowed his hands to settle on her shoulders. She stiffened momentarily, then he felt her frail composure snap. Kerry leaned into him, and the feel of her yielding body nearly undid him. He curved his arms around hers, pulling her back against him, dipping his head to settle his cheek against hers. His usual quick wit having deserted him, he could only continue to hold Kerry, their heartbeats indistinguishable.

"You could never be an embarrassment to anyone," Jace reassured her at last.

"Edward would disagree with you."

"Edward is a first-class idiot. God help us, he'll probably end up president one day." His lips grazed her cheek. It had the texture of warm velvet. "My poor little Night Dove. In some ways, you're one of the strongest women I've ever met. Yet you stay here, hiding as though you were the guilty one."

She turned in his arms to face him, denial leaping like flame within her. "I'm not hiding. This is where I belong."

Jace kept his voice steady only with the greatest effort. "Why? Just because your marriage failed? It doesn't seem to me you lost all that much."

His words shattered the moment of intimacy. Kerry flashed him a look filled with fire. "You don't know anything about it. You've no right to judge."

He ignored that objection. "You could leave any time you want. You don't have to stay here."

"I like The Junction."

"You're safe here," he countered. "Nobody gets too close, do they, Kerry? Nobody disturbs your world. But there are places out there—"

"Do you think I haven't lived in that world? I spent two years trying to fit into the Washington scene."

She drew a quick, steadying breath, and in the depth of her eyes he saw the dark reflection of remembered pain. When she spoke, her voice was calm, yet distant. "At first Edward was determined to mold me into a proper political wife. I tried to be everything he wanted. Making friends with people just because it was 'politically prudent,' ignoring those who couldn't further his career. But I hated it. All the whispers and rumors. Who's moving up. Who's on the way out..."

Her voice drifted to a standstill, and he thought she was barely aware of his presence, that she had withdrawn to a place he couldn't follow. The skin over her cheekbones had gone ashen, and as though he could coax color into them, his thumbs slid along her tense flesh. "I know Washington. It's filled with uptight, power-hungry people. I wouldn't expect someone like you to be happy there," he said softly.

"There just wasn't any room for a small-town girl who didn't know how to play the game and couldn't measure up to the standards they set. Edward never understood or accepted that. We argued constantly. And all the while he was—"

She broke off, pulling out of his grasp to put distance between them. Her hands moved along her arms, as though she were cold. Jace latched on to her, swinging her back to face him before she could shut him out completely. "And all the time Edward was what?"

He'd miscalculated her pride and spirit. She didn't flinch from the truth, but instead, met his gaze squarely. "Having an affair, of course," she said in a tumbling rush. "With someone completely opposite of his half-breed wife. Someone with class and political influence and ancestors who came over on the *Mayflower.*"

It struck Jace with a pang of sadness and fury that there was nothing, nothing he could do to ease this hurt. He shook his head in disgust. "The man was a fool."

"I learned valuable lessons from Edward. I suppose I should thank him."

Jace looked at her skeptically. "What lessons?"

"I can't be anyone but who I am. There are some places I just don't belong. And you can't place your trust in people, no matter how much you want to believe in them. My father. Edward . . ."

"You're wrong, Kerry."

"I don't think so."

"You can't cut yourself off from life."

She frowned in sharp displeasure. "I haven't done that. I've simply found a way to keep life less painful."

He curbed his desire to take her by the shoulders and shake her. Hard. "Sounds very logical. But by avoiding the pain, you're missing the pleasure, too. That's a big mistake."

The wine had left a sour taste in her mouth. How had the conversation taken such an unwelcome direction? She didn't want to argue. Jace had been kind tonight. He was easy to talk to. Maybe too easy. But he was mistaken if he thought he could change her mind. Kerry had worked too long and hard to see her convictions eroded.

"Really?" Kerry retorted. The barest hint of a smile curved her lips to mock him. "Let's take you for instance, Jace. You want my trust, but how honest have you really been? Aren't you still keeping secrets? Just a few?" A weighty silence followed her questions, and although Jace did not try to fabricate an acceptable denial, Kerry could see he felt the bite of discomfort as her words struck a nerve. "When you showed up here two days ago, I should have refused to help you." Her brows knit in thoughtful bemusement. "I keep asking myself why I didn't."

"Kerry . . ." Her name was a plea.

He looked so completely miserable that Kerry almost felt sorry for him. "It's all right," she said. "I'm not expecting explanations. You're paying me very good money to find Gator. That's all.''

The silence became a clumsy barrier. Jace offered no excuses, no confessions. He was not a man given to hiding his emotions, but though she saw weary resignation in his expression, his thoughts were unreadable.

"It's late," she said tiredly. "We need to get an early start tomorrow. Good night, Jace."

With only a whisper of movement, he crossed the room. Kerry felt suffocated by his nearness, forgetting for a moment the cool facade she was striving to maintain. Galvanized by the fear that he might feel compelled to confront her, Kerry began clearing the coffee table of the empty glasses and wine bottle. She could feel his eyes on her, but refused to meet his gaze.

She went into the kitchen and ran water over the glasses. As she turned off the tap, Kerry heard the front door open, then close as Jace let himself out into the night.

Chapter 6

The rented Camaro bounced onto the crushed shell-and-pine needle-covered road that led to Jace's remote campsite. Relocating had been the smart thing to do, just in case Burkhardt's men hadn't given up on finding him, but this far into the Everglades the night was black and damp and unfriendly. The idea of trying to sleep on the cold, hard ground, protected only by the shelter of a nylon tent and a sleeping bag, didn't hold much appeal. Jace sighed. If he'd had his way this evening, he would have spent the night in front of that warm, inviting fire at Kerry's lodge. With Kerry. Snuggled under a blanket and sipping the last of the wine. Making discoveries.

But he'd completely botched that plan. Somehow Kerry had turned the tables on him.

Those eyes. Cool blue and guileless and world-weary beyond her years. If he never had to meet Kerry's eyes, Jace figured he'd be all right. The problem was, the damned woman had a way of looking at him, direct and uncompro-

mising, that made him feel like an errant schoolboy. Only
when he forced her into conversation about her own life did
she withdraw.

It was that straightforward manner of hers, he decided.
A delightful change from most of the women he knew, but
exasperating, too. She didn't trust him. Hell, maybe she
didn't even like him. Maybe he imagined an attraction that
wasn't there. The spark of desire that seemed to arc between them every time they got close might be a wishful
figment of his own imagination.

With piercing resignation, Jace conceded that Kerry
wasn't likely to promote a relationship as long as there were
secrets between them. She didn't deal well with subterfuge.
It wasn't in her nature. He frowned into the darkness, remembering the disclosures she'd made about her marriage,
her father's hidden past. Considering her history, mistrust
wasn't surprising.

The Camaro's headlights picked out the eerie solitude of
his camp. Two pairs of golden eyes winked into the light,
and a pair of raccoons scuttled away. The greedy beggars
had probably ransacked his supplies, but Jace was too tired
and distracted to care. The tent zipped up against the night,
he pulled off his boots and stretched out on the sleeping bag.
With his hands cushioning his head, he stared into the
darkness.

Tomorrow. They'd find this Gator James. They had to.
And then Jace would know what his next step should be.

At that point, Kerry's involvement would end. They'd
talk. He'd tell her the truth. All of it. Even the part likely to
turn her against him. She would understand. He'd make her
understand.

Jace rolled over, pulling the sleeping bag's thick warmth
around him. The wind sobbed through the trees like a lost
child. *Understanding? Who are you trying to kid, Jace?
Kerry might understand why you want Burkhardt so badly,*

might even agree with you, but she'll never forgive you for lying to her. He'd never make her see that he'd distorted the truth for her own good. Kerry would damn him to hell for his deceit, for turning out to be no better than every other man in her life.

Engendering someone's anger had never bothered Jace before. He'd stepped on a few toes over the years, and as an investigative reporter he'd given more than one criminal reason to curse his name. He didn't mind a good fight. A worthy opponent made victory that much sweeter.

Growing up, the three Warfield kids had fought among themselves. But threatened by an outsider, they'd closed ranks. He'd run interference for Joel and Joanie all his life, and never given a damn who got their nose out of joint because of it. And women. Looking back, there were probably one or two who would cheerfully have run him down with their car if they got the chance.

No, he wasn't concerned by the idea that someone might hate him. He just didn't want that someone to be Kerry.

She was becoming too important to him—taking away the emptiness that had begun five months ago, altering the fabric of his life with her smile, her integrity. That infuriating, contradictory behavior of hers that gave Jace hope that maybe, just maybe, she was as lost in the wild turbulence of new emotions as he was.

A spasm of worry crossed his face. No. He'd never willingly take a chance of destroying this tentative bond between them. Instead, he'd make her care. He'd set fire to every nerve in her body the same way she set fire to his. The truth could stay buried a little longer. Until it just didn't matter anymore.

When Jace returned to Paradise Found the next morning, Kerry was at the dock waiting for him, ready to cast off. His eyes met hers in silent inquiry before he jumped aboard.

She offered a luminous smile, evidently having no desire to erode the pleasantry of the morning with reminders of last night's disagreement.

They maneuvered through the brackish inland waterways, cutting noisily through the sunrise mists that cloaked the earth with wisps of white. It was bright, but pleasantly cool. Jace decided he liked the way Florida wound itself down to winter with a clear crispness instead of the bone-jarring cold he was used to in Denver.

Exhilarated, he inhaled deeply. Maybe today they'd get lucky. They were getting close. He could feel it in his bones. Today might be the day. Hell, even Kerry had smiled at him this morning. Things weren't all bad.

But their first stop proved to be a waste of time; they reached a secluded, trackless marsh inhabited by a company of pelicans and little more. There were signs indicating that Gator James had once hacked out a small nursery, but it hadn't been tended in years. The sight of the overgrown camp mocked their efforts.

Back at the airboat Kerry unfurled a map and pointed out their next destination. "There's a fellow named Bill Christian who might be able to help us. He and Gator work for the Parks Department every spring counting gator nests. It's worth a shot."

Jace nodded grimly. Both were aware few places remained to look for the old man.

Witnessing the smoldering frustration in Jace's eyes, Kerry offered, lamely, "Sooner or later, we'll find him."

He gave her a tight smile, but said nothing.

It was almost noon before they reached Bill Christian's camp. Kerry cut the motor and they slid alongside a wobbly dock that staggered out from the land like a kid's erector set gone haywire. It was easy to see that Gator James and this Christian fellow were kindred spirits. They'd built identical tar-paper shacks on the edge of the swamp, and the surrounding area boasted the same ramshackle assortment of rusting metal, boat skeletons and fishing equipment left about the yard like forgotten toys. Jace's nose wrinkled under the pungent smell of boat oil, fish and dead things left out too long in the hot, Florida sun.

He jumped to the dock and it swayed under his weight. Kerry joined him. As he tied off to an anchor cleat held by one bolt, she said in a low voice, "Let me do the talking. Okay?"

He tossed her an arch look. "Why?"

"Bill doesn't like strangers."

"Does anyone like strangers in this neck of the woods?" His tone shimmered with sarcasm.

"Just play the strong, silent type, John Wayne."

He shrugged. "It's your swamp."

They approached the compound slowly, their shoes sinking in the soft, trampled earth of the meandering path bracketed by high grass. Beneath a shelter of trees, a black man stood at a rickety wooden table and he glanced up as they drew nearer. His mouth split into a huge grin. It was a boxer's toothless smile, but friendly enough. He waved at Kerry. Sunlight flashed off the knife he held in one hand.

"Is this guy wanted by anybody?" Jace asked in a low voice.

Kerry looked at him, her features serious. "Not in Florida."

A good-sized turtle lay on the table, upside down and quite dead. The poor creature was methodically being separated from its shell by Christian, the wicked-looking knife slicing through muscle with a quick, chilling expertise. It didn't look like an easy task. The man's obsidian features glistened with sweat. Beneath the corded muscles of his bared arms, veins popped and rolled as he bore down for increased leverage.

"'Lo, Kere. What you doin' out this way? You lost?" The man's soft, lilting speech reminded Jace of rum punches and Calypso bands, but somehow he couldn't picture this man as an advertisement for the Caribbean Tourist Board.

"I started to think I was," Kerry replied. "Took me awhile to find you."

"Don't usually like to be found."

Kerry spent the next few minutes in casual conversation with the man. Jace kept silent as requested; his presence went unacknowledged. He didn't mind.

Huge turtle shells littered the area around the table. One wall of the shack boasted the biggest alligator hide Jace had ever seen. Probably the only thing holding up the miserable little building.

He listened as they talked about fishing and the expected rain and whether someone named Bobby was ever going to convince someone named Maya to marry him. Kerry handled the conversation well. She didn't push for information about Gator James, and her interest in Christian's responses seemed genuine. Jace watched her, noting the clean lines of her profile. He tried to imagine her growing up in this crude environment, having friends whose faces looked as if their pictures ought to be hanging on some post-office wall. In spite of his suspicion that Kerry was hiding out in Flamingo Junction, licking her wounds from a bad marriage, he was amazed by her ability to build a life in such a harsh, unforgiving place. He respected her perseverance.

Jace fixed his eyes on the worktable and tried to recall the last time he'd been interested in a woman who wouldn't faint at the sight of a little blood, the last involvement that hadn't become an endless litany of complaints about the latest fashions or diet talk or petty gossip. He'd always been attracted to women who were soft and unassertive and rather dependent. Funny, to find himself now fascinated by a self-sufficient female, who preferred a simple life-style. And who, he reminded himself, didn't seem to care about him one way or the other.

The mention of Gator's name brought Jace's attention back to the conversation.

"Have you seen him?" Kerry was asking.

"See him all the time."

"Recently?"

"Maybe." Christian's polished onyx eyes flickered toward Jace for the first time, then back to Kerry. "Who's the turon?" There was no meanness in his tone, only curiosity. He laid aside the knife, shoved his hands under the turtle's flesh and pulled. With a sucking pop the creature gave up its fortress.

"A friend."

"You vouchin' for him?"

"Yes."

The man looked at Jace again. "What you want with Gator, mon?"

"Answers to a few questions."

The knife began dissecting the turtle meat into manageable pieces. "You ever had turtle?"

"No."

"No better eatin', mon. Fry up a mess with grits and puppies, you got a feast."

"I believe my friend might be interested in *buying* some," Kerry said. Her glance settled meaningfully on Jace. "He said just the other day he wanted to try a few native dishes."

Jace didn't need to be hit over the head. He'd paid informants often enough in the past to know when a deal was being struck. Fishing out his wallet, he tossed a few bills onto the work-scarred table. A squadron of flies buzzed away for a few moments, then resettled. Jace tried to summon an interested smile. "I'm looking forward to trying some."

Bill Christian flashed the gaped-tooth grin at him. "That so! Well, I cut you a fine piece then." He sliced off a large portion of the unappetizing meat.

Being from Colorado, with its abundance of corn-fed beef, turtle didn't hold much appeal. But Jace made no comment as the man plucked a wad of crumbled newspaper off the ground and slapped the piece into the center of it.

With the proficiency of a butcher wrapping the finest filet, Christian folded the classifieds over the meat and presented it to Jace as though offering a gift. "Gator's in Miami," he provided at last.

"Gator never goes to Miami," Kerry remarked in surprise.

"Gone to talk to some big men up at the college. Them orchids of his is more important then most kinfolk. Said there might be research money for him if he showed his latest pretty."

"When will he be back?"

"Mornin', most likely, if they don't give him the wire brush treatment. You know, Gator even got his hair cut for them guys. 'Spec he'll be madder than a rabid coon if he don't get that money."

"Where's he likely to be tomorrow?"

The last of the turtle meat plopped into a bucket at Bill Christian's feet. "Might try East Duck Key. He's been babyin' them pretties there for three months now."

"Thanks, Bill," Kerry said. "You come by the house soon. I've put up some mulberry jam you won't be able to resist."

"Will do it. You stay out of harm's way." Christian turned his attention to the next turtle scheduled to meet his knife.

Kerry and Jace walked side by side down to the dock. "Interesting guy," Jace commented as he unlooped the rope from its tenuous anchor. "What's a turon?"

Kerry tossed a grin over her shoulder as she jumped aboard. "Local name for strangers. A cross between a tourist and a moron."

Jace scowled.

"Looks like that's all we can do today," Kerry said as they approached the dock at Paradise Found.

Jace didn't reply, but Kerry didn't expect him to. The return from Christian's camp had passed without conversation and she knew the loud roar of the boat's engine hadn't been the only reason. Perched on her seat above and behind Jace, Kerry hadn't missed the dejected slump of his shoulders.

She didn't blame him for being disappointed. The last few days had been frustrating. Used to having her clients happy and excited, or at least satisfied after a day spent in the Glades, Kerry experienced a shadowy sense of guilt over the delay in finding Gator James. If she'd used her head, she might have thought to go to Bill Christian earlier. Jace could have talked to Gator by now, instead of spending the past three days on a wild-goose chase.

Impatient with this sudden lack of confidence in her own ability, Kerry made a disgusted sound. This wasn't her fault, so why berate herself? She cast a sullen glare at the back of Jace's head. The noonday sun glinted so brightly off the wind-tossed halo of his hair it was almost painful to look at. It wasn't natural for a man to have hair like that, she thought resentfully. Just one more thing about him she found annoying.

She wished he would give up this foolishness and go home. There were other criminals in America besides Eric

Burkhardt. Why didn't he go after them? Why did he have to stick around *her* Everglades?

She didn't want him here. In spite of her determination to remain cool and unresponsive, Jace Warfield had the power to turn her world inside out. Every time he came near, she went jittery inside, like a teenager on her first date. It was alarming to realize her mind had so little control over her body. She'd told Jace she wasn't looking for a relationship, and she meant those words. She certainly didn't intend to get tangled up with an unknown quantity like Jace Warfield. If she ever did get interested in a man again, and that was a big *if,* it would have to be someone she trusted one hundred percent. A man who wouldn't try to mold her into someone she could never be. So why wasn't her body getting the message?

Last night, sleep had proven impossible. At first Kerry thought she was still in the grip of her emotions. Reliving past history with Jace had been a mistake, the result of a long, tiring day and too much of the wine she seldom drank. But as she lay in bed tossing and turning, Kerry realized it wasn't her past that kept sleep at bay. It was the present. The remembrance of Jace's hands on her shoulders, the hard warmth of his cheek pressed against hers, the way he could look at her, delve deep into her soul with those hazel eyes, until she went breathless with anticipation.

It was crazy.

Scary.

Yes. He should definitely end his search and go home.

Even as she had that thought, Kerry knew how pointless it would be to voice the idea. Whatever his reasons, he was a stubborn, determined man who wouldn't give up. To get Jace Warfield out of her life, she'd probably have to find Burkhardt herself. Then maybe they'd both know a little peace.

She cut the motor and they drifted toward shore. Kerry studied Jace as he stretched to bring them alongside the dock. Under his shirt the muscles bunched, making the material across his shoulders pull snug, defining the lean, hard strength of his body. She felt her nerves jump. Ignoring him would definitely be a lot easier if he weren't so darn well-built and handsome.

Barney barreled down the grassy slope to dance happily around them as they unloaded the boat. Their arms full, they walked up the slight incline that led to the lodge. At the shelly drive, Kerry turned toward Jace. "I guess I'll see you tomorrow, then. Same time as this morning. We ought to get to East Duck Key by ten."

She turned away and started toward the lodge.

"Kerry, wait."

She swung around, a spark of uneasiness jabbing the base of her stomach.

"How about lunch?"

The spark spread along her insides. She floundered for an excuse to keep him at arm's length. "My pantry's a little low right now," she offered, then chided herself for such a feeble objection. She pointed to the package he held gingerly in one hand. "I could fry up that turtle."

His mouth molded into a smile. "I'll pass. I meant, me taking you to lunch."

"Oh."

"So? Will you go?"

"Well, I have a lot of things to do. . . ."

"Like what? Maybe I could help."

"Like . . ." She latched on to the first lifeline she could grasp— Barney, still snuffling in circles around them like a demented bloodhound. "Feeding Barney. And he needs a bath. And I wanted to get some spring housecleaning done before the season starts. The lodge is a mess."

His look conveyed disbelief, but he pretended to give her objections serious thought. "Well, I think your place looks fine, and Barney's just going to get dirty again, and as for feeding him..." He opened the newspaper-wrapped turtle meat and let it drop to the ground.

Realizing Jace's intent, Kerry began, "I don't think he likes turtle..." then subsided as the traitorous beast zeroed in on the meat and wolfed it down.

Jace's mouth broke into a grin, and one brow lifted to give him a particularly devilish look. "That takes care of that. Anything else?"

With a disdainful grimace, Kerry lifted her chin. "Don't you ever give up?"

"Give up what?"

"Pestering women who don't want to have anything to do with you."

He flashed her a challenging glance. "Don't you think you can handle it?"

Hackles rose. "Of course I can handle it." *And you.*

"Fine. Then it's settled?"

Lunch. Should be easy. What could he do to her emotions over a sandwich and a few potato chips? He'd be wasting his time. "All right."

"Great! I'll be back in thirty minutes to pick you up." He started off for his car at a loping jog.

"Wait a minute!" she called after him. "Where are you going? I can set these things down and we can leave now. The diner in town serves a pretty good lunch."

"I'm sure it does," he called back over one shoulder. "Just give me thirty minutes to get ready."

"Jace—"

He was behind the wheel of the Camaro before she could voice another word. Ready for what? she wondered, watching him spin out of the drive.

Chapter 7

Thirty minutes later, Kerry gazed down into the opened trunk of Jace's rental car, her mouth agape at the sight before her.

A foam cooler held containers of potato salad, coleslaw and baked beans. Maya Nichols's fried chicken took up nearly one side of the ice chest. With a flourish, Jace pulled back a plastic lid to reveal twin slices of Maya's specialty, cheesecake flavored with Amaretto. Kerry's mouth watered even as her senses flared with annoyance. It was plain to see he had more in mind for lunch than a simple sandwich.

"Well, what do you think?" he asked, slamming down the trunk lid.

"You said lunch," Kerry replied accusingly.

He looked genuinely surprised by her reaction. "This *is* lunch."

"*This* is a picnic."

"You still have to eat, don't you?"

"You set me up."

"Maybe a little. I wanted to arrange something special. The woman who owns the diner suggested a picnic. Very accommodating lady."

"I can see I need to have a talk with Maya."

"Are you refusing to go?" The challenge was back in his voice.

She wanted to. For her own peace of mind, Kerry knew she should. But he looked so appealingly boyish standing there. More at ease and happy than she'd seen him in days. Refusing seemed churlish and cowardly. She could handle this. "Why should I refuse?" she responded. "I'm starving. Can we go now, or do you have more surprises to spring?"

She settled into the passenger seat. When Jace got behind the wheel, Kerry was immediately aware of a certain intimacy. On the airboat, the motor's whine had made conversation difficult. But silence now seemed unthinkable. Relax, she willed her stomach muscles. It's just a picnic. You can handle this. You can.

"Where to?" Jace asked.

She glanced at him, her pulse picking up speed at the sight of his shaded features, the heart-melting smile he offered. Close. Too close. "You mean you didn't plan the location, too?"

"How about Shark Tooth? You said it was interesting."

If you find mosquitoes interesting, she thought with a secret grin. "Uh, that area's not very conducive to picnicking. Let's head toward the Park. You might want to take a few pictures at Mrazek Pond."

The drive to Everglades National Park was short, although to Kerry it seemed to take an eternity. She kept the conversation light and general, but she was always aware of Jace seated only a foot away—aware of the limber strength of his hands on the steering wheel, corded thigh muscles as he downshifted the Camaro, the soft, rumbling sound of his voice when he laughed. Her brain refused to concentrate on their discussion, and instead, soaked up every skittering sensation created by his nearness.

They rented a canoe for the afternoon, wedging the foodstuff into the center well, along with a blanket, Jace's camera case and a pair of binoculars. Stroking out from the outfitter's marina, Kerry in the bow of the craft, and Jace steering from the rear, they wound their way along the quiet waterways. She was pleased to note he handled his paddle adeptly, with little wasted motion.

They passed several spots along the shoreline perfect for picnicking, but he urged her on. After rejecting the third one, Kerry shipped her paddle and frowned back at him over her shoulder. "Is there some particular place you're looking for? I'm hungry."

"I'll know it when I see it," he said mysteriously. "Keep paddling."

Kerry made a face at him, but slid her paddle back into the water. She didn't know what he had in mind, but a little hunger wasn't going to weaken her resolve one bit. *I can handle this.*

Paddling through a labyrinth of red mangroves, they came to a shady hammock canopied by mahogany trees. Jace pronounced it the ideal spot and they bumped ashore.

While Kerry spread the blanket, Jace secured and unloaded the canoe. Under her lashes she observed him, liking the way his muscles shifted and bunched, and dismayed that every lithe movement drew a sexual response from within her. The breeze toyed with his hair, that golden hair that was really quite extraordinary. She had to make her attention focus elsewhere, concentrating on setting out food and plastic ware. She hand-ladled ice into foam cups. Anything to avoid watching him.

When he plopped down beside her, she handed him a cup of iced tea. He took it with a grateful look, their fingers touching briefly. "Your hands are cold."

"It's the ice."

"Cold hands, warm heart," he quipped.

"You can lead a horse to water, but you can't make him drink," she shot back.

"Are you implying I led you here for some specific purpose? Other than a simple picnic?"

"There's nothing simple about you. Now, can we please eat?"

Except for occasional sounds of appreciation for Maya's cooking, they ate quietly. Kerry watched Jace out of the corner of her eye, but he seemed genuinely interested in polishing off a third chicken leg, with nothing more up his sleeve than satisfying pangs of hunger. Her nerves began to settle.

When there was nothing left but empty containers, Jace fell back against the blanket, staring up at the trees overhead. "Whew! I'm stuffed." He turned his head. "How about you?"

Kerry stopped replacing the empty cartons into the cooler and glanced at him. In the filtered sunlight his hazel eyes had become liquid caramel, clear and warm and probing. In spite of the afternoon heat, a barrage of shivers went through her. "Me, too," was all she could manage.

"This is a beautiful spot, isn't it?"

"Yes. But so were the others we passed."

"I didn't want anyone invading our privacy."

She smiled at that.

"What's so funny?"

"The Everglades is about as private as you can get. Haven't you realized that yet?"

He sighed. "I'm beginning to. I never dreamed it would be so difficult to find a crazy old coot like Gator James."

"I'm sorry it's taken so long. We'll find him tomorrow."

Jace's hand reached out and ran lightly along her lower arm. Her breath stumbled. Pleasure flared at the contact.

"You have nothing to apologize for. I never could have found him on my own. I seem to be getting deeper and deeper in your debt." His fingers drifted down, tracing feathery patterns across the back of her hand. "You know, there's a part of me that doesn't want to find this James fellow."

"Why?"

"Because your involvement will be over. I'll be on my own."

His touch, barely perceptible, sent electric currents ricocheting through her, so thrilling that she barely suppressed a shiver. She tried for a nonchalant expression. "You'll manage."

"I'll miss having you for a sidekick," he said in a soft, throaty voice.

A victim of nerves, Kerry forced a laugh, using her scornful expression as an excuse to withdraw her hand from his reach. "Do you want dessert?" she asked, anxious to attain safer ground.

"Still too full." He sat up. "Why don't you show me this pond you think I'll find so interesting?"

Glad for an excuse to move away from Jace's distracting nearness, Kerry plucked the binoculars off the blanket and rose. "Great idea. I'll teach you how to bird-watch." She slipped away from him. "Bring dessert," she called over one shoulder.

They wound their way down to the pond, trekking through mangrove forests and a narrow saw-grass prairie. Mrazek was one of the more popular spots in the park, but on an off-season weekday like today, there wasn't another human being in sight. Kerry found a grassy opening along the water's edge, a spot where the trees hugged the shore-line and created a cool, private place.

She sat down, drawing her legs up so that her elbows rested on her knees. Jace followed her example. "Well? Isn't it terrific?" she asked in a low voice.

"It's small," he observed.

"Of course it's small. It's a pond. But be quiet and watch."

In a short time, Jace began to see why Kerry liked Mrazek. It was a photographer's paradise. With a telephoto lens, he captured on film ibis, pink roseate spoonbills and hundreds of other spectacular species that Kerry supplied names for. The birds fished and fought and called noisily to their neighbors. He used up the film he'd brought and wished for more. As a journalist, he recognized a good nature story and he felt a pang of bitter regret that J.D. was not here to participate.

Beside him, Kerry remained silent and helpful, nudging his knee to hand him the binoculars when she spotted something he shouldn't miss. He began to see how she could love the Everglades. In spite of the heat and mosquitoes, it had an elemental beauty that reminded him of the disappearing wildness of the West.

Surreptitiously, he stole a glance at Kerry. In the dappled sunlight her face was soft, but her features had never looked more Seminole to him. There was striking individuality in the understructure of bone, the proud tilt of her head. Her hair sifted down her back like a midnight stream, straight and silky. Against the soft-worn fabric of her blouse, her breasts rose and fell gently. She was relaxed now, where before she had been nervous and wary.

In his throat, Jace felt the percussion of his heartbeat.

"Look over there," Kerry said softly, pointing to a clump of buttonwood trees,.

It was a distraction he welcomed. She handed him the binoculars and he brought them to his face quickly, knowing the longing he felt would be blatantly obvious. He tried to concentrate on the flock of blue herons squabbling in the trees, but all he could see were Kerry's eyes.

She could tell Jace liked the subtle beauty and quiet peace of the pond. She felt more comfortable with him now than she had all day. Away from their tense search for Gator James, he was finally allowing the Glades to work its magic on him.

His delight pleased her. Edward had hated the Everglades. Her father had tolerated it. Sometimes Kerry felt only she and her Seminole relatives recognized the true beauty and power of the swamp. She watched Jace's mouth quirk into a smile beneath the binoculars, and she felt a warm flush of pleasure steal over her. As though aware of her perusal, he turned to look at her. Some deeper emotion sparkled in his dark eyes for the briefest of moments before he turned his attention elsewhere.

He opened the plastic container containing Maya's cheesecake and offered Kerry a slice. "The perfect ending to a lovely afternoon," he said, slipping out his own wedge. "We'll pretend it's wine."

"You'll think this is better than wine," Kerry predicted. The cake was firm enough to eat without a fork. She nipped off the pointed end, letting the nutty sweetness slide around her tongue. The taste of it made Kerry close her eyes with delight. "Mmmmm..."

"You're right," Jace agreed. "Much better than wine." He laughed around a mouthful. "No one back home would believe me if I told them I spent an afternoon sharing cheesecake in a bird sanctuary with a beautiful woman."

"It doesn't seem strange to me." And surprisingly, she meant those words. It felt natural to be here with Jace, alone on the edge of the swamp, as relaxed and peaceful as she could ever remember being.

He finished his dessert. Although Kerry savored every morsel, she was still full from lunch. One lone bite of cheesecake remained and she caught Jace gazing longingly at it.

"Did you want the rest of this?" she asked.

"Only if you don't," he said, trying to sound only mildly interested.

"Go ahead," she encouraged, extending it toward him between thumb and forefinger. "I can't stand to see a grown man beg."

He grinned his thanks, then shocked her by guiding her hand toward his mouth. His lips closed around her fingers, cheesecake and all, as his tongue slipped forward to lave the creamy delicacy farther into his mouth. Kerry's breath slipped a notch. The act was warmly sensual. Consummately erotic. And when the last bits of cheesecake had been licked away, Jace's tongue continued a gentle exploration along the tips of her fingers. Sliding along their length, then replacing it with his lips to press soft, nibbling kisses across the fleshy pads. Sensation shimmered within Kerry, even as caution whispered into her brain.

"What . . . are you doing?" she managed at last.

"No napkins," Jace replied in a husky murmur.

"We can wash our hands in the pond."

"We could," he agreed lazily. "But I like my way better. Don't you?"

Yes. . . . No! Unable to manage an appropriate response, Kerry remained silent. Their gazes met in quiet communion, and they studied each other, long moments broken only by the sounds of the birds at the pond and a flirtatious breeze sifting through the trees. Jace's eyes were filled with wanting and need. She knew her own must be wide and startled, yet she was no longer afraid. He must have sensed her acceptance of his touch, because his mouth lifted in a small smile. "Kerry, this is crazy...." The words whispered against her captured fingers.

"I know."

His lips found the inside of her wrist, connected with the pulse thrumming to life there, but his eyes never left hers. "Wonderfully crazy."

"Yes..." She gasped as his mouth found the inner bend of her elbow and he drew swirling patterns across the delicate flesh.

"What should we do, little Dove?"

"That feels nice," Kerry remarked dreamily.

He chuckled, then tipped closer to drop a kiss at the corner of her sun-warmed mouth. "And this?"

"Very nice."

His lips drifted across the distended fullness of hers, seeking entry. She welcomed him, eager to sample the heat of his kisses. With a whisper of urgency she called his name, wanting his mouth on hers, and he obliged, kissing her again and again. His tongue stole between her teeth to tease with wild hunger—a tantalizing invitation. He tasted of almonds and lemon and the hot spice of passion too long denied.

Gently he pushed her backward to the grass. His muscled chest pressed hard against her. His fingers brushed along the tops of her breasts, caressing, impatient as he sought to free them from her blouse. Her breath quickened at the invasion, and Jace's hand stilled immediately. Eyes gone dark and heavy-lidded with desire searched hers. "Relax, sweet Kerry. Invite me in," he implored her. "I won't go any further than you want me to. I swear it."

You've already gone too far, she wanted to protest, but Jace's touch, though light and undemanding, vanquished all thought, wobbling the earth beneath her resolve. Anticipation shot through her. Kerry's body refused to take orders from her brain. Already her arms were slipping over his shoulders, eager to draw him closer. Already her hips arched to meet his, begging release from sweet torture.

His lips trailed fire up the arch of her throat. He found the delicate curve of one ear and nuzzled the soft lobe, then explored the inward swirl with his tongue until her stomach contracted and her heartbeat pumped faster, as though her blood had been infused with a new, richer mixture. "Want me, Kerry...." Jace's voice came quietly, thickly, a low groan of pleasure. "Want me the way I want you."

She did want him. Needed him. This man, so unlike Edward, so unlike any man she had ever met, made Kerry feel alive for the first time in years. She gave free rein to endless possibilities. Perhaps she wasn't too unsophisticated for Jace. The very differences that had shattered her marriage seemed not to bother him at all.

"I want..." Kerry's voice faltered as her will dissolved inside Jace's embrace. Such clever hands. Touching her breasts with featherlike strokes one moment, scorching patterns across the engorged peaks the next. His lips still exploring the curve of her throat, Jace's fingers separated her blouse. She felt the cool caress of fresh air, then his hands glided downward to warm her rib cage. Her body quivered in response.

Lost in tumultuous feelings, Kerry was barely aware when he levered his upper body away to look down toward his hands. "What's this?" he asked in a voice hoarse with desire.

She glanced down, realizing Jace had encountered the sheathed knife she always carried under her blouse. It was part of her wardrobe, a necessity in the Glades, and it was often forgotten until she undressed for bed. Small, but sharp, it served Kerry handily.

"Not meant to discourage *me,* I hope," he teased, amusement lacing his tone.

"I forgot to take it off when we got back this morning," she said, wondering why she felt the need to explain a habit she'd always considered good sense. At her reply, she felt laughter rumble through his body. "What's so funny?"

His mouth nipped at her throat in a trio of playful kisses. "I expected to encounter a bra, not a knife."

Like a bath in freezing water, Jace's words doused Kerry's ardor. The torch of passion he'd ignited fizzled. She knew he found her desirable. But though he might want the momentary release of casual sex, would he ever come to think of her in terms of a deeper involvement? The truth was, she suspected that in the blond, ordered existence of his life, she had no place.

What did it matter? Kerry asked herself. She liked Jace, but she wasn't looking for a relationship. Certainly not marriage. A quick, temporary interlude held the promise of pleasure for two mature, consenting adults. So why had the excitement ended? Why did this bitter knowledge drive a wedge of pain into her heart?

You want more. More than Jace will ever want or be able to give. Foolish Kerry. Don't be so greedy. But she couldn't help herself. For one final moment she savored the feeling of his embrace, before she reassembled her mind, attempting to gain control of her emotions.

He sensed her withdrawal. His hands ceased their delightful magic and his eyes lifted in frowning confusion. "What is it, Kerry?" When her gaze slid away, he brought his fingers to her chin. "I meant what I said, little Dove. Whatever you want. Tell me."

You. I want you. Heart and soul. Always. Embarrassed by unexpected emotions, stunned to recognize this felt an awful lot like love, Kerry flushed scarlet and squirmed beneath him. *I can't be in love with him. I can't.*

Jace interpreted her uneasiness as rejection. "It's all right, Kerry," he said quickly. His hands stroked the hair away from her brow. "Calm down. I won't hurt you."

He pulled away and sat up. She followed suit, rebuttoning her blouse. Jace's back was to her, and Kerry placed a hand on his arm. She felt the hard muscles jump and tense. He didn't acknowledge her touch. His profile might have been carved from stone.

"Jace, I'm sorry. I didn't mean—"

His fingers were suddenly against her lips as he swiveled to face her. In his eyes lay a shadowy pool of regret and frustration, and maybe the tiniest bit of hurt. "Don't." His voice was rough, but surprisingly tender. "My fault. I have to keep reminding myself what a low opinion you have of me."

She felt her cheeks go white with sudden crystallized perception. He believed she still distrusted him. How could he think that! Couldn't he feel the way her body responded to his slightest touch? Her misgivings lessened every day she knew him, giving way to deeper understanding, closer friendship. She couldn't remember the last time she'd been able to be close to him without her heart banging against her rib cage. With a kind of surprised anger, she wondered how he could be so blind.

"Jace..."

Before she could say anything more, he stood, brushing bits of grass from his jeans. "It's getting late. We should get back."

He kept his tone carefully neutral, and he thought with wry regret that it was the *only* thing he could control. Willing his limbs to relax, his pulse to settle, took longer. A lot longer.

He offered his hand, and Kerry felt so miserable to see the afternoon end on such an unsatisfactory note, she did nothing but allow him to draw her to her feet.

* * *

Please let Gator be here, Kerry prayed as they reached East Duck Key. If Bill Christian's tip didn't pan out, she didn't know where they'd go. Jace would have as much luck sticking pins in a map while blindfolded. He had yet to criticize, but Jace probably thought she was the most inept guide who ever had the gall to hang out a shingle.

At least he was still speaking to her. In spite of yesterday's awkward moments, their relationship hadn't changed. They remained friendly and excited by the prospect of finding Gator James at last.

Yet Kerry was restless. Another sleepless night behind her, with no answers to the questions that continued to plague. Her emotions felt stretched to near-breaking point.

Could she be in love with Jace Warfield? A man she'd known for such a short time?

Impossible. *He's not my type at all.*

Unthinkable. *It would never work out between us.*

Illogical. *We belong to two different worlds.*

Oh, God, how could I have let this happen to me!

Kerry pulled back on the throttle. Shading her eyes against the morning sun, she scanned the overgrown shoreline. When she saw the boat bumping against the grassy hammock, her heart went into trip-hammer rhythm. "There!" she shouted over the low roar of the engine. Jace had seen it, too. He straightened, then shot her a questioning look. She nodded. "It's his!"

They slid against the shelly sand and Jace pulled the airboat out of the sluggish current. Together they approached the yellow skiff. Using her hands as a megaphone, Kerry called the old man's name. Her voice ricocheted off nearby slash pines, startling a flock of herons from their roosts, but garnering no response.

"He's probably so wrapped up in his work he can't hear us," Kerry said, nodding toward a meandering path that led deeper into the brush. "Shall we see where that goes?"

She led the way along the trampled grass trail. The undergrowth became thicker, more determined to block their passage. Palmetto fronds slashed at their legs, and in some places the vines were so possessive of the trail that Kerry and Jace had to duck to proceed. They left bright sunlight behind, as overhead the tall pines formed a cool, quiet tunnel.

At last the path widened into a shady clearing. "Gator?" Kerry called again. "It's me, Kerry Culhane. Anybody home?"

There was no answer. Like the rest of the old hermit's camps, this one seemed deserted. Numerous plants in every kind of pot imaginable—coffee cans, plastic jugs, a discarded sink—cluttered the area. The scent of orchids hung in the air, rich and heady. A wobbly table made of driftwood stood beneath a pine, and a few feet away a lean-to had been erected. In the gentle breeze its blue plastic roof lifted with a crackling whisper.

"There's probably another camp like this close by," Kerry said. She ambled off toward a row of potted orchids suspended at eye-level beneath an arbor made of discarded wood and chicken wire. "He'll come back here sooner or later."

Jace wandered over to the table. A loose-leaf notebook, grubby and filled with copious scribbling, lay on it, the pages fluttering slightly. He flipped to the last entry. It was dated today. Excited relief filtered through him. Gator James had to be close by.

Kerry lifted the petals of a flowering orchid to her nose. "Mmmmm . . . come over here and smell this."

With an indulgent smile, Jace glanced her way, his interest caught by the sight of her, the irresistible lure of Kerry's lips, parted just slightly. Just enough to make a man imagine there could be invitation there. The dark fall of her hair lay in silky torrents down her back. She looked beautiful among the flowers and dappled sunlight. Innocent, yet decidedly sexy.

His gaze raked along her body. He felt the renewed stirring of his manhood, such quicksilver heat that he nearly lost his grip on reason. He was making himself crazy inside, wanting her. But even if the lady had been agreeable—and yesterday's fiasco had shown she definitely was not—this wasn't the place for romance. Before he embarrassed himself with a blatant display of male interest, Jace looked away.

An icy numbness clutched his belly when he saw the blood.

The pine beside the table was a monstrous relic of the past, as thick as two men standing abreast. The bark was scarred and ravaged by wild animals, and as Jace drew closer, he realized his initial suspicions had been right. Blood. A wet, weeping smear of it across its gnarled trunk,.

He paced forward with measured tread, wishing he could rid himself of the cold, hollow dread that had settled within him. Instinctively, he slipped a hand into the small of his back to remove his gun. Inches away from the ugly stain, Jace's peripheral vision caught sight of a patch of yellow, its brightness out of place amidst the greens and browns of the hammock. He rounded the trunk.

At the base of the pine lay a man, his head thrown back, his arms and legs sprawled in an awkward pose of death.

Jace knew they'd finally found Gator James.

Chapter 8

The road back to Flamingo Junction from the county sheriff's office was like all those in this part of the state—boring and arrow-straight. Dry scrub grass hugged the pavement on both sides and stands of pines dotted the sparse emptiness. Brahman cattle, raised by Seminoles at Big Cypress Reservation, regarded the Camaro's passage with lazy disinterest.

Surreptitiously, Jace glanced at Kerry, wondering if she was even aware of her surroundings. He worried about her. She was a tough lady, but Gator's death had shocked her. Since leaving the sheriff's office, she'd been silent. What was she thinking? Feeling? He hated the thought she might hold him responsible. Or that she regretted supporting the story he'd given Sheriff Crant.

The old man's death had been reported and their statements given. They told the police they'd come on the body by accident, that Kerry had been hired to escort Jace around the swamp for an article he was writing. The sheriff seemed to accept that explanation.

The long afternoon of waiting put them both on edge. They were relieved when the police eventually returned from the hermit's camp with their report. Gator James had been murdered by one shot to the heart. No immediate suspects, no witnesses. Kerry and Jace were free to go, but should remain in the area should they be needed for further questioning. Anxious to be away, Jace hurried Kerry into the car.

There was no doubt in his mind that Eric Burkhardt had ordered the old man's execution. There had been no attempt to make it appear a suicide. No gun. No note. Murder, plain and simple. Was the killer getting careless as he tried to sever ties that might harm him? Jace wondered. He'd better reevaluate his options and find Burkhardt soon. Right now, tired and dispirited, he couldn't think. But sooner or later, the two men would meet. He'd made that promise to J.D. months ago, and nothing would stop him from keeping it.

Jace stopped for gas in Flamingo Junction before they made the turnoff to Paradise Found. While he pumped fuel into the tank, he watched Kerry through the dusty back window of the Camaro. She hadn't moved. She sat staring out the passenger window, her body frozen in misery. Fear curled through his gut. He wanted to offer her words of comfort, but he sensed that whatever he said would only make it worse.

He got back into the car, and when Kerry gave no indication she was aware of his presence, he asked, "Are you all right?"

"Yes."

She's sorry she supported me back there. I asked her to, and she did, but now she's having second thoughts. It registered that he hadn't won Kerry's trust yet—not completely—and that knowledge left Jace feeling disappointed and unaccountably sorry. "We couldn't come clean with Crant," he said into the silence.

She didn't seem to notice the intensity of his tone.

"I've told you, he can't be trusted."

"I know," she agreed, not bothering to glance his way. "Sheriff Crant doesn't exactly have a sterling reputation in Flamingo Junction. He's never been caught doing anything that would get him fired or arrested, but that's probably because no one's bothered to look real close."

"Then . . . what?" Frustration made his words abrupt. "What are you thinking, Kerry?"

She turned to look at him then, with eyes that were suddenly old and dull with pain. "I've known Gator James all my life, but I never knew whether James was his first name or his last." Her throat closed on the words and it was a long moment before she could continue. "You'd think a person would take the time to find out something like that."

She hurt. He could hear it in the rawness of her voice, see the strain in tense muscles along her jawline. A knife blade of anguish twisted into his heart and made him feel ashamed. He'd done this to her. His interest in her as a woman had blinded him to common sense, had made him involve Kerry in his private war. It had been a mistake from the beginning.

Silence slid between them. No words of remorse came from Jace's lips. Nothing he said could change the situation. With his eyes still on the road, he did the only thing he could think to do. His hand drifted across the seat to find hers, desperately taking advantage of her stunned inertia. Her flesh was cold; the bones felt fine, like fragile porcelain. An awesome gladness filled him when Kerry made no move to pull away. His hand cradled hers, and after a long moment, she twined her fingers in his. Aching emotion dammed his throat. Forgive me, he begged silently. *I never meant to hurt you like this. I never wanted you to share my hate.*

He wanted his touch to be a balm, a communion of support, and perhaps he succeeded, because after a time, though she continued to remain silent, some of the tension seemed to leave her.

Dark had fallen by the time they reached Kerry's home. No pink flamingo moon tonight. The moon flitted bashfully behind clouds, painting the landscape with pale, eerie light. Barney trotted out to greet them. Kerry gave the dog an effusive hug, as though glad to find a friend in the darkness.

Jace wanted to be with her tonight, but he couldn't quite drum up the courage to ask. When she straightened, he said, "I'll talk to you tomorrow, Kerry. Get some sleep."

She nodded. "You too. Good night, Jace."

Disappointment filtered through him as he climbed back into the car. But before he could pull away, there was a light tap on the passenger window. He leaned over and rolled down the glass.

Kerry offered a tentative smile. "How about some coffee?"

At the sheriff's office they had both drunk endless cups of coffee. Whatever Kerry's reasons for this invitation, it wasn't the need for more caffeine. And it didn't matter.

"I'd like some company," she added by way of explanation. "Barney's not much on conversation."

He wouldn't examine her motives any deeper. Relief came with the knowledge Kerry wasn't directing her anger and hurt toward him.

He shifted the Camaro into Park and got out.

In spite of his protests, she made dinner. Over steaming omelets they talked, keeping the conversation general. By unspoken agreement, neither mentioned Gator's death or the long day spent with the police. As though by avoiding the subject they could somehow change the outcome.

Afterward, Jace insisted on drying the dishes she washed. Silently they worked side by side. Annoyed to discover nerves shimmering along her spine every time their shoulders touched, Kerry was grateful for the steaming heat that curled upward from the sink to alibi the color in her cheeks.

By the time they finished, it was nine o'clock. Kerry realized suddenly it was Tuesday, the night she and Charlie played cards, yet he hadn't shown up. Had he come to the lodge, suspected she had company, then left? She should go and apologize. Besides, he'd liked Gator. He'd want to know what had happened.

Pulling the dish towel through the refrigerator handle, Kerry glanced at Jace, who was trying to coax Barney into sitting up for a dog biscuit. "Can you entertain yourself for a few minutes? I want to walk over to my uncle's cabin. I should tell him what happened to...what happened today."

"I'll come with you."

"There's no need. It's just through the woods behind the lodge. I often take a late-night walk."

"Not tonight," Jace replied firmly.

She flashed him a surprised look. Was he just being gentlemanly? Or implying it wasn't safe?

She started to protest, then subsided. She'd seen that determined look before. Without further argument, Kerry allowed him to hold open the front door as she pulled a colorful Seminole jacket from the coatrack. Barney bolted out the front door with them, eager for an evening romp.

The path was wide and straight. So familiar. Kerry loved the peaceful secretiveness of the tall trees, the pungent smells of damp leaves and raw earth that flooded the senses, the muted stirring of night creatures. Even the rustle of undergrowth beneath her feet sounded like playful, whispering children.

No. That wasn't true anymore. The swamp was no longer playful *or* peaceful. She'd tried hard all evening to shelve the memory of Gator's death, but it flared again with painful insistence, raising goose bumps along her arms. Why Gator? He was just a harmless old man. The Glades, never hospitable and often deadly, had always encouraged secrets. Unpredictable. Wild. But never had it brought death so close to her door. It seemed suddenly alien to her.

A cool breeze kissed her cheeks like a lover's caress, and Kerry lifted her face to encourage its touch. She didn't want to think about today, the way she'd skirted the truth with Crant, a man Jace had told her he didn't trust. The hard, flat intonation of the sheriff's voice had angered her, and seemed to relegate Gator to some forgotten notation on a police report. The old man had deserved better than that.

Deliberately, Kerry turned those thoughts away and slid a glance at Jace beside her. He looked distracted. She wondered where his thoughts had taken him. The sensitivity he'd shown today surprised her, his depth of understanding for her feelings, at the sheriff's office and later on the drive back home, leaving her more confused than ever.

But death and secrets and Jace Warfield walked hand in hand. His presence here wreaked havoc on her life, her friends, everything she'd tried so hard to build for herself. She had known it would be difficult for her heart and mind to find common ground when it came to her involvement with Jace, but instead of coming to terms with *any* of it, she did her best to keep her head buried in the sand. Such cowardice annoyed her.

Through the lacy curtain of branches overhead, Kerry counted stars, wondering if ever again she'd know tranquility in her life.

* * *

His legs stretched before him, Jace lounged on the top step outside Charlie Longtooth's cabin. Barney shambled up, and with a whine, plopped down beside him. Sensing Kerry might want to break the news of Gator James's death to her uncle alone, he had decided not to intrude on their privacy. Although he and Longtooth exchanged polite greetings, he recognized an aloofness in the older man more than just Seminole reserve. The Indian's dark, solemn eyes had raked him up and down, and Jace knew he'd been found lacking.

Absently he stroked the silky fur behind the beast's ear, wondering when Kerry would come out. Wondering if there was a chance in hell he'd be able to mend the damage. Not likely. Maybe if he explained to Kerry—

Jace hurled those thoughts away. What was he thinking! He couldn't involve Kerry in his life any longer. Not now. Maybe not ever.

The plans he'd made months ago lay at his feet like dusty autumn leaves. Gator James's murder rested uneasily on Jace's conscience, adding to the burden blanketing his shoulders—a stifling cloak of guilt. Nothing was working out the way he'd anticipated.

Certainly not his involvement with Kerry Culhane. And before *she* became Burkhardt's victim, he had to end their relationship, once and for all.

The cabin door opened with a creak of protest. He stood as Kerry came out, followed by her uncle. She waved farewell to the older man and Jace nodded goodbye. Charlie Longtooth dipped his head in acknowledgment, but didn't smile.

With her head down and her hands rammed into her jacket pockets, Kerry started down the path. Her stride was purposeful, preoccupied. Frowning, Jace fell into step beside her. Was she angry? Upset? What had Longtooth said to her? His mind took up a restless chase for answers.

"Everything all right?" he asked.

"Yes."

"What did your uncle say?"

"About what?"

"About Gator."

"He knew."

"How?" he pursued with straightforward diligence.

"Doc called. And swamp grapevine has spread the word."

"Is that anything like sending smoke signals?" Kerry's lack of communication created a gnawing disquiet, but he wouldn't give up without a fight. Unfortunately, he didn't know who or what his opponent was. *Come on, Kerry. Talk to me.*

She tossed him a sharp look. "By tomorrow morning the entire county will know what happened to Gator."

"So?"

She snapped to a halt, her eyes cutting to the depth of him. "You believe Burkhardt killed Gator, don't you?"

"Yes."

"Then, doesn't it seem likely Burkhardt will disappear now?" Her tone told him she considered his lack of understanding irritating. "Everyone in town is going to be suspicious. First that man in the Park, now Gator. Sheriff Crant's been forced to start a full investigation. Burkhardt would be crazy to stick around."

Some of his uneasiness receded. She wasn't angry with him. Just worried Gator's killer would slip away. Justice wouldn't be served. Jace understood that emotion. Far too well.

He shook his head, offering her a small smile of reassurance. "That's not going to happen."

"Why not?"

Jace lifted two fingers. "Two very good reasons why Burkhardt isn't going anywhere. One, he's developed a reputation as a man who laughs openly in the face of danger. If he turns tail and runs, he'd lose respect. His ego would never allow that. Two, this is the biggest deal he's ever made. Even if he wanted to, he can't pull out now."

"How do you know all this about Burkhardt?"

"My informant."

"Then, why don't you go to your informant," she said logically, "and have him tell you where to find Burkhardt?"

Jace's heartbeat became uneven. *Oh, God, I wish I could. I'd listen, J.D., I swear I would.* "I can't. He's dead." Bitterness like an acid etched his tone.

Stunned, Kerry watched as mingled rage and pain crossed Jace's face. His informant. Gator. How many others had died? She looked away, sensing this wasn't the time to ask questions. She tried to center her attention on Barney scratching through dead leaves on the trail ahead. Tried to make the dog the focal point of her reality.

Jace stared at Kerry's moonlit profile. Emotions warred on her lovely face. She looked battered—as tired and helpless as he felt inside. Silver edged her features, and he caught the sparkle of unshed tears.

"Kerry, we have to talk...." If he didn't tell her the decision he had come to now, he might never get the words out.

She turned tortured eyes to him. "Why did he have to kill Gator, Jace? He was just a..."

The sight and sound of her pain slipped past his defenses. He gathered her to him, and when she dived deep into the shelter of his arms, Jace knew he was in trouble. Holding on to Kerry Culhane and his common sense just never seemed to go together at all. He tried to tell himself this was right. She needed comforting now. But even as his mind justified this action, a lacerating contempt for his own weakness filled him.

Like two children lost in inhospitable darkness, they clung together, drawing strength from one another's nearness. She didn't cry, but he heard the difficulty of her strangled breathing. With desperate tenderness, his hands moved along her back in anxious, consoling motions. His lips sifted through her hair, planting kisses between a soft litany of regret. "I'm sorry, Kerry. Forgive me. I never thought Burkhardt would kill the old man. I swear it."

They stood together for a long time, until her breathing calmed. Warm and pliant against him, Kerry's scent filled Jace's nostrils, her lips brushed the hollow of his throat. He stood frozen. Unable to move or speak, his best intentions evaporated under the delicious feel of Kerry's body pressed to his.

"What can we do, Jace?" Kerry murmured against his throat. "We can't let him get away with this."

We. The word hit him like a two-by-four between the eyes. What was he doing? He stiffened, putting distance between them before his resolve floundered completely. His mind rummaged hastily for the right words, then realized that the truth, no matter how sharp-edged and painful, was the only acceptable explanation.

"Kerry, I made a mistake," Jace began. "I shouldn't have brought you into this. I had my own selfish reasons, but it's not too late to put it right. I want you out of this. Now."

"What do you mean?" Surprise spiked her tone.

"I mean, your involvement is over."

"Because of Gator?"

He nodded. "I won't risk your safety."

"I can take care of myself."

The last word landed harshly, a sure sign Kerry found his decree difficult to take. She looked hurt, but he clamped down on the impulse to draw her into his arms once more and prepared to deal with her objections. "I know you can," he agreed in a reasonable tone, "but that's not the point. This has never been your fight."

"You made it my fight. You hired me to do a job."

"Which you did. Tell me how much I owe you and I'll settle up now. Tonight."

"I don't want your money," Kerry snapped, letting the syllables fly like sparks. "The job isn't over. We found Gator too late. But we can still find Burkhardt."

Jace sighed. "In that case, you're fired."

Her gaze narrowed in that dark, menacing expression that made him feel like he'd just latched on to the tail end of an alligator. Anger flashed in her eyes. Beautiful. So beautiful. His arms ached with the effort it took to keep from pulling her into them.

She smiled suddenly, and he was immediately suspicious.

"Suppose I told you," she said in a soft, goading voice, "that I know exactly how to find Eric Burkhardt."

The more
you love romance . . .
the more
you'll love this offer

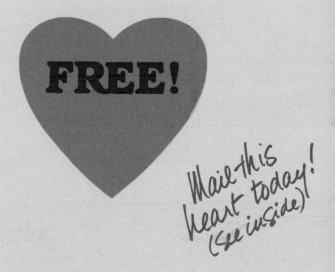

FREE!

Mail this heart today! (See inside)

**Join us on a Silhouette Honeymoon
and we'll give you
4 Free Books
A Free Victorian Picture Frame
And a Free Mystery Gift**

IT'S A
SILHOUETTE HONEYMOON—
A SWEETHEART OF A FREE OFFER!
HERE'S WHAT YOU GET:

1. Four New Silhouette Intimate Moments® Novels—FREE!

Take a Silhouette Honeymoon with your four exciting romances—yours
FREE from the Silhouette Reader Service™. Each of these hot-off-the-press
novels brings you the passion and tenderness of today's greatest love stories…your free passports to bright new worlds of love and foreign adventure.

2. Lovely Victorian Picture Frame—FREE!

This lovely Victorian pewter-finish miniature is perfect
for displaying a treasured photograph. And it's yours
FREE as added thanks for giving our Reader Service a
try!

3. An Exciting Mystery Bonus—FREE!

You'll be thrilled with this surprise gift. It is useful as well as practical.

4. Free Home Delivery!

Join the Silhouette Reader Service™ and enjoy the convenience of preview-
ing 4 new books every month delivered right to your home. Each book is
yours for only $2.96* each, a saving of 33¢ each off the cover price per book—
and there is no extra charge for postage and handling. It's a sweetheart of
a deal for you! If you're not completely satisfied, you may cancel at any time,
for any reason, simply by sending us a note or shipping statement marked
"cancel" or by returning any shipment to us at our cost.

5. Free Newsletter!

You'll get our monthly newsletter, packed with news about your favorite
writers, upcoming books, even recipes from your favorite authors.

6. More Surprise Gifts!

Because our home subscribers are our most valued readers, when you join
the Silhouette Reader Service™, we'll be sending you additional free gifts from
time to time—as a token of our appreciation.

START YOUR SILHOUETTE HONEYMOON TODAY—
JUST COMPLETE, DETACH AND MAIL YOUR FREE-OFFER CARD

Get your fabulous gifts ABSOLUTELY FREE!

MAIL THIS CARD TODAY.

DETACH AND MAIL TODAY!

GIVE YOUR HEART TO SILHOUETTE

Yes! Please send me my four Silhouette Intimate Moments® novels FREE, along with my Free Victorian Picture Frame and Free Mystery Gift. I wish to receive all the benefits of the Silhouette Reader Service™ as explained on the opposite page.

PLACE
HEART STICKER
HERE

NAME _____
(PLEASE PRINT)

ADDRESS _____ APT _____

CITY _____ STATE _____

ZIP CODE _____

240 CIS ADMW
(U-SIL-IM-01/92)

SILHOUETTE READER SERVICE "NO-RISK" GUARANTEE

—There's no obligation to buy—and the free gifts remain yours to keep.

—You pay the low subscribers-only price and receive books before they appear in stores.

—You may end your subscription any time by sending us a note or shipping statement marked "cancel" or by returning any shipment to us at our cost.

© 1991 HARLEQUIN ENTERPRISES LIMITED

PRINTED IN U.S.A.

START YOUR
SILHOUETTE HONEYMOON TODAY.
JUST COMPLETE, DETACH AND MAIL YOUR
FREE-OFFER CARD.

If offer card below is missing write to:
Silhouette Reader Service, 3010 Walden Ave.,
P.O. Box 1867, Buffalo, NY 14269-1867.

Chapter 9

"How?" The moment he asked he regretted it.

He should have told her he wasn't interested. But he was. He should have said he didn't care. But he did. So much so his heart went into a pounding rhythm.

Common sense battled with desperation. He wanted Kerry away from potential danger. Burkhardt's coldly calculated methods of ensuring his own security had crumbled to reckless behavior impossible to predict. Jace was willing to take risks with his own safety, but not Kerry's.

But you need Burkhardt. Soon.

"I have the key, Jace," Kerry stated calmly. "I've had it all along. I just didn't think of it until a few minutes ago."

Her words played with his temper. Didn't she know how dangerous this was? She should be wanting to put distance between them, eager to cut him out of her life. She should be scared, because, by God, he was. Irritated for showing an interest, he captured Kerry's arm, shaking her slightly. "Dammit, this isn't a game," he said with soft vehemence.

"I'm well aware of that." In frigid tones she asked, "Do you want to find Eric Burkhardt? Or go home empty-handed?"

Their gazes locked. Jace shook his head grimly. "I'm not going back without him."

"Then just listen for a moment, will you?"

Kerry had his attention, and she knew it. He couldn't afford the luxury of refusing to hear her out. Releasing an oath, he demanded reluctantly, "Tell me."

She began moving toward the lodge. "We have to get word to my grandfather. He'll know where Burkhardt is."

"How?"

"Chi-ke-ka and his tribe live deep in the Glades."

"So."

"He and others who wanted to preserve the old ways splintered off from the reservation in direct defiance of laws regarding Seminole land occupation. The government's tried to force Grandfather back to Big Cypress, but they could never find him." She smiled, remembering wild tales of Chi-ke-ka's ability to disappear before the eyes of the law. His exploits were legend to her people, her grandfather as revered in his own time as the untamed ancestor he sprang from. "Eventually, they gave up. I think the government was embarrassed because they couldn't find a handful of middle-aged Seminoles. But the point is, Chi-ke-ka's been everywhere in the Glades."

"So you think your grandfather would know where to find Burkhardt," Jace returned, sounding not quite convinced.

"Honestly! Haven't you heard a word I've said?" Kerry asked sharply. "Of course he'll know. Charlie said Grandfather knew about Gator's death before we even got back to the lodge. Nothing happens in the Glades that Chi-ke-ka isn't aware of."

"And you think if we just ask him, your grandfather will tell you?" His tone conveyed skepticism.

"Well…" Kerry hedged. It was an admission that she was sure of no such thing. "He might. If it's put to him by the right person."

"You?"

She lifted her chin. "I *am* his granddaughter. Initially his response might be negative," Kerry mused out loud. "He wouldn't want me involved—"

"He'd be a wise man."

"But I know I can convince him. Grandfather's very territorial. Normally, the tribe keeps a low profile. They just want to live out the rest of their lives in the old ways. Burkhardt's a threat to their existence, too."

They reached the lodge's front porch. Kerry whistled for Barney and the dog appeared, panting from exertion. She bent to pluck twigs and leaves from his thick coat. Jace watched her movements silently, envious of the loving touches she lavished on the animal and wanting Kerry in his arms. He thought how easily she could be hurt, how unbearable it would be to see her come to harm. In spite of the hope Kerry offered, he felt compelled to make one more attempt at reason.

"You don't need to be involved. Tell me where to find this grandfather of yours," he said. "I'll convince him."

She straightened with a laugh, tossing silky black tresses away from her face to favor him with a disdainful look. "He'd never agree to meet with you. He's distrustful of outsiders."

"Kerry…"

"It's true! He never even warmed up to my father."

"Take me to him."

"I'm not sure I could find the camp. I've only been to it a few times. It's isolated, and for the tribe's protection, outsiders aren't welcomed."

He didn't doubt that. He wanted to shake her for being so damned obstinate and determined to put her own welfare in jeopardy. Spurred by frustration, his tone was harsh. "Then, how do *you* propose to persuade him?"

"I can't," she retorted. "At least, not alone. Tomorrow Uncle Charlie comes over to do yard work. I think I can convince him to help. With both of us on your side, it might influence Chi-ke-ka. Grandfather listens to what his son has to say."

"Your uncle didn't look like he'd be a big fan of mine."

"He's not," Kerry said in a soft, low voice. "But he liked Gator." She sighed, suddenly tired. "Admit it, Jace. You haven't got a clue where to go to from here. Have you?"

By six o'clock in the morning, Charlie hadn't come. That fact worried Kerry. Preferring the early hours when the Florida sun was less brutal, her uncle should have been here by now.

She wondered if he was still angry with her.

Last night had been the first time she could ever remember seeing Charlie upset. At first Kerry believed Gator's death was responsible for his abrupt comments and dark scowls, but she'd soon realized he was displeased with her. He unleashed a quiet fury that left her openmouthed with surprise.

Accustomed to his protectiveness, Kerry was still stunned when he accused her of taking unnecessary risks, for foolishly trusting Jace Warfield and for becoming involved in something sinister that was none of her affair. Kerry had called forth every ounce of her persuasive powers to calm the older man and get him to listen to her side of the story. Even then, Charlie still wanted to step outside the cabin and beat Jace to a bloody pulp for exposing his niece to danger.

In spite of such dire threats, Kerry was certain she could convince her uncle to help. He could be as territorial about the Glades as her grandfather. He had liked Gator James and been greatly distressed by his murder. And the most compelling argument of all, Kerry had made it abundantly clear she would continue to help Jace Warfield.

Kerry frowned down at her watch. Forty-five minutes till she was supposed to meet Jace at the diner. Hopefully, with encouraging news regarding a meeting with her grandfather.

All right, she decided, when another five minutes trickled away. *Stubborn, just like his father. If Uncle Charlie won't come to me, then I'll go to him.*

Kerry set off through the woods. In her mind she rehearsed a dialogue designed to sway. It wouldn't be easy. It had been too long since the days when she'd been able to manipulate her uncle with no more than a child's smile.

At the cabin's front door, she hesitated a moment, squared her shoulders, then rapped the pine surface commandingly.

"Uncle Charlie?" There was no answer.

Seminoles didn't believe in locks so Kerry wasn't surprised when the door yielded to her slight push.

She stepped into the gloom and drew breath sharply, stunned by the sight before her. Uncle Charlie's sparse furnishings lay smashed about the room, as though lifted high and then thrown down by a giant's hand. Glass sparkled from shattered pictures and a broken mirror. Couch cushions had been ripped, their foamy contents disemboweled. Her uncle's handcrafted coffee table lay upside down, reduced to kindling.

Finally comprehending what this destruction meant, Kerry stumbled forward, her heartbeat pounding in her ears. "Uncle Charlie," she called again, the same moment her eyes found the flecks of blood drying on the pine floor. The spots formed a macabre trail leading into the kitchen. Her mind skittered in horror. With a trembling hand, she shoved open the kitchen door.

Blood drained from Kerry's face. She heard a low, tortured groan and recognized it as her own.

Jace squeezed the Camaro between cars parked haphazardly in front of the Flamingo Junction Diner. Through the grease-streaked front window he could see Maya Nichols scuttling through a sea of hungry patrons.

So much activity surprised him, but he supposed all small towns had a local haunt where residents gathered to discuss crops and baseball and what was wrong with big government.

Slamming the car door, he bet those weren't the *only* topics of conversation. This town was full of lawbreakers. Two or three of those good old boys were bound to be involved in something shady. He pushed open the screen door, his eyes flickering over the occupants. He wondered if any of these men worked for Burkhardt, supplementing sugarcane profits with quick money made by running guns.

He found a table, the Formica top still damp from a hasty swipe of Maya's rag. With a glance at his watch, Jace willed Kerry to appear soon. He disliked meeting in a public place and he already regretted the decision to consider her solution.

Niggling doubts had pestered him all night. Cautionary voices warned him not to put his faith in one ancient Seminole with no use for white men.

Coffeepot in hand, Maya cut a path to his table. She looked frazzled. "You're waiting for Kerry, aren't you?"

He smiled an acknowledgment.

"You'd better go over to the clinic. There was trouble out at the lodge—"

Jace didn't hear any more. He vaulted out of his chair, shoving it back so suddenly that heads turned in his direction. The screen door slammed against the wall as he sprinted out, pounding across the hard-packed sand with the same thundering rhythm as his heartbeat.

No no no please! Not Kerry...please, God! Not Kerry! His mouth went dry. He stopped breathing. The front entrance of the clinic swam into focus, yet he was hardly aware of it.

All he could see, all he could feel, was Kerry. Kerry, so seldom in his arms, but sending his gut into a backflip every time he held her. Her sense of decency. The rare smiles that touched his heart and left him hungry for more. In his mind's eye he saw her—vital and alive—and the knowledge of how easily that could change brought a rise of panic in his chest.

Burkhardt suddenly didn't matter. Revenge didn't matter. All that mattered was finding Kerry safe. Keeping her that way. *Please let her be all right...please...not like J.D.*

He threw open the clinic's front door and immediately saw Kerry huddled on the couch, her long hair sifting forward to obscure her features. Her hands, splattered with dried blood, supported her head. Jace's belly took a hard, quick drop. "Kerry..."

She heard his ragged whisper and looked up. Her face was tearstained, the dark eyes brimming. A sob escaped her lips. "Oh, Jace..."

He gathered her into his arms, running trembling hands over her to reassure himself she was in one piece. He felt her anguish, her fear and a fragility he'd never thought to see in one as self-possessed as Kerry Culhane. His hands tightened around her and Jace knew a moment of quiet despair because the truth came swift and sure.

God help him, he loved her.

So clear. Devastating in its strength, the realization took his breath and drove knife-edged pain into his heart. He marveled that he'd been so blind to his own motives. And even as he gloried in the recognition of such an elemental truth, fear flowered. Because loving Kerry Culhane now, when his entire life had been reduced to the lowest common denominator, was wrong.

Impossible.

He tilted her face upward. "What's happened, Kerry? Are you hurt?"

She shook her head violently. "No. It's Uncle Charlie. He's been beaten."

"How bad is it?"

"I don't know. I found him unconscious this morning. The cabin was ransacked. Doc's sewing him up now, but I'm so afraid—" She broke off with a whimper, burrowing into his chest.

"Shh," he whispered, stroking his hands along her back. "It's all right now. I won't let anyone hurt you. Everything will be all right."

Hollow words. Frustration ripped him with the realization of how completely powerless he was to keep her from harm. By involving her, he'd torn Kerry from her safe existence, and there was no going back.

They waited together, sitting side by side and clutching each other's hands in the clinic's austere reception area. The quiet shredded their nerves as another half hour slipped away.

Kerry spread her hands in front of her, as if noticing the dried blood for the first time. "There was so much blood," she said in a distant voice. "The cut on the back of his head needed stitches, but I was shaking so hard, Doc said I was doing more harm than good."

She leaned into Jace's strength. Her head rested against his shoulder, the place where his life's blood met in a throbbing rhythm. It reverberated in her ear, quick and sure and vibrantly alive. Kerry didn't know exactly what she felt for this man. What she did know was that she didn't ever want to leave the safe harbor of his embrace.

"Hold me," she murmured wretchedly. "Don't let me go."

His hand caressed the curve of her cheek. "Never, little Dove," he said in an urgent, loving tone. "Rest. We'll know something soon."

Gradually he felt the tension within Kerry loosen its hold. Her breathing slowed. Her lashes fluttered against the bare skin at his throat. Her clenched fingers uncurled and she fell into an exhausted half sleep.

Tenderness welled in Jace, a tide so strong it threatened to overcome. He wanted to hold Kerry and never let her go. He wanted to erase the past six months, meet Kerry again—without deception or hurt this time.

He wanted to do all those things. And he knew without question, such things were beyond his power.

"He'll have a headache, but there's no permanent damage. I'm going to keep him a few days. Just to be sure."

"Thank God!" Kerry cried on hearing the doctor's prognosis. She hugged Jace fiercely, then Doc Sanders. "I want to see him."

"He's asleep."

"I promise not to wake him. Please, Doc."

"All right," the doctor agreed. "But let him come back around naturally. Don't wake him up."

She nodded quick agreement, then glanced questioningly in Jace's direction. "Go ahead," he encouraged. "I'll wait."

Kerry threw him a smile, then hurried toward the ward. Doc Sanders moved to the steel desk and began scribbling notes into a leather-bound journal. After a moment he closed the book with a snap, turned and glared at Jace. "Is this your idea of making Flamingo Junction a safer place?" he accused. "Longtooth could have been killed."

Wearily Jace closed his eyes. "Don't, Doc. I can't change what's already happened."

Doc snorted in disgust. "You know this was Burkhardt's doing, don't you?"

Jace turned his head sharply with sudden interest. "Did Longtooth say that?"

"He wouldn't confirm it to me, but he did say the two men who beat him said they were acting on orders. And they warned him to keep his mouth shut regarding anything he knows about what's happening out in the Glades."

Jace's body prickled. He ran his fingers along his jaw, thinking there might be answers here if he looked close enough for them. "How friendly were Gator James and Longtooth?"

The old man shrugged. "I don't think they were that close. Gator hunting a few times, perhaps. And last summer they both hired out to the Parks Department, so I suppose there could be some connection." He removed his glasses, then rubbed the redness across the bridge of his nose. In a quiet, solemn voice he added, "This is getting out of hand, Jace. I think it's time you brought in some help."

He jarred his glance loose from the doctor, unwilling to consider that option. "Just give me a little time to think this through, Doc."

Sanders gave him a look that said he doubted time would make any difference at all. "From the looks of things, you'd better work fast."

Jace felt a tap on his arm and shook his head groggily, then bolted upright when he saw Kerry standing over him.

"He wants to see you," she said.

He didn't ask why.

By unspoken agreement, Kerry remained in the waiting room. He made his way to Charlie Longtooth's bedside. It was the same bed Jace had lain in only days before, the same room where Kerry had tended his own wound. It seemed a lifetime ago.

Charlie Longtooth's dark, healthy skin tone had deteriorated to a muddy color. His lower lip was split and puffy, his eyes nearly swollen shut. Bandages swathed his head. But Jace glimpsed the fire in the older man's eyes and realized, more than anything else, the Indian was angry.

To Longtooth's credit, when he spoke, his voice was controlled. He wasted no time in getting to the point. "You want this man Burkhardt."

Jace didn't pretend not to understand. "Oh, yes. I want him." His voice was firm and bitingly cold.

"Good."

The approval in the older man's voice didn't surprise him. He knew what it was like to want revenge. To be visited by hate. What did startle him was the look of absolute calm and certainty on the Indian's mangled features. Burkhardt's downfall had been settled. The deadly quiet of that one word left no doubt.

"I will see . . . that you have the help you need. He will be yours," Charlie said on a little hiss of air. No attitude of arrogance. A statement of cold, hard fact.

"Why did he come after you?"

The Indian appeared to consider the question, or maybe he just needed an extra moment or two to draw a less painful breath. "Perhaps he is nervous," he said. "He fights the shadows, thinking there is danger for him there."

Jace's gaze sharpened. "What would he have to be nervous about, Mr. Longtooth?"

"Gator stumbled into Burkhardt's operation in the Glades. The morning he was killed, he came to see me, to

Flamingo Moon

ask my advice. He thought he could make this man pay him for his silence. I told him it would be a mistake.''

Jace shook his head. Gator James had found out quickly enough just how foolish that decision had been. ''Burkhardt would never let himself be blackmailed.''

''My friend was a desperate man. He needed money.''

''He didn't get it,'' Jace replied in a flat voice. ''Why did he involve you?''

''I feel certain Gator was forced to admit he had spoken to me. This,'' the older man's fingers lifted toward his battered face, ''is your enemy's warning that the conversation should go no further.''

''Do you know where Burkhardt's base of operation is?'' Jace asked, then frowned at his own question. ''No. If Burkhardt thought you were a real threat, you would have been dead by now.''

''I do not know where this man is. But there are ways...'' The Indian fingered the bruise that had swollen the side of his face. The movement drained the color from his cheeks, but his eyes were resolute. ''He may wish he had not been so generous with my life.''

''I'm sorry. You shouldn't have been involved in this.''

''You involved me the moment you asked my niece for help.''

''I wish to God I hadn't.''

''You realize, she is determined to help you. Now more than ever.''

''I can't allow it.''

The dark eyes assessed Jace bluntly. ''No, you cannot.''

''Does Kerry know why you were attacked?''

''I've told her nothing,'' he said, his voice trembling with exhaustion. He paused to bring it under control.

''The men who caused you this pain won't go unpunished.''

Longtooth shook his head sharply, paling as the movement brought renewed pain. "It is not important." His eyes leveled on Jace in a searing stare. "You understand my help does not come without a price."

"I understand," Jace said quietly. "I had planned to take care of it this afternoon."

Charlie Longtooth looked pleased for the first time. "She can be . . . stubborn."

"So can I."

Satisfied, Kerry's uncle closed his eyes. In another moment, he was asleep.

With a heavy sigh, Jace left the sickroom.

Just short of the waiting room he stopped, studying Kerry from the doorway. Her eyes closed, her lips slightly parted, she looked relaxed, but weary. Her head rested against the back of the couch, revealing the exotic beauty of her features.

His heart twisted at the sight of her vulnerability. He tried to find some thread of logic in what he was about to do, but it eluded him. *Don't hate me, Kerry.* With helpless and increasing dread, he moved forward to bring about the destruction of his own future.

Chapter 10

Persuaded by Doc that her uncle needed at least a day of uninterrupted rest, Kerry allowed Jace to usher her over to the diner where Maya poured them both a cup of her strong coffee. The breakfast crowd had come and gone. The only people remaining were a few of Flamingo Junction's unemployed, and the ever-present Bobby Michaels.

"And you don't have a clue who did it?" Maya asked incredulously.

Kerry kept her face carefully neutral. "No. I can't imagine why anyone would think Uncle Charlie has anything worth stealing."

Maya's red curls bobbed as she shook her head in disgust. She nodded in the direction of a customer. "Duty calls. You give your uncle a big kiss for me when you see him. Tell him I said hurry up and get well."

"I will." Kerry turned her attention back to Jace, who had remained oddly silent during Maya's inquisition. His features were bland, but in the depths of his eyes he seemed preoccupied, distant. She chalked it up to weariness. "I still can't believe it happened." When that comment elicited no response, Kerry gave him a curious look. "You're very quiet."

"There are a lot of things on my mind right now."

The chilly tone in Jace's voice pulled Kerry upright. "Things Uncle Charlie told you about the attack?"

"No."

"Don't lie to me."

"It's a little late for that, isn't it?"

It was an odd admission. Odder still was the way his lips twisted in a nasty, cynical imitation of a smile. He seemed unnaturally calm. Kerry experienced a niggling discomfort. What was wrong?

"It was Burkhardt's men, wasn't it?"

"Probably."

"He's running scared. We must be getting close."

He gave her a mirthless smile. "You underestimate him. He's just playing with us."

"Then it's time we made some new rules. No one hurts a member of my family and gets away with it." She took a sip of coffee. "Charlie may be out of commission, but I can find Grandfather myself. You can bet he's not going to let some thug get away with using his son for a punching bag."

"No. It's over, Kerry."

"Not for me," she said, shaking her head vehemently.

Jace leaned across the table. "You don't get it, do you? I don't *want* your help."

"That doesn't matter. Jace, we've already had this discussion—"

"This isn't a discussion, it's a decision. I'm leaving, taking the first plane out of Miami back to Denver."

"What!" The cry burst from her as she regarded him with shock. Heads turned in their direction, and Kerry struggled to bring her voice back to deep, sure tones. "You can't be serious. What about the job you have to do?"

"The government wants Burkhardt, but I'm not here to help them get him."

"What are you talking about?"

"I lied to you."

"I don't believe you. I trust—"

Jace's eyes flared in anger. "You little hick," he growled through clenched teeth, "of course you trust me. I worked hard to *make* you trust me. But I don't need your help anymore. You have no further use."

Something's not right. I can't be hearing what I'm hearing. He couldn't have fooled me. He couldn't. Stunned and confused, Kerry's lips parted in an effort to draw air into lungs that suddenly seemed too small. Her eyes searched Jace's, desperate to see into his soul. But what she saw in his features chilled her blood. "Then tell me the truth now."

He shrugged. "Why not? You can't do me any harm." His voice dipped. "Eric Burkhardt and I were partners."

"No," Kerry exclaimed in mingled rage and pain.

"He and I have been smuggling guns to Third World countries for years. A very profitable and agreeable partnership, until he got greedy and took off with all our working capital to go into business for himself. It's taken me months to track him down." He gave her a hard, implacable look. One that implied he no longer cared if she found the truth distasteful. "I'm not interested in what he's got going now. I just want my investment back, with interest. That attack on your uncle was his way of telling me to forget it."

"You're lying. I don't know why, but you are," she accused flatly, barely able to speak for the knot of grief forming in her throat. Nausea churned her stomach. Each word he spoke was a savage blow, leaving behind the shards of a beautiful dream.

Silence fell between them, deathly still, yet palpitating with emotion.

She nearly shattered his control. He couldn't hold her unwavering gaze, and his eyes strayed around the diner until he gained mastery over his emotions. He knew this was the right thing. Why, then, did it sting so much to see condemnation glistening in Kerry's hurt-filled eyes? *This is for your own good, dammit. Don't look at me like that.* For one awful moment he was afraid he'd said the words aloud out of his own anguish. He gave himself a hard mental shake, schooling his features into lines of rigid scorn. "You were right about me all along," he said. "I'm not John Wayne. I'm not even one of the good guys."

A dark tide of color rose in Kerry's cheeks. "Why are you telling me now? I could go to the police." Feigning a bravado she didn't feel, she amended, "I *will* go to the police."

"And tell them what?" His low voice slashed. "You don't have proof and I've done nothing illegal. If anything, your own actions have compromised your own validity."

"Why..." Kerry swallowed around the bitterness blooming within her. "Why did you want my help?"

"I needed someone who knew the Everglades, someone fairly manageable. I thought it could be Doc. Believe it or not, he and my father really are old friends. Then you came into the picture. The fact that you're a woman suited me very well. I hoped your lack of sophistication would make you easy to manipulate, but unfortunately, it hasn't worked out that way."

"I'm sorry to disappoint you."

"Not a total loss. Believe it or not, if I thought you'd agree, I'd still take you to bed. I'd even have been sorry if Eric's men had killed your uncle."

"You bastard!"

He didn't allow himself to react. The trick to deception was in acting natural, Jace decided. No matter how much it hurt. "Don't take it so hard. I still intend to keep my promise." Aware of outsiders taking interest in their conversation, he pulled out his wallet and set a healthy sheaf of bills on the table. "You'll understand my need to pay in cash." He gave his voice a ring of finality.

"Neither you nor Burkhardt is going to get away with what you're doing." She caught her bottom lip between her teeth, unable to control the quiver in her voice.

"I haven't *done* anything yet. And Eric can take care of himself. I'm not through with him. I have fewer men on my payroll, but they're just as deadly. My time will come."

"Not if I can help it."

Jace rose, stopping beside her chair. Kerry refused to look at him. "Let me give you a piece of advice, little girl. The same one I've been given." He leaned low, so close his breath brushed against her cheek. "Go home. I know where your uncle lives, too, and I don't believe in subtle warnings."

Kerry's color faded. To her credit, she gave no other sign she'd heard the implied threat. A hollow, acid dread clawed at the base of Jace's skull. He knew he'd probably just destroyed any hope of repairing the damage he'd wrought. He walked out of the diner.

Stunned, Kerry sat immobile for a long time. Caught in the savage grip of hurt and outraged pride, she tried to sort through his words. He'd destroyed the faint illusions she'd created. Had she been that wrong? No. There must be another explanation for what had just happened.

There had to be.

Kerry pressed her fingers to her eyes, willing tears to stay concealed as aching emotions clogged her throat. Bitterly she recognized that in spite of everything Jace had just said, hope hid itself in a hollow place in her heart. Her trust had been destroyed, but the feeble flame of love remained. Despite the coldness of truth, one pitiful ember struggled to remain alive.

She hated herself for allowing it to survive.

She stayed at the clinic most of the day, helping Doc as an excuse to remain close to Charlie. As an excuse to keep from thinking. Neither Charlie nor the doctor mentioned Jace Warfield's absence, and Kerry's attitude kept them from asking questions. She couldn't bring herself to tell Doc the truth about his friend's son. Not yet.

Absorbed in her own thoughts, her movements throughout the day were mechanical, distant. She stayed busy, allowing herself no time to mourn what was lost.

By the time Doc convinced her to go home, Kerry had fallen into a moody, dreamlike rhythm of listless malaise. As though pulling herself from a deep sleep, she kissed her uncle goodbye, then headed for Paradise Found.

She bumped the car along the back roads, hating the way she couldn't shake memories of Jace Warfield from her mind. Had he left yet? Perhaps even now he'd boarded a plane back to Denver. Her inability to hate him made her that much more miserable. What was wrong with her? He was a criminal. He'd admitted using her. He had left her with the threat of harm to her family. He didn't deserve love.

She was just shocked. Grieving for half-formed dreams that could never have been. With a snarled curse, Kerry dashed tears from her cheeks. "I don't love you, Jace Warfield. *I don't.*"

Her mind was caught in the grip of such dull anger that at first she didn't see the car parked in the driveway. Mac's police cruiser. Her brow clouded at the thought of what this visit might mean.

The burly patrolman approached her as she got out. Hoping he wouldn't be able to tell she'd been crying, she said, "Hello, Mac. What are you doing out my way?"

His pale blue eyes took in every detail of her appearance. He didn't return her smile. "Do you have a few minutes, Kerry? I'd like to talk to you about Jace Warfield."

Her heart, which had previously been lodged somewhere in her throat, sank right to the bottom of her toes.

Ten minutes later Kerry brought a tray bearing iced tea and cookies into the living room. MacGruder had settled comfortably on the couch, his muscular frame causing the cushions to sink almost to the floor. In spite of the fact she'd known Mac for years—had even dated him once—he looked big and intimidating. A nervous warning fluttered in her stomach.

She handed him a glass of tea, then moved to the end of the couch, one leg drawn up so she could face him, her arms crossed.

"Aren't you going to have a glass?" Mac asked mildly.

"Not thirsty."

He gave her a wry smile. "Too nervous to drink, huh?"

"I'm not nervous."

"You sure look it."

"Well, I'm not."

He downed half the tea. "Took a continuing ed class recently. How to 'read' a suspect's body language. Know what crossed arms mean?" He didn't wait for her answer. "Suspect's hiding something. Getting ready to stonewall."

Kerry kept her arms crossed in sheer defiance, unwilling to let Mac bully her into saying something she shouldn't. What was she worried about? She hadn't done anything illegal. On the defensive, she attacked. "Is that what I am— a suspect?"

"Nope. These are good cookies. You make them yourself?"

"No." Anxiously, Kerry added, "You said you wanted to talk to me about Jace Warfield."

"Yeah." He washed down a cookie with the rest of the tea. With a satisfied sound, he set the empty glass on the tray. His eyes caught hers in an unwavering gaze. Very softly he asked, "What kind of mess have you gotten yourself into, Kerry Culhane?"

She had to swallow twice. "I don't know what you mean."

He looked disappointed in her answer. "I've known you a long time. This guy must really have your heart in a ringer if you're willing to lie for him."

Kerry flushed. There was a logical reason why she so seldom lied: she wasn't very good at it. "It's not what you think. I know I didn't say anything the day you met Jace, but at the time, it seemed justified."

"I'm not making judgments. I'm not even here in an official capacity."

"Then, why are you here?" she asked in surprise.

"I read the report on Gator James's murder and asked a few questions that put two and two together. Doc confirmed my suspicions." Mac refilled his glass. "Did you know Warfield's got a lot of cops looking for him?"

"I do now."

He leaned toward her. "Damn it, Kerry! I can understand Doc letting the son of an old friend talk him into helping him, but how'd you get tangled up with a guy like that?" She remained silent. Evidently, his eyes found the answer he was looking for. His gaze was troubled, but understanding flickered in their ice-blue depths. He sighed heavily. "Lord, you really are in love with the man, aren't you?"

She couldn't talk about that part of their relationship. "What's going to happen now?"

"Can you take me to him?"

"No."

"I know about Charlie. After something like that, you're still willing to protect this guy?"

Her anger flared. "If you think that," she said in clipped tones, "then you don't know me as well as you think you do."

Beneath the tight collar on his uniform shirt, Mac's neck reddened with embarrassment. "Sorry. I'm just not used to seeing you act this way. You realize, don't you, what happened to Charlie wouldn't have, if you'd stayed out of it?"

Wearily, Kerry slid forward so that her elbows rested on her knees. "Don't make this any harder for me."

"Do you know where he is, Kerry?"

"By now he's probably on a plane back to Denver."

"Well, that will make the feds back in Washington happy."

She turned her head sharply to look at Mac, her breath inhaling raggedly. "Is he going to be arrested?"

Mac shrugged. "I'm sure the cops are anxious to explain a few things to him about police procedure."

Kerry continued to stare at him, puzzled. "In other words, they don't have anything on him."

"Half a dozen law-enforcement agencies would like to string him up, but what do you do with a guy like that?" Mac's brow furrowed as he gave a scornful laugh. "He thinks he's John Wayne, for God's sake."

His words brought Kerry upright. "I don't understand," she said blankly. "I thought Jace Warfield is a criminal."

"It's not a crime to want to see justice done."

"Would you mind telling me everything you found out about Jace?" The question carried swift suspicion.

"Some things I can't discuss. The rest you already know."

"Then tell me what you can. I need to know just how far he stretched the truth."

"Well, he's a free-lance journalist. Pretty good, too."

"He won a Pulitzer."

"Yeah. Six months ago. About the same time his partner, Joe David, turned up dead."

"Joe David, the photographer? I read in the paper that he overdosed on drugs in a Miami hotel room."

Mac broke a cookie, then swallowed the larger half in one bite. "Not according to Warfield. He said his partner never did drugs. Said it was murder. He told the police David had called him a couple of days before his death, all excited about uncovering some gun smuggling going on in the Glades. He wanted Warfield to drop everything to come down here and investigate."

"But Jace didn't come...." Kerry supplied, the pieces beginning to fall swiftly into place.

"No. And two days later David turns up dead." The remainder of the cookie disappeared. "Unfortunately, the police didn't buy Warfield's story. No proof. Your friend wouldn't leave it alone, and seeing as how he's worked for government agencies, he headed right to the top to find someone who'd listen. I can't discuss what the feds told him. But they didn't move fast enough to please him, because he ended up here, poking around on his own."

"Then he's not working for the government?"

"If he is, we haven't been told." Mac tilted his head, running one beefy hand along his chin. "Come to think of it, that wouldn't be too unusual." He frowned, rejecting that idea. "Nah. Warfield's just a frustrated civilian interfering with police procedure. He'll get his butt shot off if he doesn't keep his nose out of it. Sheriff Crant knows something big is going down in the swamp."

"Then, you know about Eric Burkhardt."

Mac looked suddenly sheepish. As though thinking better of it, he replaced the last cookie on the plate and stood. "Already said more than I should. I was just hoping you might know where I can find him. I'd make a few points with Crant if I could convince Warfield to back off. But if he's left the area, maybe he finally realized the danger on his own."

"If he was still here, could you arrest him?" Kerry asked with deceptive casualness. "For his own good, I mean. Until whatever's happening in the swamp is over."

"You mean like, for interfering with a police officer in the performance of his duty."

"Something like that."

Mac shrugged. "Probably." A grin split his features. "Make him madder then hell, though. Just as well he's gone."

"Yes," Kerry agreed. "Just as well."

She saw MacGruder off with a wave, forcing a smile with effort. As soon as his cruiser bumped onto the main road, her lips solidified into a thin, tight line.

How dare Jace try to make her believe he and Eric Burkhardt were partners! Telling her he'd used her for his own foul purposes. Worse, threatening her if she didn't cooperate. Oh, what arrogance! He'd manipulated her more easily than a child. With a soft curse, Kerry pivoted from the front door, feeling more foolish and furious by the minute.

She collected the tea tray from the coffee table, her movements so abrupt that the empty glass fell and broke. Depositing the pieces in the trash, she wished she could dispose of her anger as easily. But every time she thought of what Jace had put her through, Kerry felt her blood pressure rise.

It didn't matter that he'd enacted that horrible scene in the diner to keep her safe. After what had happened to Charlie, she wanted Burkhardt captured as much as he did. By what right did he make the decision to exclude her?

She tried to ignore the logic that whispered into her brain, but it stubbornly persisted. *Maybe because he cares about you, Kerry.* Giving the idea calmer consideration, she nibbled on her bottom lip uncertainly. No. That couldn't be it. He'd never given her the slightest reason to hope for more than a brief affair. Jace Warfield was just hung up on that macho image of himself. Used to having complete control over a situation, he hadn't liked it when she started calling the shots.

And don't forget, he lied from the very beginning, she refuted that annoying little voice murmuring in her mind. Why couldn't he have trusted her with the truth? Jace's lack of faith in her hurt more than anything else.

She decided at that moment that he wasn't going to get away with it.

She checked her watch. At least another two hours of daylight remained. She didn't buy Jace's tale of taking the first plane back to Denver. He was still here. Maybe not at Shark Tooth any longer, but he couldn't have gotten far. She was a pretty decent tracker, and he wouldn't be expecting her.

Kerry strode into the living room to pull her shotgun off the gun rack. She shoved shells into both chambers, then closed the barrel with a snap. She smiled more easily as a thought took hold. He'd scared the hell out of her this morning; now it was her turn. *And maybe, just maybe, I won't rearrange his anatomy for him.*

Chapter 11

Jace's camp proved ridiculously easy to locate. No one at the National Park would ever suggest camping at Shark Tooth Hammock, and locals knew better. When Kerry saw the broken branches where a car had struggled through the underbrush cloistering either side of the road, she knew she'd find Jace's camp up ahead. She only hoped he'd be there.

She nudged her car into a shady tangle of kudzu vines. Like one of her ancestors stalking invading Spanish conquistadors, Kerry set off silently down the grassy path, the shotgun wedged securely in the crook of one arm. The late-afternoon sun warmed her back as she shooed sand gnats away.

Fifteen minutes later she saw Jace's Camaro. Beyond it lay his camp. The sight of his equipment brought relief and anger. Evidently he was so sure of this morning's work, he didn't fear she'd come after him. Oh, she couldn't wait to see his face!

Crouching low, she peered around the fender of the car. Thirty feet away, Jace stood with his back to her. Hands on his hips, he stared into the undergrowth, apparently absorbed in his own thoughts. She wondered if he thought of her, then scolded herself for even daring to hope such a foolish thing.

She crossed the campsite on silent feet. He never moved a muscle. When the distance between them had shortened to ten feet, Kerry stopped. "Thinking up a new set of lies?"

Jace swung around. For a brief moment Kerry saw hope and longing flare in his eyes. He could pretend all he wanted, but in that heartbeat of time, he was damned glad to see her and she knew it.

"Kerry..." Disbelief crept into his expression. His smile died a quick death. "What are you doing here?"

Furious, she attacked. "Did you think I'd just let you walk away?"

"I thought I made myself clear this morning. I don't want your help. I don't néed you."

"Try another song. I'm getting tired of that one." When he stepped toward her, she brought the shotgun up. "No. Don't come any closer."

A grin twitched at the corners of his mouth. "Didn't your father ever teach you not to point a gun at someone unless you intend to use it?"

"Yes." She pumped a shotgun shell into the earth between Jace's boots and the ground exploded in a shower of sandy dirt. "Want to know where my father said I should shoot a man first?"

"Dammit, Kerry, that's not funny!" The words thundered from him.

"Do you see me laughing?"

"Look," he said, recovering his composure, "you have a right to be mad—"

"The only reason I haven't already blown a hole through you is because I don't intend to go to prison for killing such a low-life weasel. But you'd better start talking. I'm not adverse to sending you back to Denver singing soprano the rest of your miserable life." She aimed the shotgun just below his belt.

Jace's dark eyes held hers for a long moment. At last he sighed heavily. "All right. You have the advantage here. What would you like to know?" His head tilted back insolently. His arms locked across his chest.

Remembering Mac's observation about crossed arms, Kerry's temper soared. So! Even with a gun pointed at his most prized possession, Jace was still willing to brazen it out. Oh, she really ought to shoot him and get it over with! He stood there as if he didn't have a care in the world, with his shirt pulling tightly in all the right places and his wind-tossed hair shaded to spun gold in the fading light. *In about a hundred years I ought to be able to resist that smile of his just fine.*

Kerry struggled to put steel in her voice. "I want the truth. Not that garbage about working for the government. And not the lies you trotted out for me this morning."

"You didn't believe me?"

She shot Jace a venomous look. "I hate you for treating me like some kind of idiot."

"It was for your own good."

"You had no right to make that decision for me."

"I wanted to protect you."

"You're not John Wayne!"

"And you're not Annie Oakley!"

"Maybe not, but do I look like I need protecting now?"

They studied one another with brooding anger and smoldering frustration, finding no common ground.

"I didn't want to see you hurt," Jace said at last.

His tender tone caused Kerry to drop her mask of outrage for a moment. "Well, you hurt me a lot, damn you."

"How?"

She wasn't ready to discuss the damage he'd done to her heart. "You called me a hick."

"You called me a bastard."

"Guess that makes us even."

"Guess it does," he agreed, a thread of laughter in his voice. "So where do we go from here?"

Remembering her grievances against him, Kerry arched her chin defiantly. "That puts us right back where we started. The plain, unvarnished truth. You owe me that much, Jace."

"You won't like it."

"I can handle it."

"It goes against everything you believe in."

"*You* went against everything I believe in."

His gaze sharpened. "What does that mean?"

"It means I let you in. You made me feel things I haven't felt in a long time. I opened up to you, but you shut me out."

What was she saying! She hadn't meant to reveal any of that. She stared suspiciously at him, as though he'd somehow tricked the words from her. The look he gave her brought a momentary panic. Consuming, compelling, his eyes delved past her armor of anger, reading the truth written on her heart.

He shook his head slowly. "All I ever meant to do was keep you safe. When your uncle was attacked, I couldn't think of anything but getting you out of this."

She dismissed his argument with a wave of the shotgun. "The truth, Jace."

Silence yawned unbearably, filled only by sounds of the swamp settling into night. Crisp sunlight had dissolved into a dusky pink and gold sunset. The tall pines issued a faint moan of protest as the breeze began to assert itself.

Kerry watched as Jace's lips lost their hard, uncompromising line and his manner changed subtly. A taut, brooding expression appeared in his eyes. They regarded her intently, refusing to allow Kerry to look away.

"The truth is," he said in a low voice, "I want you. All I can think about is having you in my arms."

She rejected the words with a small shake of her head. "Don't..."

"I want to make love to you."

"Don't..." His gaze held hers. Unable to bear such scrutiny, Kerry closed her eyes, rejecting Jace's words with another shake of her head. "Don't try to sway me that way."

"You wanted the truth. You're hearing it."

There was fire in his voice, tinged with a quiet despair. When she opened her eyes again she saw he was closing the distance between them. Kerry watched his approach like a sleepwalker held in a trance. She made no move to stop him.

"I care about you so much it scares me," he continued. "I look at you and see such honesty and inner strength, and I think how ironic it is, when those things are missing from my own life."

Oh, how unfair, Jace! Saying things that made desire cloud rational thought. Knifing through her composure to ignite the passion. He stopped in front of her. A small turn of her head and she could press her lips to his. His breath rained soft and warm on her cheek. Though his features were shadowed, she could read the appeal in his eyes, the intensity.

With one hand under her chin, he turned her face toward his. "I feel like I've spent the last few months in a dark, deep hole, and there you are, offering me a hand out. But I don't want to take it, because I'm afraid that instead of getting out of that hole I'll just pull you in with me."

"All I want to do is help you, Jace," she said softly. "Can't you accept that?"

"I don't want to. I want...to be able to let you go." His fingers lined her lower lip. The expression on his face was troubled. "I can't seem to do that."

He replaced his fingers with his mouth, brushing it lightly across the fullness of her bottom lip, inflaming her senses.

Her head snapped back. "Stop that!"

"Stop what?"

"That."

"This?" His tongue teased the barrier of her teeth. She tried to give him nothing, but he gripped her jaw with enough pressure that her lips opened under his. She tasted his breath in her mouth as his tongue stole forward. Desire soared. With a groan, her tongue met his, dancing away shyly at the first heated contact, then playing with increasing warmth.

The barrel of the shotgun dangled uselessly at her side, and she felt him nudge it away to pull her close. One arm came around her supportively. The other tunneled into the silk of her hair. Jace tugged a handful of it and their lips separated, their lungs hitching for oxygen. Only a breath apart, their eyes found each other. His glittered with passion. Kerry knew her own must be wide with yearning.

"Don't hate me, Kerry." Jace's voice vibrated with emotion. One finger traced her lashes, smoothing away the dampness she hadn't known was there.

"I can't. I want to, but I end up wanting you instead...." Kerry's throat closed. Jace's mouth found hers once more. Nuzzling into her hair, nipping at her ear, his lips passed languorously over Kerry's sensitized flesh until she lost pace with her breathing again.

His hand molded her closer. His hips rotated against hers slowly, frankly, making her intimately aware of his desire.

"Were you really going to shoot me?" he murmured against her throat. The rumbling feel of his words reverberated warmly against her skin. Kerry shivered.

"I . . . thought about it." She tried to sound stern.

"Do you still want to?"

His tongue flicked against the pulse of her throat, making her thoughts scatter. Her head draped back. "Only if you stop."

It was the welcome he sought, and they both knew it. He tasted the sweet headiness of her surrender. Blood pounded dizzily in his brain. Senses demanded release.

Sliding his hand under her knees, he lifted her in his arms. Through a cloak of darkness he carried her to the tent, stopping only long enough to see the shotgun propped securely out of harm's way.

Scattering hot, open kisses across Kerry's mouth, he laid her on the sleeping bag. The tent was small, still warm from the afternoon sun. Remembering the ferocity of the mosquitoes at night, Jace backed away to zip the screen opening into place.

She groaned in protest at the loss of his touch and came up on her knees. The interior of the tent was darkened velvet. The only illumination came from the moon, a silver crescent too new to offer much light. "What are you doing?"

"Keeping the mosquitoes at bay." Sitting face-to-face, thigh to thigh, one hand reached to capture a thick lock of her hair. "I'm sorry this isn't more romantic. I want this time between us to be special."

"It will be," she replied huskily, following the pull on her hair to find his mouth with hers. "Because it's with you." The wet silk of their lips blended in gentle exploration. "Besides, a tent makes me have such . . . basic urges."

"Mmmm . . . I like those urges."

He followed her lead, marveling at the pearlized satiny texture of her skin as he tasted the warmth of it in his mouth. His lips dallied leisurely down her neck. He felt her swallow, and he smiled, wondering if she could be half as nervous as he was.

Kerry had managed to touch his heart from the very beginning, and had stolen it completely such a short time later. This was the woman he'd been searching for his entire life, yet it frightened him to realize how easily this could be destroyed. Anxiety gnawed at him, even as the unexpected gift of herself made his blood pump with renewed vigor. *Please, God, for once let me say and do all the right things. Don't let me hurt her anymore.*

He discarded the barrier of her blouse. Tracing one finger over the practical simplicity of Kerry's bra, he said, "I want to see you."

She removed it, and fire lapped at Jace's senses. Small, perfectly shaped, Kerry's breasts rode high with each ragged breath, the nipples already engorged. Dipped in diffused moonlight, they were smooth, yet firm, inviting his touch.

Before he could act on the impulse, Kerry said with a toss of her hair, "Now you."

He shucked the shirt with a quick movement that ruffled his hair like sifting gold dust. Kerry hadn't seen his chest since those early days in the clinic, but, oh, the memory had remained true. Jace's torso was a dark wall of strength, sable hair covering contours and planes that made her hands itch to explore. With delicately searching fingers, she tested one flat, pebbled nipple. She heard him inhale quickly in surprise, then heard herself moan in pleasure as he abraded her own breasts with the pads of his thumbs.

His caressing, circular motions made her heart beat with excitement. Blood rushed just beneath the surface of her skin, leaving her in a fever of impatience, burning for more. Engulfed in a new, hidden domain where only passion ruled, she was eager to make discoveries.

Smoothing down the satin flatness of her abdomen, Jace found the sheath that held Kerry's knife. He chuckled in the darkness, remembering. "Still trying to discourage me?" he asked.

Her fingers stole beneath his waistband to slide across his hair-dusted belly. "Does this feel like discouragement?"

He didn't answer. He couldn't. The breath had vacated his lungs in a gush of air that left him reeling, fighting to conquer the demands of his body.

By unspoken agreement they each helped the other slip out of their clothes. They made a sensual exploration, teasing responses with hands and lips.

Murmuring an endearment, Jace eased Kerry to the sleeping bag. She opened her eyes to find him poised over her, his face close enough she could see the dreamy contentment in his gaze, the wet sheen of passion-sated lips. His hands scorched a path over her body, his mouth chasing after them, intent on learning and relearning every part of her until Kerry was certain she could take no more. Her fingers slid around Jace's back. His muscles rippled beneath her touch, making her aware of his power and strength, the effort he made to control his own need.

She felt his manhood pressing against the junction of her thighs, and still he held back. Kerry groaned in frustration. She shifted her hips, inviting, begging release.

Her mouth found his. "Jace, so help me, if you don't finish what you've started, I'm going to die from wanting."

He grinned and ground his pelvis against hers until she moaned with pleasure. "Don't you like this?"

"Yes . . ." Kerry said, panting. "But I think I could like . . . even more."

She felt the soft rumble of his laughter as he entered her slowly, nestling inside her with infinite gentleness. Kerry glanced up into his eyes, saw the desperation there, the effort he made to allow her body time to accommodate him. A fine mist of perspiration stood out across his brow. She felt his corded, straining muscles along the length of her.

She kissed him quickly, greedily. "Jace, don't. It's all right. Stop trying to protect me," she ordered in a soft, loving tone. "I want to feel you inside me. Don't hold back."

Her legs lifted over his back, urging him on. With a muffled groan, he plunged deep. Deep into the dark, welcoming warmth of her. He was afraid he'd hurt her. He tried to force himself to be still, but Kerry writhed instinctively and pulled him closer. His control splintered. With a low growl of pleasurable pain, Jace buried himself within her, capturing her cry of satisfaction with his mouth.

He fit against Kerry, and into her, as he knew he would—perfectly and completely, like the whole of two parts. No fumbled learning of new rhythms, only a certainty of right, of belonging as neither had ever belonged before. Their gazes locked in a unity of purpose as they moved in perfect counterpoint.

Kerry met each thrust. His every movement engendered a like response. There was no need for the passionate encouragement he whispered into her ear. No need for gentle coaching. She was beyond it. Beyond anything except the delicious swirl of sensations floating out from the center of her being in hot, heavy waves of fulfillment. Her breath trapped in her chest, her heart sending the blood singing in her veins, Kerry clung to Jace fiercely as her world tilted.

With a deep shudder, her body blossomed, spreading fingers of contentment throughout her like cool water seeping through parched sand. Her limbs became liquid; her mind free-floated.

She heard Jace's harsh intake of air, one breath, then another. She felt his final convulsive tremor before he relaxed against her. Her hands stroked his sweat-slick back as their lungs struggled for oxygen.

She smiled, listening to the thunder of his heart against hers, pleased to know the pleasure had been shared.

They cuddled close, basking in the afterglow of healthy, satisfying lovemaking and the wonder of newly acknowledged longing. In years past, Jace had sometimes fought the eagerness to escape a lover's arms once passion's delirium had been gratified. The need to distance himself from any hint of commitment. Now the thought of leaving Kerry's side, even for a few moments, was more than he could bear.

He needn't have worried. Kerry was content where she was. There was no awkwardness, no shyness. She loved Jace. She trusted him not to harm her. And she hoped to change his mind about going after Burkhardt.

With Kerry nestled in his arms, and feeling relaxed and content for the first time in months, Jace was surprised when the nightmare came. It visited him as it always did, catching him with his guard down, peppering his sleep as it had so many nights before.

He stood in front of J.D.'s casket—

Jace's eyes flew open. He'd recalled himself from sleep, and he felt grateful that some unconscious side of his brain was looking out for him. He wished it could always be so.

Slowly he inclined his head, wondering if he'd awakened Kerry. Her hair was a shadowy silken mass fanning across his chest. Her breath pattered warm and even in sleep. Carefully Jace shifted his hips until he rested on one side, so that more of Kerry's long, sleek body curled against him. Lightly he ran his hand up the flare of her hip, allowing his fingers to rest along the underside of one breast.

He considered fondling it, teasing her awake with a few well-placed kisses, then decided to let her sleep undisturbed. The day had been difficult. Just because he couldn't sleep was no reason to deny Kerry a few hours' rest. In some dark, quiet corner of his mind, he knew they might soon need this respite.

He stared into the darkness, listening to the faint hum and buzz of night insects outside the tent. He wished their time together could always be like this—quiet, undemanding—but no matter what discoveries he and Kerry made this night, there were decisions to be made tomorrow, plans to put into action. He still wasn't happy with Kerry's involvement. In fact, Jace was absolutely certain that accepting her help was the biggest mistake he'd made thus far, a disastrous decision conceived in a state of a lovesickness bordering on insanity.

Oh, yes. He loved her—and he'd never been happier.

Or more miserable.

I wasn't there for J.D. when he needed me. It could happen the same way with Kerry. Could he ensure her protection and still bring Burkhardt to justice? *I can. I have to.* But the gnawing uncertainty made the hair on the back of Jace's neck stand up.

Chapter 12

Kerry awakened to the feel of Jace's arm lying across her breast, a reminder of sweet passion shared. She stretched lazily against him, turning on her stomach so that her eyes could find his. "You're not asleep," she said softly.

"No."

His tone was pensive, and something in the way he held her, protectively, almost too tightly, suggested a certain seriousness. "What is it, Jace? What's the matter?" Her fingers stroked the fine hair matting his chest.

He sighed. "Nothing. Everything. I was just lying here, thinking." He lifted her hand from his chest, planting a kiss in the center of her palm.

She wanted to ask him where his thoughts had taken him, but would he answer? She couldn't be sure. For now, she was content to forget everything except how good it felt to be in his arms. She lay her head on his chest, listening to the strong, steady pounding of his heart. "What time is it?"

He lifted one arm to read the luminous hands of his watch. "A little after 10:00 p.m. Are you hungry?"

"Yes." Playfully, Kerry dipped her head, nipping at the taut, muscled flatness of his belly. "Hungry for you." His stomach growled, and she rewarded it with a light slap. "Stop! That's not the response I was hoping for."

His laughter drifted over her bared flesh. "I can't help it. I'm hungry. Shall I see what I can find?" She nodded, and he added, "Don't expect too much."

He made a hasty foray outside the tent. When he returned, his arms were laden with a variety of foodstuff that he juggled in order to zip the screen back in place. From his wrist, a battery-powered lantern dangled wildly, creating elongated shadows against the walls of the tent. Sitting cross-legged on the sleeping bag, Kerry enjoyed the way light played with the contours of his lean, granite-hard body.

"How hungry are you?" he asked with a wry smile.

"Why?"

He sat across from her, spreading his cache like jeweled offerings placed before a queen. "Your choices, madame. Peanut butter and strawberry jelly, or squeeze cheese on crackers. Warm beer. And for dessert—stale chocolate-chip cookies."

She favored him with a look of mock-disappointment. "How many shots did it take to bag this stuff."

"I'll have you know I had to wrestle the peanut butter away from a squadron of kamikaze mosquitoes."

She sighed dramatically. "My hero."

They ate lustily, as though enjoying the grandest feast. Outside the tent, night insects hummed and buzzed, but inside, it was warm and cozy, as intimate as a clandestine midnight supper.

"How can you eat that stuff?" Kerry asked as Jace squirted cheese from a plastic tube onto a cracker.

"What's wrong with it?"

She made a face. "It's full of chemicals."

He popped the cracker into his mouth, then tilted the plastic to read the ingredients. "There's cheese in here, too." He frowned. "Somewhere." When Kerry continued to regard him skeptically, he added, "Well, I like it."

Kerry shook her head in disgust. "How could my first impression of you have been so wrong?"

"Which was?"

"The first time I saw you I thought, now here's a guy who works out in a gym regularly, probably runs a mile every morning and wouldn't eat anything that wasn't organically grown."

Using his finger like a stalk of celery, Jace ran cheese along its length. "I don't have time to work out. I think running is a bore, and I love junk food. Sorry." He slipped his cheese-covered finger between his teeth. "Want to know what my first impression of you was?"

"I'm not sure."

He continued on as though she hadn't spoken. "I thought you were the most beautiful woman I'd ever seen. I thought you needed kissing. And I thought you'd be crazy about me once you got over being so stubborn."

"You egomaniac. You were drugged at the time."

"Drugged, not stupid." His eyes glittered with amusement. "Admit it, you were crazy about me."

She merely lifted her chin. "I admit I'm crazy—"

He tilted forward to tease her mouth with his. "About me," he coaxed huskily.

His tongue slid between her lips—a slow and easy exploration. She tasted salt and strawberries and the sharp edge of hot desire as their mouths merged, spawning delicious tingles along her spine. "About you," Kerry conceded with a groan.

"Mmmm . . . you taste delicious."

"It's the jelly."

"Is there any left?"

She indicated the opened jar. "Help yourself."

She should have guessed he would have an ulterior motive. Gently Jace pushed her back until she rested on her elbows. Before she was fully aware of his intention, he dipped two fingers into the jar, withdrew a large dollop of strawberry jelly, then slathered it carefully across each of her breasts. Her breath quickened, partly because the substance was cool and wet and unexpected, but mostly because his touch created such delightful sensations. "Jace, what are you doing?" she asked in a slightly dazed whisper.

"Isn't it obvious? A taste test. We'll see just how good this jam is." His fingers swirled the mixture carefully, painting her aureoles a dark pink.

"It's jelly." Her breath caught as she had difficulty getting the words out. "Not...jam."

"What's the difference?"

"Jelly..." she gasped out, "has no fruit in it."

He grinned. "Then you're wrong. It's jam. See," he said, rubbing one of her nipples between two fingers, "there's a ripe little strawberry right here." Lowering his head, his lips pulled it into his mouth, sucking, tasting, laving his tongue over the distended bud. "Mmmm...sweet. Like warm sugar."

"Jace, stop!" Kerry cried, thoroughly aroused. "I concede."

His lips moved upward to capture hers in sensual delight. Eager and impatient, Kerry pulled him closer, her body already responding to his touch, and her mind willing, so very willing to set aside thoughts of hunger and taste tests and strawberry jam.

During the night the temperature dropped. They snuggled close, arms and legs entwined, occasionally falling into

a light sleep only to awaken to a caressing touch, a soft
sigh—the only communication they needed to renew interest. By the time dawn clutched the horizon with the faint
pink and purple fingers of first light, they felt alternately
exhausted and exhilarated.

"Kerry?"

"Hmm..."

"I'm going to do everything I can to see that no harm
comes to you or any more of your family."

Nestled on his chest, Kerry tilted her head upward. She
lifted the back of her hand to his cheek. "I trust you, Jace.
Everything will be all right."

He turned his head to brush a kiss across her knuckles. "I
wish I had your faith." Fleeting shadows crossed his brow
as he shook his head. "You don't know what we're up
against."

She gave him a searching look. "Then, tell me, Jace. Let
me in. Please."

He took a calming breath. An eternity passed before he
spoke. "I have a personal score to settle with Burkhardt."

There was raw anger in his tone, but Kerry didn't flinch
from it. His words were the opening she needed, had waited
for. If they were ever to have a relationship—a week, a
month, a lifetime—however long it lasted, there had to be
some basic truths between them. She could see it was difficult. The pale light of dawn muted his features, giving Jace
the illusion of softness, but there was nothing soft about his
eyes. They were cold, dispassionate, as though his soul had
been stripped away. If Kerry had not known how alive they
could be in the midst of passion, those eyes would have ter-
rified her.

She forced tranquillity into her voice. "Mac came by the
lodge yesterday. He told me about Joe David. You didn't
come down to help with his investigation and a few days
later he overdosed."

Jace's head swung viciously back and forth. "It wasn't an accident."

"How can you be sure?" she asked gently.

"The coroner said his system was full of cocaine. But he never did drugs."

His breathing roughened. She felt the expanding rush of it as he drew in deep draughts of air. Beneath her ear, Kerry heard the quickening heartbeat. Her hand stroked his chest anxiously. "Even partners can't know everything about one another. Every person has a darker side—"

"He would never have taken that willingly," Jace interrupted, his tone so emphatic Kerry lifted her head to stare at him. "In college his best friend overdosed on heroin. The grief nearly tore him apart. After that, he never touched anything remotely illegal. Hell, he even quit smoking."

His words surprised her. "I didn't realize your friendship went back so far. How long were you two partners?"

His response was a long time coming, as though he tried hard to bring emotion under control. His eyes fixed on the tent's ceiling. A muscle worked along his jaw. "All my life," he murmured. "He wasn't just my partner. He was my brother."

Kerry jerked upright. "But your brother is—"

"Joel David Warfield," Jace supplied. "Joe David was his professional name. We started working together after he graduated from college." He smiled slightly, remembering. "He didn't want anyone in the business to think his big brother was handing him assignments, so he dropped the 'Warfield.' He thought Joe David had a more powerful ring to it. My father almost threatened to disown him when he—"

He broke off and looked away. Her heart aching, Kerry remained silent, sorting through pieces that should have been so obvious before—his deliberate avoidance in discussing his family, his single-minded pursuit of Eric Burkhardt, his troubled sleep that first night in the clinic. His brother. The younger, bright-haired boy in that picture she'd seen. *Oh, Jace. no wonder.* Tears welled in Kerry's eyes. She bowed her head to choke back a sob of regret for such a foolish, miserable loss.

Jace heard her swift intake of breath. He drew her to him in an embrace that gave comfort even as it begged solace of its own. His hand found her cheek and came away wet with tears. It shook him to realize someone outside his own family could care so much about J.D.'s death, and it blurred the cynical edges that surrounded his heart.

His fingers sifted long strands of midnight hair away from her face. "Kerry, don't. Please, sweetheart."

The tone he used was gentle, so caring, it brought a wash of fresh tears. "Jace, I'm so sorry."

"I know. Please don't cry."

Her head rested heavily against his bared chest. He murmured reassurances in her ear, offering comfort, as though the loss of his brother had somehow cut as deeply for her.

In hushed tones, he painted word pictures of his brother's life: the childlike pleasure he took in organizing family camping trips, J.D.'s determination to see his work taken seriously, the deep, hurting ache his death had created in his family. As he spoke, the weighty burden of grief lifted a little, as though sharing his loss with Kerry somehow lessened it.

Nestled close, Kerry's hand trailed lightly up and down Jace's arm, an endless rhythm meant to communicate understanding and compassion. His words of regret and bitter sorrow flowed over her. Though it broke her heart to hear the pain and wintry emptiness in his voice, she sensed his need to find release in remembrance. The part of him she'd never seen, the vulnerability hidden behind a protective wall of isolation, was crumbling brick by brick.

"You dream about it a lot, don't you?" she asked when his words had dwindled to a halt.

"Sometimes."

She smiled at him encouragingly, not surprised by that evasive answer. Kerry lifted her fingers. With the lightest pressure she trailed the slope of Jace's cheekbone. "From the first day you showed up at the clinic you've looked tired, as though you don't get enough sleep."

"I've been worried about finding Burkhardt...." Dissatisfied by such a poor excuse, his words slid away.

"You talk in your sleep," Kerry said gently.

She felt the tension gather in him, the strain in his voice when he spoke. "That last conversation with J.D. keeps replaying in my dreams. I should have realized he was really on to something down here. I would have, if I hadn't been so self-absorbed by all that Pulitzer garbage."

"So you blame yourself," she stated calmly.

His silence was the only answer she needed.

"You couldn't have known what would happen."

"Doc saw him just the day before he was killed. J.D. told him he had pictures. Solid evidence. He couldn't wait to get back to Miami to develop them and call me. I should have been there for him." The words were rigidly controlled.

"Because you've always been there in the past."

"Yes."

Such pain in that one word. "And finding Burkhardt now will atone for that sin?" Kerry tried to reason with him.

Jace shifted abruptly. "Don't, Kerry," he ordered tersely. "I know what you're going to say."

She shook her head. "I don't think you do." Catching his chin in her hand, Kerry forced his eyes to meet hers. "Do you think I don't understand the need for revenge? I'm not the turn-the-other-cheek type. I want the men responsible for Gator's death and Uncle Charlie's beating put behind bars as much as you do. But that's what civilized countries have police departments for. Taking his own revenge destroyed my father's life, the career he could have had as an artist. He probably *did* kill the man who murdered his fiancée, but he died that same day. His act of revenge never brought him any peace.''

Jace frowned, but responded without anger. ''I don't want revenge. I want justice. I want Burkhardt in prison and knowing every day of his life why he's there.''

''The police want the same thing, don't they? Why can't you let them do their job?''

''I told you, I can't trust Sheriff Crant. Burkhardt's got more than one cop in his pocket. If he's picked up, I can't be sure he wouldn't walk within twenty-four hours. But there are agencies in Washington who won't let him off the hook—if I can get hard evidence.''

''Did they ask you to get that evidence?''

''No.''

''Then, you're interfering with their job.''

''I don't look at it that way.''

''They do.''

Jace's arms dropped from around her. With brisk, efficient movements he sorted the tangle of clothing piled in one corner of the tent. ''The sun's up. Let's find your grandfather.''

There was no anger in his tone, only the grim determination Kerry expected. For a brief moment, she considered refusing to take him to Chi-ke-ka, but, seizing her emotions in hand, she realized the foolishness of that idea immediately. Jace would simply revert to the methods he'd used before she met him.

''Let it go, Jace,'' Kerry whispered in frustration. ''Get on with your life.''

He looked down at her, with eyes that softened for just a moment as his finger stroked her cheek. In a barely audible voice, he said, "I can't. Until this is over, I don't have a life."

Barney bounded out of the woods to meet them as they arrived back at the lodge. Kerry bent to ruffle the dog's thick coat. Warm from the sun, it smelled comfortingly familiar with the lusty odor of the earth.

She glanced at Jace, who was removing his camera case and her unloaded shotgun from the back seat. "There's dog food in my pantry. Will you feed him while I take a quick shower?"

"Sure."

Together they walked up the crushed shell path. "I wouldn't mind a shower myself," he said. "I feel like I've been bathing in a coffee cup lately." A gray scrub lizard scuttled quickly out of their way. Barney followed the creature's journey with interested eyes, but made no move to chase after it.

"I'll set out an extra towel. Try not to use all the hot water," Kerry said.

He threw her a mischievous look. "Showering together would take care of that problem."

"No time. I want to call Doc and see how Uncle Charlie's doing. Then I think we should head out."

His smile turned into a grimace. "Sometimes I really dislike that practical streak of yours."

She tossed him a teasing glance over one shoulder as he followed her up the trio of wide steps. Her hand was on the doorknob, but it suddenly swung away from her reach. She jerked back in alarm, and felt Jace's arm come around her in the same instant she saw the man standing in the doorway.

Burly, with the mean, small eyes of a wild ferret, he held a gun in his left hand. He smiled, but there was nothing pleasant about that faint twisting of thin lips. "Please come in," he said. "Mr. Burkhardt's been waiting for you." Barney growled and the man's grin faded. "Shut him up in one of the bedrooms, or I'll get rid of him."

She made a quick grab for the dog's collar, then kneed Barney forward as another armed man stepped into view to escort her to one of the back bedrooms. Over one shoulder Kerry threw a worried glance toward Jace. A third man had come up behind him to take the unloaded shotgun. A few moments later, Jace's gun, a weapon she hadn't known he possessed, was pulled out of the waistband of his jeans.

His features might have been set in concrete. Wary, but calm, he didn't attempt to resist the body search. Her eyes found his, and only then did Jace's face change. His lips lifted in a small sign of encouragement.

The initial shock vanished and Kerry bit her lip as full realization hit her. Burkhardt was here at Paradise Found. The blood slid through her veins like cold needles. She knew his decision to confront them could only mean one thing.

The man beside her prodded Kerry to keep moving. She led Barney into the darkened spare bedroom, gave him a consoling pat, then shut the door. Her guard indicated she should precede him to the living room. Behind her Barney scratched and whined at the door.

Jace sat stiffly on the love seat, an armed guard directly behind him, a gun leveled at his spine. In back of the couch stood the man who had met them at the door, his gun held with an odd nonchalance. He had the kind of face that might never have known a smile and wasn't looking for one.

But it was the man who sat on the couch who drew Kerry's full attention. The man she knew must be Eric Burkhardt.

He didn't fit the image she'd created in her mind. Expecting a crude, vicious barbarian, Kerry was surprised by the look of a mild-faced intelligence as the man turned to watch her enter. Somewhere in his late forties, he had a pleasant handsomeness. Tall, blond and neat—to the outside world he could have been an accountant on a golf outing.

Not a cold-blooded killer.

And then, none of that first impression mattered, because he smiled at her and fear threatened her fragile control. He had white, even teeth, but that grin didn't reach his eyes. Those eyes—so pale a blue they were nearly colorless—were hard, analytical and edged in cruelty. This was a man who looked at people and saw bugs writhing on the point of a pin. Maybe had even put a few of them there himself.

"Ah, Miss Culhane. Please, sit down and join us," he coaxed. "No, not there," he said when she moved to the seat beside Jace. "Here, beside me. I'd like to ensure Mr. Warfield's cooperation." His head jerked to indicate the man behind her. "I know your reputation, Miss Culhane. If you carry a weapon, please give it to Collins and save yourself the indignity of a body search."

Panic surged, but Kerry kept her face blank, refusing to allow fear and loathing to show. She didn't want to lose their only weapon. One look at Collins's face, however, and she knew it was lost. There was a bright eagerness beneath his robotic stare. He wouldn't mind performing a body search at all.

She slapped the knife into her captor's hand, who dismissed its threat with a sneer, then slipped it under his belt. In spite of its small size, Kerry felt the loss keenly.

As ordered, she sat on the couch next to Burkhardt. His hand reached to capture one of hers, as if they were teenagers on a first date. There was wiry strength in his fingers. Though they were laced lightly through hers, Kerry knew if she tried to move away he could easily prevent it.

"You look disappointed, Miss Culhane," he said in a voice spiced with amusement. "Were you expecting a raving maniac?'' He gave Jace a disapproving glance. ''For shame, Mr. Warfield. Just what have you been telling this young woman?''

Jace remained utterly calm. ''Nothing. She doesn't know anything about you.''

''Oh, please. Spare me your lies.'' He sighed. ''You know, I was quite disappointed when I discovered you were still alive.'' His gaze lifted to the man behind Jace. In a voice edged with steel he added, ''Especially when I'd been assured you hadn't survived our search.''

''So how'd you find out?'' Jace asked.

''Sheriff Crant described you to me after you reported Mr. James's death. Not too many men have your particular hair color. And though you've lost the beard, I got a close enough look at you that day in the Park to know you were the same man.'' Burkhardt scowled. ''You're a very determined man, Mr. Warfield. Why is that?''

Jace favored him with a noncommittal shrug. ''You seem to have all the answers.''

''All but one. Why you're here. I've checked into your background, and I know your reputation as an investigative journalist. But this single-minded pursuit of me for the past five months isn't part of any assignment.'' Burkhardt's features took on a sudden conceited arrogance. ''Surely my business activities haven't made me so famous....''

''Don't flatter yourself,'' Jace interrupted curtly. ''You're relatively small potatoes, Burkhardt.''

A short, unfriendly silence fell. The grandfather clock in the hallway suddenly took over the conversation. Through the connection of their hands, Kerry felt an awesome stillness come over Burkhardt, as he struggled to control his fury. While he had yet to say or do anything overtly threatening, Kerry was afraid of that tightly leashed anger.

"Then what spurs this devotion to duty, Mr. Warfield?" Burkhardt asked at last.

Jace remained mutinously silent.

"Please don't be stubborn," Burkhardt advised with a long sigh. "I assure you, Miss Culhane will be the one to suffer."

The words were ridiculously courteous, but the threat came through, followed by the increased tightening of Burkhardt's hand on hers. He remained still; his eyes regarded Jace with lazy interest. But with steady pressure, the grip on Kerry's fingers became viselike. She blinked in surprise to realize his hold could carry such punishing strength. Her head came up, her mouth parting slightly to draw a fortifying breath,.

Jace saw her wince and realized Burkhardt's intentions immediately. He didn't doubt this man would crush Kerry's hand to make his point. He enjoyed inflicting pain.

"Don't!" Jace snapped. "There's no need to hurt her." His eyes burned bitter hatred. "Five months ago you killed a man in a Miami hotel room. You rigged it to look like an overdose."

Immediately, the pain in Kerry's hand subsided. The wave of cold nausea washing over her slowly settled. The adrenaline level in her blood did not.

Burkhardt offered a look of blank amazement to his companions. "Did we?" he asked in a puzzled tone. Then with an extravagant smile, he added, "Oh, yes. I recall the incident now. A nosy photographer who thought he'd been very clever. A friend of yours?"

Jace's features remained granite-hard, but beneath the shadowy surface of his eyes Kerry knew a dozen complex emotions warred. His hands had tightened into fists. She cast him a worried glance, then slid her eyes to Burkhardt. Through the anchor of his hand she sensed the tension.

Every nerve within him was strung taut. He waited, obviously hoping Jace would react.

Kerry nearly panicked then. Jace's lips were pressed into a hard slash of anger. He was teetering on the edge of control. With pulse-pounding certainty she knew they were on the verge of being killed. No chance of escape. No reprieve.

Don't do it, Jace. Stay calm. Give us a chance. She sent the silent communication across the room, pleading with him to stay still. After a long, tense moment, she saw Jace exercise iron mastery over emotions that were still raw and hurting.

"The man was my brother," Jace replied tightly.

"Ah. A family matter. I was afraid it would be something like that." Burkhardt turned toward Kerry, his voice bland. "Righting a family wrong—it's often impossible to dissuade a man with that kind of purpose. Am I right, Mr. Warfield?"

"Yes."

"I thought so." He made a derisive sound. "What a family of crusaders. Your brother had a similar attitude. That unwillingness to compromise made it impossible to let him live."

Afraid Burkhardt's mocking tone would drive Jace's temper past the point of good sense, Kerry quickly filled the silence. "Why did you kill Gator James?"

Burkhardt turned his attention to her, seemingly pleased by her interest. "What a strange man. To love flowers more than his life. The university turned down his request for a grant, so he thought he could blackmail me into financing his little enterprise. Such a foolish notion."

"You can't go around executing people. Eventually the law will be breathing down your neck," Kerry said on a bitter note.

Burkhardt smiled. "You forget where we are. The Everglades is an excellent environment for my kind of operation, and Sheriff Crant knows when to look the other way." He laughed. "For that matter, for the right price, you can buy cooperation from every law enforcement agency in South Florida. But the moment my planes and boats are refueled, I'll be out of everyone's way. Now, then, there's only one more problem to be resolved. Unfortunately, my dear, your association with Mr. Warfield makes your fate as easy to settle as his."

He looked directly at her, his features pleasantly regretful, but his watery-blue gaze was as cold and lifeless as the eyes of a beached sand shark. No doubt what their "fates" were to be. Somehow, she managed to breathe.

Jace shifted forward. "Let her go, Burkhardt. I can ensure her silence."

"Ah, but you can't," Burkhardt said with a malevolent smile. "She's a very dangerous thing—a woman in love. The war you've waged has become her own, I'm afraid. Try to take comfort from the fact you'll die together."

Chapter 13

They were going to die.

Nausea fisted in Kerry's stomach. It was only by the greatest determination her knees supported her. Ahead, Jace walked calmly toward the dock behind Burkhardt and one of his men. Somehow she managed to follow, but in spite of her best intentions, she was shivering with fright.

This isn't happening.

The words exploded over and over in her mind, the blasts ripping at her ability to think, as raw emotion fought bleak reality. *This isn't happening . . . not happening . . . can't be happening. A nightmare. I'll wake up in a moment and everything will be fine.* But that small, frightened inner voice was easily muzzled by the rioting panic within. Everything was not all right. She and Jace were going to die. Two more victims of a man who gave less thought to killing than he did to what he'd have for breakfast.

Anger whipped through her. No! She wouldn't go peacefully to her death—dying in slow stages of anticipation before Collins could carry out Burkhardt's orders. She wouldn't let him have that satisfaction. *Don't give in to it, Kerry.* Clamping down on a panic that made her want to run and keep on running, she searched the fringes of her mind for an answer.

She stumbled as her knees wobbled. The man behind her jerked her upright roughly. She winced as his fingers ground muscles into the underlying bone. He shoved, hard, and she plowed into Jace, who swiveled to prevent her fall.

One arm came around her and his fingers lifted her chin until their eyes met. "You all right?" he asked. His voice was unbelievably casual, but his eyes were dark with concern.

She nodded, her insides quivering as she recognized the ridiculousness of that inquiry. Of course she wasn't all right! Everything had gone wrong. Everything.

His fingers moved imperceptibly against her cheek. The look in Jace's eyes spoke of love and sorrow and regret. In a mere whisper he said, "Hang on and try to be ready."

Ready for what? Did he have a plan? Common sense and a feeling of fatalism told her she was looking for hope where there was none.

Burkhardt swung around to pierce them with a sudden, suspicious look. His eyes traveled angrily to the man behind Kerry. It was the first real emotion Burkhardt had shown. "Keep them apart," he ordered. "Under no circumstances are they to talk to one another."

The guard behind Kerry jerked her away from Jace.

At the dock, a long, sleek powerboat glinted in the morning sunshine. Behind it bobbed another craft, less impressive but more practical. Collins and a second man nudged Kerry and Jace aboard it, indicating they should sit across from each other at the stern. A short time later, Jace's camera case and Kerry's shotgun were also stowed.

Dazed, Kerry listened as snatches of conversation between Burkhardt and Collins drifted down from the dock.

"An *accident,* Collins," Burkhardt explained again. "Our poor Sheriff Crant has a hard enough time explaining two bodies with bullet holes. Think of something clever. Something that will make me willing to forgive your earlier transgressions." Though mildly put, the words carried enough menace that Collins swallowed hard. "When you've finished, meet Rayburn at the drop-off point. There's still work to do tonight if everything's to be finished by Saturday." He glanced down at his prisoners, his features once more a carved, disinterested mask. "I'm afraid this will have to be goodbye." His lips twisted in a malicious smile. "Perhaps you'll be a more challenging adversary in your next life, Mr. Warfield."

He jumped aboard the powerboat and one of his men switched on the motor. It roared to life like an ill-tempered lion, the water churning dark and furious beneath the engine's propellers. As the craft slid away from the dock, Burkhardt settled a wide-brimmed hat on his head.

He did not look back.

Squinting against the sun, Jace watched Burkhardt disappear from sight. He suppressed a sigh of relief. The odds against him and Kerry had been cut by half. As he suspected, Burkhardt wouldn't stick around for the execution. The man liked the feeling of superiority, the power of menacing his victims, but he left the dirty work to others.

Jace cast a glance at Collins and the other remaining guard, a thin-lipped ruffian without a grain of intelligence apparent on his sun-wracked face. Neither he nor Collins worried Jace the way Burkhardt had. They were manageable. His mind raced, discarding one plan after another.

His gaze flickered to Kerry. Alarmingly pale, she stared at her hands in her lap as though seeing them for the first time. He wondered if she'd given up. Jace hoped not. Be-

fore the day was through, he'd need her strength. Her
tongue slid across her bottom lip. She was scared. Not such
a bad thing, he thought. It made the primal instinct for sur-
vival that much stronger.

While his partner kept his gun trained on Jace and Kerry,
Collins jumped aboard the boat, his stocky build making
the craft rock crazily. He wasn't a man comfortable on water, and it showed. His gun jerked upward, an indication
that Kerry should rise. "I don't much like airboats, so
you're going to drive this thing while Dawson follows us in
that toy of yours. You take us where I tell you to. Mr.
Burkhardt would prefer no bullet holes, but I can always
come up with a reasonable explanation. You understand?"

Kerry nodded and took the wheel. At Collins's instruc-
tion, she steered the vessel into the shallows. Dawson followed close behind in her airboat. With his gun trained on
Jace, Collins took the seat she'd vacated.

Over the noise of the engine, Collins shouted curt commands. The remainder of the time he stayed uncommunicative. Occasionally she heard Jace's voice, but she was
unable to make out the conversation.

It was almost noon by the time the man told her to shut
down the engine. Nearly three hours had passed since they'd
left Paradise Found. Little gas remained in the cruiser's
tank. Kerry suspected they traveled the isolated waterways
near Hyacinth Key, but she couldn't be sure.

Nearby, Dawson cut the airboat's motor. Across the short
distance separating them, he threw Collins a puzzled look.
"Do you know where we are? I thought we'd do the job at
Copperhead Bay."

"We still can," Collins replied. "What's your hurry?"
Kerry turned to look at him, and he jerked his head toward
shore. "Get us over there," he directed her.

Jace sat up straighter, unhappy with this change in plans.
Collins had something more than a quick execution up his

sleeve. Whatever it was, Jace knew he wouldn't like it. Tension crackled through him. He could make a move on Collins now, but Dawson was still too far away. He didn't want to risk Kerry's life in a badly timed attempt. He forced himself to remain still, concentrating on how best to get Dawson within range.

Collins took that worry away from him, though not in the way Jace hoped.

Both boats bumped against gravelly sand, and Collins motioned to Kerry with his gun. "Get out." When Jace started to rise, the man shook his head and leveled his gun. "Not you. You stay put. Dawson, get over here."

Collins's companion trooped over to the boat, his face wreathed in puzzled displeasure as he pulled the craft onto the sand. "What the hell's going on?"

Jace knew, and the first real tendrils of fear licked up his spine. He should have seen it coming. Back at the lodge Collins hadn't been able to keep his eyes off Kerry. He was a man with an appetite begging to be assuaged. A man who saw the perfect opportunity to have a little fun before he got down to business. Jace's glance flew to Kerry. He saw her swallow convulsively, the look of absolute hatred on her face as she stared at Collins. She knew as well as Jace why they'd stopped.

"Baby-sit our friend here," Collins said to Dawson, "while me and Pocahontas take a walk. I won't be long."

Dawson, cursed with being as stupid as he looked, didn't seem to like the idea of not following orders to the letter. His features screwed up in annoyance. "If we cross Burkhardt again, he'll kill us. The boss said—"

"I know what the boss said," Collins shot back irritably. "That doesn't mean we can't have a little fun. Open your eyes, Dawson. She's the best-looking thing I've seen in this swamp since we got here." He jerked his head toward Jace. "If loverboy moves a muscle, shoot him."

"Burkhardt said no bullets," Dawson whined.

Collins ignored him, shoving Kerry forward with a rough hand. She stumbled against the boat's fiberglass sidewall, planting her feet firmly. "I'm not going anywhere with you."

Her eyes connected with Jace's once more. She tried to find strength in the look he gave her, but the feeling of hopelessness had returned. This was the end. The lines had been drawn. She was never, ever, going willingly into the woods with Collins. Even if he shot her right now.

And then suddenly, there was something in Jace's hazel eyes Kerry hadn't seen before. His gaze shifted, took on an animated expectation. His mouth hardened imperceptibly. *What do you want me to do, Jace? Tell me,* she begged silently.

And surprisingly, he did.

He gave Collins a smug look. "Good luck, pal. This woman doesn't do anything she doesn't want to. Not without a scene."

Collins looked surprised. "You don't sound much like a man in love."

Jace's laugh was a short, ugly sound. "*She's* in love. I was in lust."

For a moment his words stunned. Then her mind clicked into focus, interpreting his intentions. She knew what he wanted. Her hands settled on her hips. "You bastard!" Kerry shouted at Jace. "This is all your fault."

"My fault! If you hadn't stuck your nose in my business, you wouldn't be in this jam. And probably, neither would I!" He shortened the distance between them, aware that Collins and Dawson were so stunned by this sudden eruption of anger, they made no move to stop him. *That's right, boys. Pay attention.*

"You ungrateful moron." Kerry allowed righteous anger to creep into her voice. "I should have let the gators have you. If it wasn't for me, you'd be bait by now."

"Just what I'd expect from a woman. One good screw and you think you're indispensable."

Behind him, Jace heard Collins laugh. The man was enjoying the quarrel between them so much he'd almost forgotten his own desire. On the other side of the boat, Dawson watched them with open-mouthed amazement, his gun muzzle tilted toward the ground. *Come on, you bastard,* Jace coaxed mentally. *Come on. Just a little closer. Join the party.*

"You self-centered snake!" Kerry shrieked.

"Bitch."

Kerry read the demand in his eyes, and though her nerves gathered into wary knots, she complied. Her hand swung to connect with his cheek, as loud and sharp as a rifle shot.

Everything happened quickly. Collins voiced an annoyed complaint and Dawson stepped forward to intervene. The boat shifted against the sand. Jace, his cheek stinging, brought his hands up to push Kerry out of harm's way. *Good girl*—she let the momentum carry her over the side of the boat, tumbling to the sand in a tangle of arms and legs.

He lunged toward Dawson. The expression on the killer's face was still jelled in shock. He hadn't brought up his gun. Jace's fingers clamped around it. He didn't take time to aim. He couldn't because the element of surprise was nearly behind him now. Collins was coming out of his stupefaction, his gun leveling on its target, as he tried to keep from hitting Dawson by mistake. Jace could almost *feel* the bullet slamming into his back. *One shot to put Collins out of the picture, and make it count, Jace, because you're not going to get a second chance.*

With Dawson's finger still on the trigger, Jace pulled the gun up and fired.

The sound of the gunshot reverberated in the air. Collins's face crumpled in astonishment, then he spun backward as the bullet took him high in the left shoulder. The gun cartwheeled out of his hand to land in the water with a soft splash. He crashed to the boat's deck like a felled tree, down, but definitely not out.

Jace buried his elbow into Dawson's soft belly. The man bent double in pain, air leaving him as quickly as a deflating party balloon. Jace wrenched the gun away and hit him again.

There was a movement behind him—Collins trying to get his feet under him in a last desperate attempt to regain control. Suddenly Kerry was vaulting over into the boat, charging the killer like a bull on a rampage. The man never stood a chance. He slammed into the engine with back-breaking force and a bellow of pain, then slid to his knees.

Without a gun, Dawson's menace became a thing of the past. He settled quickly on the sand, his hands raised in supplication. "Don't shoot me," he whined, in such an annoyingly pitiful tone that Jace was tempted to shoot him just for the hell of it.

With one eye on Dawson, Jace turned back toward Collins. He was so relieved by what he saw, he nearly laughed aloud. Scratching, biting, her arms and legs pummelling in a mixture of kick-boxing and slugging, Kerry had the killer on his back, cowering to protect himself from her blows. Gasping for breath, his shoulder flowering bright red, the man's hands clutched his groin. Jace knew one of Kerry's kicks had been well placed.

Keeping himself out of her striking range, Jace pointed the gun at Collins. "I think you can stop now, sweetheart."

Collins's face carried the mark of Kerry's nails. One eye was already swelling shut. He latched on to the sight of Jace with the desperation of a drowning man clutching a life raft. "Get her off me!" he screamed. "She's crazy."

Jace smiled. "Kerry, please don't kill him. I'd like to ask him a few questions."

Kerry plopped down on one of the boat cushions, her knees drawn up to support her arms, her lungs hitching noisily for air. Her hands trembled as she tossed hair out of her vision. She looked up at him with eyes feverishly bright and still dark with menace. "What took you so long?"

"For the last time," Dawson protested wearily, "I don't know where Burkhardt's camp is. We meet at a drop-off point. A man picks us up and takes us a different way every time. Burkhardt doesn't trust anyone."

Jace sat back on his heels, discouraged. Using the boat's nylon anchor rope, he had tied the two killers back to back. Collins's shoulder injury had been bound tightly, but the man lapsed in and out of consciousness too much to be informative, and Dawson was as ignorant as he looked. Both men were merely hired help. Jace sighed, rubbing weariness out of his eyes with raw knuckles. He glanced toward Kerry. She was siphoning gas between the two boats, trying to scrape together enough fuel to get them back to civilization. The air was redolent with fumes.

He gave his captive a wry smile. "Maybe I ought to get my friend over there to talk some sense into you."

Dawson flung him a look of bitter contempt. "She just got lucky with Collins."

"Which means you two just got unlucky, pal," Jace said, a soft note of danger in his voice. "Looks like you'll have plenty of time to get to know one another."

"You're not going to leave us here!" Dawson objected, his features drained to the color of school paste. He jerked his head toward Collins. "He could bleed to death."

"Possible, but not likely."

"Can't we make some kind of bargain?"

"Do you know where Burkhardt is?"

"No, but—"

Jace's voice was velvet lined in steel. "Then I guess we're through talking." He left Dawson to sputter protests to the empty air.

At the water's edge, Kerry perched on the foredeck of the cruiser, idly coiling and uncoiling a length of rope. Jace's boots crunched against the coarse sand. Hearing his approach, she glanced up and offered a brief smile. Shielding her eyes, she turned her gaze toward the open channel. The morning was gone, the sun a blinding dazzle across the wide expanse of water. Between the two boats a rainbow sheen of gasoline swirled, then separated with every slight tug of the tide.

"You okay?" Jace asked.

"Yes."

Something in her voice created misty doubt. "Truth?"

"Yes."

"You're still shaking."

She turned to look at him. "I can't help it. It's not every day someone tries to kill me."

His eyes held hers, probing. He smoothed a wayward lock of midnight hair over her shoulder. "You'd never know it. You were pretty impressive, tiger."

She smiled. "You weren't so bad yourself."

He lifted her hand. When he saw red roughness along her knuckles, he frowned. "Did you get this decking Collins?" She nodded. He made soothing sounds and touched his lips to the spot. "When I think of what could have happened—" He tried for a lighter tone. "You have to admit, we make a great team."

Kerry couldn't suppress a shudder. "I wouldn't have minded missing this game, Jace." She sighed. "Lord, I was scared."

"I know." He pulled her toward him. So good. So good to feel Kerry alive and warm in his arms. "Don't think about it anymore. How much gas do we have?"

"Not enough to get us home."

"Do you know where we are?"

"I know where we aren't."

"Take a guess. We sure as hell can't stay here."

She glanced toward the horizon as though directions were written across the faded blue-jean sky. "I think if we head east we'll eventually end up near Dobb's Landing. It's just a fish camp, but they have a phone. We could call the police."

He shook his head. "You heard what Burkhardt said about the police in town. We can't count on Crant. I don't think we can count on anyone."

"There are good men in Flamingo Junction, Jace. Not everyone's in Burkhardt's pocket."

"When this is over, I'll apologize to every one of them if that's what you want, but right now, I'm not willing to put our safety in anyone else's hands. We can't go back to town until this is over, Kerry." Her gaze had dropped to the sand. He lifted her face, forcing her eyes to meet his. "You know that, don't you?"

"Yes," she acknowledged with a grimace. Her head jerked toward Collins and Dawson. "What did those two have to say?"

"Nothing's changed. We're no closer to finding Burkhardt than we were this morning. Those two are grunt workers. They're picked up at various drop-off points and taken blindfolded to the main camp. Burkhardt plays it cagey."

"When they don't show up at the drop-off point, won't he know something's gone wrong?"

"Probably. But he knows they can't hurt him, so I don't think he'll panic. He's too far down to the wire to pull out now. You heard him. The day after tomorrow—Saturday—everything will be finished. We'll have until then.''

Because it used less fuel, they decided to keep Kerry's airboat and set the cruiser adrift. Collins was still unconscious, and Dawson bellowed objections from shore as they roared away from the sandspit. They headed east toward Dobb's Landing, intending to refuel the boat and continue with plans they had made that morning—finding Kerry's grandfather. That idea seemed a lifetime ago, but it was still the only one they had.

Right now, they had to reach Dobb's Landing before running out of gas. They'd survived worse today, Jace reasoned optimistically. Maybe their luck would hold.

It didn't.

When the engine emitted its first wheezy cough, they were still miles from any discernible landmark. They exchanged glances. Kerry swung the craft to follow the shoreline. If the airboat shut down, they'd at least be close to land.

Jace scanned the area. Not good. Nothing in sight but waving saw grass and unconnected stands of dense hammocks. A walk overland to Dobb's Landing wouldn't be easy or short.

The engine cut to silence with an abruptness that mocked their predicament. They slid toward shore like a ghost ship.

Splashing into the shallows, Jace pulled them ashore. The narrow strip of sand wasn't much of a beach. The sun had baked and cracked the muddy gravel so dry it resembled a jigsaw puzzle. The breeze had died and the air smelled unpleasantly of dead fish and rotting vegetation. Discouraged, he sat down and waited for Kerry to join him.

She settled beside him. Silence lengthened between them like a thread unwinding from a spool. Twenty feet from shore a pelican swooped to pluck a fish from the water, reminding Jace they hadn't eaten. "Well, Pathfinder," he said at last. "You got any ideas?"

"I guess we walk."

"I was afraid you'd say that."

She gave him an encouraging smile. "We've got a compass and maps. And believe it or not, this all looks familiar to me."

"How long before we could make it to that fish camp?"

"Maybe by nightfall. If we don't run into any trouble."

He grimaced. "What could be worse than what Burkhardt had planned for us?"

"I wasn't thinking of the two-legged variety of trouble. Between here and Dobb's Landing there are probably enough gators to make purses for every woman in America."

How did she do it, Jace wondered?

After four hours of traipsing a pinball's path through the swamp, Jace felt reduced to a dirty, tired, sweating scrap of humanity. The back of his neck itched unbearably from mosquito bites. He'd almost pulled a hamstring trying to dance off a snake he'd been clumsy enough to trounce on. Only a king snake, Kerry had told him with a disdainful look. But to Jace, a snake was still a snake, and he hadn't liked it one bit. In his parched mouth, his tongue felt swollen to twice its size. Every few minutes his stomach growled noisily enough to bring every alligator within fifteen miles running.

He decided he'd been wrong. He didn't like the Everglades.

He threw a resentful glance ahead where Kerry picked a cautious path through dead vegetation, rotting logs and wild ferns. So why didn't the woman look one tenth as dispirited as he felt? Except for a few attractively curling tendrils around her face, her long hair was still neatly entwined in the long braid she'd woven, her clothes looked cleaner, and her step remained gracefully energetic. She hadn't even had the decency to break a sweat. If he wasn't so crazy about her, he decided, he could actively dislike such an adaptable woman.

At least they hadn't had to hack a trail out of the jungle. Everglades deer traveled an extensive path through the swamp, grazing from sandspit to hammock by wading through the shallow water. Following their tracks allowed Jace and Kerry to cover considerable territory.

They'd seen numerous signs of alligator holes, but had run into only three of the creatures, all of them small and eager to avoid contact. They'd encountered a few snakes, a bobcat and an untold number of prehistoric-looking lizards, but nothing had tried to make lunch out of them.

Yet.

Having learned the hard way to be careful where he placed his feet, Jace concentrated on stepping well over a fallen log. He walked head on into a weaver spider's web. The strong silk welded to his face like ghostly sticky fingers. With a snarled curse he dug it out of his mouth and eyes.

Kerry stopped in her tracks. "What's the matter?"

"Damned spider web got me," Jace mumbled, scraping his fingers through his hair to remove the clinging substance.

"Is that all?" she asked in a relieved tone. "I thought you'd stepped on another snake."

He didn't care for the reminder of how inept a frontiersman he was proving to be. "And just who would you have felt sorry for if I had, Ms. Culhane? Me, or the snake?"

She laughed and backtracked to stand in front of him. In the soft quiet of the woods, where shadows played hide-and-seek with the sun shining between the trees, her eyes were twin blue pools of teasing light. Her fingertip flicked along Jace's cheek to removed a strand of webbing. "The snake, of course. A poor, defenseless creature just minding its own business.''

''What about me? I'm poor and defenseless.''

Kerry cocked her head to one side, favoring him with a censoring look. ''That's a very un-John Wayne-like remark.''

''Right now I feel like John Wayne's horse. Ridden hard and put away wet.'' He rolled his shoulders, pulling a knot out of the top of his spine. ''Yep, definitely the horse.''

Kerry's brow lifted playfully. ''Which end?''

Jace reached for her, catching the waistband of Kerry's jeans as she tried to slip away. ''Come here, you!'' He yanked her against him. She pretended to struggle for a moment, then subsided with a breathless laugh of pleasure. ''Miserable woman. Why aren't you as bone tired and sweaty as I am?''

''You forget. I do this all the time.''

''What? Lead men out into the swamp and beat them down until they beg for mercy?''

She stood on her toes to nip his chin, then lapped at the spot with her tongue. ''I'd never make you beg—for anything.''

His hands found either side of her head. He smiled down at her for a long moment, then his look became serious. In a quiet voice he said, ''Lord, I wish we had a bed handy.''

She tilted her head and mustered a smile, his frustration no more than her own. ''Hold that thought. When we get out of this, I'll remind you.''

He heard the uncertainty in Kerry's voice. ''We *will* get out of this.''

''I believe that,'' she said softly.

''How much farther?''

''A couple of hours. We're making good time.''

Jace sighed. ''Then lead on, Pathfinder.'' When she started to pull out of his arms, he stopped her. ''Wait a minute. One more kiss to restore my energy and I promise I'll be a good little Boy Scout.''

With a laugh, Kerry touched her lips to his. Their kiss might have deepened, but she suddenly struggled against him, pushing out of his reach. He latched on to her arm. "What is it? What's the matter?" Her eyes were fastened over his shoulder. Fearing an alligator or worse, Jace swiveled. He frowned into the shadows trying to make his eyes adjust.

And when they did, every nerve ending in his body went taut. "What the hell is that?"

Chapter 14

The first thing Jace saw was the gun.

Oh, God, he's found us. We're not going to make it after all. His every muscle jerked taut as he fought blind, choking fear. He shoved Kerry behind him. The man carrying the rifle stepped from the soft, secretive shadows of the forest, into the dappled sunlight.

It wasn't Burkhardt. Gut instinct told him who this newcomer was, and from the looks of him, Jace wasn't a hundred percent sure Burkhardt wouldn't be better odds.

"Grandfather!" Kerry exclaimed.

Jace watched her stride toward the old man, wondering how long the Seminole had watched them, wondering if he could possibly be as imposing as he looked.

A lot of hard years had created that network of wrinkles on a face bronzed by sun and wind, but there was ageless strength in his broad features. He carried himself with regal grace, reminding Jace of Kerry's movements. He wore traditional Seminole clothing—traditional for two hundred years ago—a fringed skirt under a colorful overblouse, soft-skinned leggings that hugged his calves and a small, plumed turban. Jace caught the glint of silver from several rows of crescent-shaped breast ornaments.

"How did you find us?" Kerry asked, placing a quick kiss on her grandfather's withered cheek.

"You are losing your Seminole ways." The Indian's eyes never left Jace. His voice was like well-worn leather. "You move noisily through the swamp, Night Dove...like a white man."

Jace was aware of the old man's scrutiny, the way hooded black eyes measured him for a long, intense moment. Kerry's grandfather didn't smile.

She looked at Jace encouragingly. "Grandfather, this is Jace Warfield. I know you don't like outsiders, but it's important the two of you talk."

Chi-ke-ka acknowledged his presence with a curt nod. "I have spoken to my son. He has told me of this man Burkhardt."

"Is Uncle Charlie all right?" Kerry cut in.

"He is worried about you."

"Grandfather, Burkhardt tried to have us killed this morning. Jace saved my life."

Something glimmered in the old man's polished mahogany eyes. "He is the one who put your life in danger."

Even Kerry heard the reproach in her grandfather's tone.

"We need your help," she said quickly. "Burkhardt must be stopped, but we don't know where to find him."

The old man looked down at his granddaughter and the stern features loosened a little. "You will return with me to camp. After you have eaten and rested, we will talk."

Jace took one look at Chi-ke-ka's face and decided even John Wayne wouldn't have asked for more commitment than that.

* * *

They reached the Seminole encampment by late afternoon. Jace could see why the old man didn't worry about government agencies locating his renegade tribe. They'd twisted and sliced through so many carpets of saw grass, he was amazed they were still in the same state. Throughout the journey, the Seminole had remained silent. His profile might have been chiseled in stone.

Chi-ke-ka led them through a primitive village, a hodge-podge collection of chickees, the open-sided huts designed to take advantage of any stray breeze. No luxuries here—a few crude, handmade pieces of furniture, hammocks strung between lodgepoles, wooden platform beds designed to offer the only dry spot in a rainy season. The inhabitants threw shy, cautious glances their way. Jace decided now was definitely not the time to ask questions about Indian culture.

Chi-ke-ka stopped in front of a chickee smaller than the rest. A Seminole woman wearing a long, sweeping skirt and a thin cape glided up to the old man. She was only slightly younger than he, but with delicate bone structure and lively black eyes. "It is good to see you again, Night Dove," she said. "The time between your visits has been to long."

Kerry greeted the woman warmly, introducing her to Jace as Lilly Jumper of the Otter Clan. He liked her immediately, mostly because she was the first friendly face other than Kerry's he'd seen in a long time.

Chi-ke-ka spoke to Lilly in low tones, and the woman hurried off. He turned back to Jace. "Lilly will bring you food, then you rest. Tonight we will celebrate the first child to be born to our new tribe. Tomorrow we will speak of Burkhardt."

Frustrated, Jace opened his mouth to press the issue. Tomorrow was one step closer to losing Burkhardt forever. But before he could speak, he saw the silent warning in Kerry's eyes. She knew her grandfather. His mouth shut with a snap.

"You will come with me, Night Dove," Chi-ke-ka com-manded. Without waiting to see if she followed, he strode back toward the center of camp.

Giving Jace a quick, backward look of regret, Kerry fell into step behind the old man.

Lilly came back, bringing Jace a wooden bowl filled with squirrel stew and several grainy squares of cornbread for sopping up the thick gravy. With a shy smile, she placed at his feet a stone jar filled with fresh water. He wasn't sure whether it was meant for drinking or bathing so he did both. At last, pleasurably full and somewhat cleaner, Jace lay down on the chickee's platform bed. Layer after layer of handmade quilts covered the wooden boards, smelling faintly of woodsmoke and spices. He wasn't going to be able to sleep, but until he could talk to Chi-ke-ka, he might as well rest.

He was asleep in five minutes.

When he woke, it took a few moments to orient himself. He had no idea what time it was, but the moon was full and high. Tree branches stood out against the pale sky like black lace mantillas. Kerosene lanterns hung from strategically located posts around the Seminole camp. Ahead, in the clearing that made up the center of the camp, a huge bon-fire blazed and crackled, sending sparks and smoke sky-ward in a strong updraft.

Not certain he was welcome among these people, Jace approached cautiously, following the sound of muted voices.

The Seminoles were seated around the fire, the men in front of the women. To one side sat the camp musicians, equipped with turtle-shell rattles, cane flutes and water drums. They set the pace for a half-dozen dancers who moved rhythmically around the fire, their voices softly chanting words in their own tongue, their faces tinted orange by the flames. The sight was primitively beautiful and mysterious.

He saw Kerry among the women, dancing at the edge of the circle. Watching her move, Jace's breath stilled in his chest. In the glow cast by the flames, she looked other-worldly, with a serene, majestic beauty. Her jet-black hair swung in graceful curves down her back, gleaming with red highlights. A colorful blouse and long skirt swayed seduc-tively as she turned and dipped on bare feet. He had never seen her in a skirt before and he decided he liked what it did for her figure. Like many of the women, she wore several layers of beads around her throat and they shone milky white in the dim light.

He was fascinated. And a little afraid.

These were her people, her heritage, and it had never been more apparent than now that she was one of them. The dif-ferences between him and Kerry went far deeper than the physical. They were from two distinctly different worlds, so far apart culturally, socially, perhaps even spiritually. Could they ever hope to bridge that gap? For the first time Jace began to understand the fears that had kept Kerry from commitment after her divorce. If he wanted her in his life, there would be hurdles to overcome. And some of them looked awfully damned intimidating.

Catching sight of him, she left the circle. The smile she gave him sent his pulse racing and his heart into overdrive.

"You're late," she said. "The celebration's almost over."

"Why didn't you wake me?" he whispered.

"You needed your sleep." She captured his hand in hers. "Come sit with us."

She led him to her grandfather and Jace settled cross-legged beside them. Lilly Jumper smiled at him from the other side of the old man. The tribal leader acknowledged his presence with a short nod. Still no sign of approval from that corner.

Food and drink were brought by the women. As tradition demanded, the men were served first. Wooden bowls and huge, hand-carved ladles, "sofki" spoons Kerry told him, were placed before them. Then came platters of frog legs, alligator-tail stew, smoked fish, biscuits with honey, tender, cooked hearts of the cabbage palm and wild fruits. The smells mingled in a mouth-watering aroma, and Jace rediscovered his appetite.

Awaiting her turn, Kerry leaned toward him and said, "Better enjoy it while you can. The man eating first is one ritual I definitely don't believe in."

"I'll leave you some," Jace replied with good-natured charity.

Kerry gave him a playful pout. "Don't let it go to your head. I'll have Grandfather take you out in the swamp and leave you."

Jace leaned close to Kerry's ear. "Your grandfather gives new meaning to the word 'inscrutable.'"

"I've spent the better part of an hour telling him how wonderful you are. Try not to make a liar out of me."

He grinned and slipped a piece of succulent wild turkey between her lips. She nibbled it off his fingertips, letting her tongue steal forward to capture the juices clinging to the pads of his fingers. In the firelight her eyes were full of smoky desire, and Jace's blood warmed in a way that had nothing to do with his proximity to the flames.

There was a maddening hint of unattainability about her this evening; she radiated an earthy attractiveness that drew him like a magnet, yet resisted his grasp. His pulse quickened like an awakened river, and with a grimace of realization that he could do nothing to calm it, he turned his attention back to the food.

Chi-ke-ka leaned toward him and said, "Night Dove has told me of the two men who tried to hurt you today. I have seen to them."

As little as he cared what happened to Collins and Dawson, apprehension for the two men skittered along Jace's spine at the look of banked anger in the old man's eyes. "What do you mean, 'seen to them?'"

"We have taken them from the island where they were trussed like hunting prizes. They remain in one of our chickees, guarded closely. Their wounds have been tended, and we will see to their needs—" he shrugged "—but I will do no more."

Jace nodded agreement. "When Kerry and I can return to town, we'll take them with us. There are people who will be very interested in hearing what those two have to say. In the meantime, I appreciate your help in this."

The Indian looked unperturbed. Considering the attack on the man's son, and how close his beloved granddaughter had come to being killed, Jace thought Collins and Dawson should consider themselves extremely lucky to be making it out of the swamp alive.

Lilly handed him a cup filled with a dark-looking liquid. To his unasked question, Chi-ke-ka said, "It is called the 'black drink.' It strengthens the soul and purifies the flesh." His dark eyes challenged. "Many outsiders find it unpleasant, but my people believe it has great powers."

Jace took a deep draught. It was like bitter tea, but not impossible to swallow. He wasn't thrilled when the old man filled his cup a second time, but he downed that, too, and Chi-ke-ka gave him a glance of approval. He slanted a wink of confidence in Kerry's direction. "I'm making headway," he whispered.

"I hope you'll remember that in about an hour."

"Why?"

"Because that stuff works as a diuretic, too."

After the meal, Chi-ke-ka made a short speech, and the expectant parents came forward. The woman wasn't young, but she postured girlishly when their leader gave her his blessing and the gift of a silver ornament for her cape. To the proud father-to-be he passed a tobacco sack made from a pelican's pouch and sandals fashioned from alligator hide. Jace felt privileged to witness the simple, touching ceremony.

The evening ended quickly after that. He listened to the soft, lulling chant of the Seminoles, enjoying the dark, warm intimacy created by the bonfire. Having Kerry within touching distance, but so unattainable, had created a longing within him he found nearly impossible to ignore.

After bidding Chi-ke-ka good-night, Jace rose, hoping he and Kerry could drift away from the tribe for a little time together. But immediately, Lilly was on her feet and beside him.

"Lilly will see you back," Chi-ke-ka said.

"I can find my way."

The Seminole barely acknowledged that he had spoken. "We would not have you wander off and get lost," he said, his eyes piercing Jace's, "or end up in the wrong chickee."

His mother and father were there, their faces knotted in grief, looking their ages for the first time Jace could ever remember. Joanie stood in the background, hanging on to her tears for their parents' sake—but angry, so bitterly angry. He could see the accusation in his sister's eyes every time she glanced his way.

"Why, Jace? Why weren't you there for J.D. when he needed you?" they seemed to demand. "Where were you?"

His throat clogged as he fumbled an explanation he knew wasn't good enough. As long as he lived, it would never be good enough.

Joanie's features shifted and dissolved, replaced by his brother's. The same gilt-blond hair. The same dark, intensity in the eyes. The same question: Why?

Confounded, Jace shook his head. "I'm sorry," he said in a voice that sounded like the opening of a door on rusted hinges. "I'm sorry." He lifted a hand to touch J.D.'s arm, but pulled back at the last minute, suddenly afraid. No, I can't. You're dead, he thought. I can't reach you. I can't ever reach you.

He awoke with a start, the breath scraping harshly in his lungs as he struggled for air. Throwing back the quilt, Jace swung his feet onto the chickee's dirt floor. He ground the heel of both palms into his eyes, trying to eradicate the last vestiges of the nightmare from his mind. Five months of this, and getting worse, he thought. If they don't stop soon, I'm going to be weaving baskets at the home with some guy who thinks he's Napoleon.

The problem was, he didn't know how to appease the night monsters that clawed his dreams and threatened to shred his sanity.

He shivered, though he couldn't be sure it was the cool night air that raised goose bumps. He lifted the quilt to his bare shoulders, huddling into its warmth like an old man hunched around a potbellied stove. Lifting his arm, he tabbed the stem of his digital watch. Barely three o'clock in the morning and he was wide-awake.

He rose, pulling the quilt with him as he swatted mosquito netting out of the way and left the chickee. Lilly had deserted her post about midnight, and there had been no replacement. If someone else had been elected sentry, and now stood watching from the inky shadows, he didn't know it. But then, he supposed that was the general idea.

Moving a few feet off the path, Jace answered the call of Mother Nature. Damn that old man and his "black drink." More like "black death." Since going to bed, he'd trotted outside the hut at least half a dozen times. If you're out here somewhere, Lilly, he warned silently, you'd better shut your eyes.

He smiled. Imagine that old swamp fox putting a bird dog on him! Clearly, Chi-ke-ka didn't have much trust. Remembering the way Kerry had looked tonight, all hot and sexy and intriguingly exotic, Jace couldn't say he blamed him. Just thinking about her now made it almost impossible to get the zipper of his jeans back up.

The moon painted the landscape in broad, varying depths of blackness touched with silver-rose. Jace looked up. A flamingo moon. The promise of romance. A lot of good it would do tonight, he thought with a grimace.

He glanced back at the chickee. It sat waiting for his return like a fat, malevolent beetle in some Japanese horror flick. No. He wasn't ready to face the prospect of another nightmare. Not yet.

He made his way along the path, toward the center of the sleeping camp. He heard an occasional cough, the groan of wood as someone moved in their sleep and the faint, lonely rustle of a breeze looking for company among the thatched palm frond roofs. No voices. He wondered which hut Kerry was sleeping in. Was she dreaming of him tonight? He wanted to believe that she was.

The bonfire had long since turned to ash. He slipped past it, across the wide clearing, to make his way down to the water. Kerry had told him their abandoned airboat had been brought to the camp earlier. Remembering the item he'd stowed under the seat before their trek through the swamp, he decided now was as good a time as any to retrieve it.

The beach was a narrow spur of silver sand. Beyond it, the Everglades lay dark and unmoving. Jace had to strain to hear the muffled sounds of life out there, the quick, plinking ripple of water as night creatures fed. A dozen aged boats of different sizes and styles lined the bank, including both of Kerry's airboats. Chi-ke-ka had commandeered the other vessel when he'd come to Paradise Found and discovered his granddaughter missing.

Dropping the blanket to the ground, Jace went to the air-boat wedged between two long dugouts. His hand fumbled along the base of the seat mounting. When he encountered what he was looking for, he sighed with relief.

The camera case.

Snagging it with one hand, he returned to the blanket, sat down, and brought the leather case to his lap. He lifted the Nikon from its nest of filters and film boxes. The camera dangled between his knees as he absently fingered the ghostly white initials on the strap. JDW—Joel David Warfield. A small legacy from his brother. Tension coiled within him, a sudden withdrawal to a dark, angry place he didn't want to go. He wanted to deny its control, but he wasn't sure he could.

Burkhardt's the key. If I can see him put behind bars, the nightmares will stop. J.D. can rest in peace and so can I.

The answer seemed so simple, but the execution had become so complicated. Burkhardt was only a day away from slipping through his fingers, perhaps for good. The months Jace had spent tracking him to the Everglades were danger-ously close to deteriorating into one, big, missed opportu-nity.

Kerry was the only good thing that had come out of any of this.

In spite of his doubts, his features eased into a smile. Deep down, in the secret part of his soul, he knew she was the one reason he foolishly continued to have hope. He needed her. She had the ability to bring his life back into focus, to as-suage the grief that had a stranglehold on his emotions.

He wondered if she could possibly know how important she was to him, yet he understood her apprehensive cau-tion. She'd been burned before. Now she wasn't willing to come near the fire again, no matter how badly she longed for heat. Trapped in a self-imposed exile from the rest of the human race, Kerry functioned, but she didn't live. Jace recognized the problem, because since J.D.'s death he'd been doing very little living himself.

Nearby, a twig snapped, bringing him out of his reverie. He entertained a momentary concern that a swamp creature had discovered his presence. His fear quickly reformed, shaping into delight when he realized it was Kerry.

Clad in the same skirt and blouse she'd worn at the evening's celebration, she made her way quietly to the water's edge. As Jace watched, she slipped the hem of her skirt into the waistband and waded ankle-deep along the shallows. Under the moonlight, her figure took on stark, simple lines, but he could make out the drifting shine of her midnight hair, unfettered now and swinging gently along her back, as though stirred by a lover's hand.

"What are you doing awake?" he called softly.

She jumped at the sound of his voice and turned. It seemed like a very long time before her stance relaxed and she moved toward him. "Lilly snores, and...I couldn't sleep."

She wasn't going to confess how quickly she'd gotten used to having him snuggled against her. "How about you?"

He couldn't tell her about the nightmare. "I couldn't sleep, either."

She felt a warm glow steal over her. "Because you missed me?"

"You were right about that 'black drink' stuff. I've been communing with nature half the night."

"Oh." So much for undying love. Didn't he miss her at all? "Well, good night," she said, making a move past him.

His hand reached out to catch her wrist. "Kerry...stay." He couldn't read her features in the darkness, but he sensed her hesitancy. "Please," he added. "It's a beautiful night and the mosquitoes aren't too bad. I'd enjoy the company."

After a moment's indecision, she lowered herself to the quilt. Jace drew a deep draught of night air, realizing with some surprise he'd been holding his breath in anticipation of her refusal. Since they'd come to the camp, he'd felt as though she were slipping away from him.

She stared out toward the water, as though she could see through the all-encompassing darkness of the evening. Far out in the tall grasses of a nearby island, there was a predatory yowl, followed by the snap and rustle of the undergrowth as something thrashed quickly through it.

Her smile found his, gripping it in a vise of longing, before it became rueful. "Panther," she said with a slow headshake. "He's missed his chance to have a late night supper of deer."

He acknowledged Kerry's words with a nod, amazed by her ability to distinguish the different sounds of the Everglades from one another. A feeling of isolation overtook him. On this moonlit curve of beach, they might have been the last two people on earth. Just Kerry and him. The scenario suggested infinite possibilities in his mind and did not seem such an unpleasant fantasy.

He studied her, aware of the sudden instability of his pulse, the clutch of wanting that spread hurtfully in his gut. Need, more potent with every beat of his heart, threatened to overwhelm him. Unsure of Kerry's response, and afraid his desire would become embarrassingly obvious at any moment, Jace sought diversion as best he could. He rotated his shoulders, stretching the kinks out of his spine.

She sensed his movement and turned her gaze to his. "What's the matter?"

"Those beds. I'm not used to sleeping on wooden slats."

"Seminole platform beds keep the tribe dry during the rainy season."

"And awake, I'll bet." He groaned and rubbed his hand along his shoulder.

"I'll—" she had to clear her throat to get past a sudden lump of excitement "—massage your back if you like."

Kerry could almost feel the grin that overtook his features. "I like."

Turning, he offered her his bare back. It was such a nice back: well-muscled, smooth. Half in anticipation, half in dread, Kerry touched her palms to Jace's shoulders. She tried to concentrate on making small circles into big, but all she could think of was the way her legs could ride so perfectly on his hips.

Too late, she realized the mistake of staying here with him. Too quickly, she rejected the little voice that told her to go.

Jace moaned in pleasure.

Kerry's hands tingled.

She tried to tell herself it was the friction of flesh against flesh.

"That feels wonderful," he said with a contented sigh. "You've got great hands." The smile he tossed over his shoulder held a spark of eroticism. "Among other things."

Because she knew where comments like that could lead— a place she very much wanted to go—Kerry asked quickly, "What do you think of Grandfather?"

"He'd make one hell of a poker player. I can't read him at all. I've just been sitting here wondering what my chances are."

"He won't let us down," Kerry said with clear conviction.

"I don't think he likes me. I get the distinct impression I've been placed in protective custody."

Kerry laughed. "You have."

"Lilly's sticking closer to me than my shadow." Jace suddenly swiveled to face her. His eyes peered through the darkness, trying to connect with hers. "However, since she's asleep now," he commented slowly, "maybe we ought to take advantage of that fact."

"What do you mean?" His meaning, of course, was perfectly clear, but Kerry wasn't sure she should acknowledge it.

He pointed skyward. "Take a look up there. Shame to let that flamingo moon go to waste." He traced the line of her jaw with one finger. "Don't you agree?"

Oh, yes. She quite agreed. Any objections she might have voiced dissolved as his hand slid down her throat until it rested suggestively in the deep vee of her blouse. *Who are you trying to kid, Kerry? You knew where this would lead the moment you offered to rub his back.*

Tugging gently on a strand of her hair, he brought his lips to hers. Lazily insistent. Waiting for her to respond. He didn't have to wait long. Her lips yielded and her tongue met his with just enough teasing impatience to make Jace want more. Their mouths merged and mated.

His hands pushed gently, trying to ease her to the quilt, but Kerry resisted. "Jace, no."

"Kerry, I swear," he said with a low groan, "if you stop me now, I'll feed you to the nearest alligator."

"I'm not going to stop you."

He kissed the tip of her nose. "Then, what?"

The front of her blouse had dipped low, exposing the tops of her breasts. She jerked the garment back into place. "This is all very nice, but it isn't what *I* want to do."

"And what—" he cleared his throat because his voice was so husky with desire it was nearly inaudible "—would you like to do?"

Lightly, Kerry pushed, and he let himself fall backward until his head rested in her lap, cushioned by her thighs. She looked down at him, her body a dark outline against the rosy moonlight. "Isn't this better?" she asked. Her hair swung forward to fall in silky torrents around them.

Her fingers whispered along his temple like the faint caress of the evening breeze. Kerry's mouth lifted. With the dreamy intimacy of a kiss, she sifted through the glinting gold of his hair, brushing a fingertip lightly across one eyebrow, tracing the contours of his lips. He heard her exhale a long sigh of happiness and recognized that his own breathing had roughened.

She trailed her hand down his chest and made the quick discovery that her fingers, drawing delicate patterns across the lean and defined muscles, brought a flexing response Jace was powerless to control. He lay still, watchful, but she witnessed the fluid ripple of strong flesh, the jump of his pulse at his throat. It was strangely exciting to be the aggressor, to know she had the power to make him ache for the fulfillment of lovemaking.

Made bold by untamed desire, Kerry brought her hand lower still, her fingers unsnapping his jeans and sliding the zipper downward. In the poor light Jace's eyes momentarily leaped with surprise before he closed them. His breathing came harsher, quicker. He made no move to stop her when her hand closed around the heated bulge. She felt a delicious shudder pass through him.

Trying to master his respiration, Jace asked, "Kerry, what are you doing?"

"You mean you don't know?" Mischief laced her voice.

"I'm getting the idea." Her sensitive fingers elicited a response that threatened to scatter all control. "Are you trying to kill me? Don't start something I'll have to finish by myself."

Her hand stroked. "Do you like that?"

"That's quite...a technique...you have there," he replied in a weak, breathless voice.

She laughed softly. "What makes you think that's all there is to it?"

The coaxing message in her fingers was clear enough. He drew a shaky gasp. "I can see that it's . . . not."

Her skilled, teasing touch incited his passion to ravenous proportions. She set fire to every jangled nerve. His interest in this playful indulgence quickly disintegrated under the force of heat Kerry created. Murmuring his desire, Jace shifted, bringing her upward with him until they knelt face-to-face. With a hunger that greedily sought a like response, he kissed her sweet mouth in savage earnestness.

"You were so beautiful tonight—like an Indian princess," he rumbled against her mouth. "Watching you dance nearly took my breath away. I wanted you so badly."

"But you don't now?" she ventured with a light laugh.

He drew his head back, and she caught the gleam of mischief in his eyes. His fingers covered hers, slipping them down between their bodies, until her hand again rested at the heated joining of his legs. "I don't know. What do you think?" he asked in a silky tone.

She pretended to be startled by her discovery. "Why, you sly devil. You've got a little technique all your own, haven't you?"

"Not so little," he protested.

She manipulated her grasp in such a way that a small, ragged cry escaped Jace's lips. "No, not so little at all," she agreed huskily.

She pulled the loose blouse over her head, while his hands gathered handfuls of her skirt, sliding it down out of the way so he could etch every fine detail of her body in his mind. His heart jolted when he realized she wore no underwear. He rocked her forward on her knees, nuzzling her breasts to inhale the fragrance uniquely Kerry—wildflowers with a hint of spice. With the touch of a feather his tongue toyed with her nipples, first one, then the other. When she pulled back in surprise, he brought her harder against him. His hands traveled down the slim curve of her spine, capturing her well-rounded buttocks and sliding toward her inner thighs.

Kerry came up higher on her knees as Jace found the dark, secret entrance of her womanhood. She arched toward the contact. Her hands gripped his shoulders tightly. Her head tilted back. Lost in a thousand pinpoints of erotic sensation, she shut her eyes and gave herself over to his wickedly skillful exploration.

Jace touched, entering her, though not deeply, then withdrawing, manipulating fingers and thumb in ancient ways that made Kerry groan in frustration. His lips, pressed against her midriff, created their own havoc. Dipping his tongue into her navel, using his mouth to tickle the fine, downy hair across her taut belly, trailing a warm, wet pattern down...down where no man, not even Edward, had ever placed his lips before.

He felt her hands tighten along his shoulders and stole a glance upward. Edged in moonlight, Kerry's head was thrown back, her eyes closed. Hair streamed past her shoulders. She was the most primitively beautiful creature he'd ever seen. Exotically sexy in her naked splendor. Wild. A statue of a proud Indian princess come to magical life could not have made him more aware of her heritage. In spite of the darkness, he continued to stare, seeing her more clearly than he ever had before. He felt wondrously blessed that this woman should want him.

Layer upon layer of sensation filled Kerry. Jace's fingers probed the core of femininity, delving deeper. Nothing in her experience had ever prepared her for this heady action, the way her pulse suddenly dropped into the very center of her body with a heavy thudding rhythm. Like a desert flower thirsting for rain, she opened to the wonder of his touch. The frictional rotation of his fingers reduced her breath to dizzying gasps. She felt the moist heat of her response dampen her inner thighs.

"That's it, sweet Dove," he whispered against her breasts. "Give yourself to me . . . slowly now . . . yes, again."

Shaken, and embarrassed by how quickly she had responded, Kerry's eyes flew open. Moon-kissed shadows hid Jace. Finding a handful of his lustrous gold hair, she tugged until their eyes met. "I believe you really do hate me, after all," she accused, the words coming with a breathless tremble, but without heat.

His free hand came up under her hair to rest along the back of her neck. His fingers stroked her flesh as his eyes glittered with mischievous lights. "How can you think such a thing? What can I do to prove my innocence?"

"Stop tormenting me. . . ." she replied weakly. Her eyes fluttered shut as his fingers did something wonderful. Funny how the most commonplace areas on a person's body could be erotically tuned by someone who knew what they were doing. And, oh, yes . . . Jace definitely knew what he was doing. . . .

"Jace . . ." She whimpered in frustration.

He lowered her slowly, supporting her gently until her back touched the worn, cool softness of the Seminole blanket. "Easy, little Dove," he groaned. "I don't want to hurt you."

She was beyond caring. The night had snatched his features, but not the feel of his hands on her, the rough-gentle hunger of his lips. Her breath purled and evaporated as his mouth charted a slow path, exploring the valley between her breasts, brushing back and forth over the cockled tip of a pouting nipple, before settling on the underside of one rosy crest. He spanned her rib cage with his hands, and she surged into his grasp, driven by pure, sweet sensation and trembling need.

"Please, Jace . . ."

His body reacted before his mind, pressing to conquer the secret place between her thighs. With a moan of pleasure he plunged into her and she arched against him with a wild grace. She was so hot and ready for him he couldn't control his frenzied reaction. He thrust into her again and again, felt himself spiraling upward with a raw, passionate madness, his heartbeat barely able to keep pace with his respiration.

Too fast.

Too soon.

But his body was a headstrong stranger who heeded none of his warnings. He could do no more than follow the feeling, ride each sweet, shuddering crest and hold on tightly to Kerry, as though he tried to hold on to a dream. And when the end finally came, and his breath pooled raggedly into the hollow of her throat, he held on to her still. Because it felt too good to stop.

Unable to speak for the ripples of sheer pleasure graduating outward from the center of her being, Kerry clung to Jace. She savored the fullness of him within her; the potent headiness of knowing how perfect their union could be.

Enervated and complete, they lay in the cool early morning air, their bodies molded tightly together. With obvious effort, Jace lifted himself on his elbows, his hands capturing either side of her head. His fingers shook with the power of what had just passed between them. "Kerry, I'm sorry," he whispered. "I didn't mean to be so... rough. Did I hurt you?"

She silenced him with a quick kiss. "Don't apologize. There's no hurt you could do to make me forget how beautiful this is between us."

He pulled her tightly against him. Once again he kissed her with warm, sweet desire, and for the first time since J.D.'s death Jace realized that, within his heart, love burned far brighter than revenge.

Chapter 15

The sun had barely risen when Jace woke, yet he could hear the muted sounds of activity coming from the camp. He sat up with a sleepy groan, blinking against the diffused morning light. The first thing he saw was Lilly Jumper, sitting on a stool just outside his chickee. Her hands efficiently worked mortar and pestle, grinding cornmeal in a wooden bowl.

"Good morning," he greeted, wondering what time the poor woman's shift had started.

She inclined her head politely. "If you are hungry, I will bring you o-sof-kee. It is like grits."

He'd never eaten grits in his life and he wasn't about to start now. "No, thanks. I'm still full from last night."

"I have brought clothes," she said, indicating a pile on a nearby chair.

Jace rose, lifting the garments tentatively. The jeans he'd slept in itched and chafed uncomfortably, but he wasn't sure he wanted to wear one of the Seminole skirts he'd seen on many of the men. He was relieved to discover a plain shirt with a drawstring neck, and a pair of soft, well-worn denims. Nearby sat the stone jar, filled with fresh water, and a cake of roughly formed soap. He couldn't help but be touched by his jailer's attention.

"Thank you," he said, and meant it. "Is Kerry around?"

The memory of last night whispered into his brain. It had been so beautiful. So right. In the light of day, their middle-of-the-night interlude held a dreamlike quality. Only the small sting of scratches along his back—Kerry's attempt to pull him closer—made Jace certain their joining had been real.

"She has gone with the women to pick the chokeberry."

He frowned in disappointment.

Lilly stood, brushing cornmeal dust off her skirt. "When you are ready, I will take you to Chi-ke-ka. He is hunting this morning and asks that you join him."

Jace tensed. The time had come.

One thing about the old man: he knew how to build suspense.

Chi-ke-ka waited at the water's edge, standing in the back of a long dugout made entirely from one piece of cypress. He indicated that Jace should take a seat at the bow. The vessel was so narrow that his shifting weight sent it rocking wildly, but a moment later they pushed off from shore, the Seminole using a long, wooden pole to move them into the current.

They slipped along the edges of several small islands. Only the occasional squawk of birds and the quick splash of leaping fish broke the stillness of the morning. Jace stared at the fresh horizon, his features schooled into an expression of indifference in spite of the way his heart hammered. Hard experience had taught him the value of silence.

At last Kerry's grandfather found the island he seemed to be looking for. With an impressive shifting of his pole, he maneuvered the dugout to shore. Jace jumped out to pull the craft onto the beach, splashing out of shallow water as cold as clay.

He glanced around. The island boasted a simple, pristine beauty. Only the marks of a haughty and self-assured Mother Nature warmed the sunlit shadows here.

"You have hunted before?" Chi-ke-ka's question suddenly broke the silence.

"A few times." Jace didn't bother to expound. He was a fair shot, but he'd never seen the sense in killing wild animals simply for the fun of it. He supposed John Wayne would have disowned him for such thoughts. "What are we after?"

The old man's dark eyes met his, an odd mingling of craftiness and amusement. "Dinner."

Jace nodded as if he understood. This could be interesting, he thought. His gaze flickered to the shallow well of the boat. No guns. Only a wire and rope snare device and a long length of pipe with a few homemade gizmos attached to one end. He hoped that the prey Chi-ke-ka had in mind wasn't going to put up much of a fight about meeting such an end.

The Seminole set a quick, steady pace through the undergrowth. He seemed to know exactly what he was looking for as his sharp eyes searched the ground. Following a pace behind, Jace had to admire the man's ability to read something in the dead mulch of leaves and twigs, the dried patches of mud zigzagged with cracks.

An hour later, when they had yet to encounter anything more intimidating than an aggressive squirrel, he wondered if Kerry had been serious last night. Perhaps she had asked her grandfather to take Jace out in the swamp and lose him.

Chi-ke-ka suddenly came to a halt. They had reached a small clearing kept shady by overhanging buttonwood trees. "The nest is ahead," he told Jace. With a slight creaking of aged bones, he lowered himself against the trunk of a pine, indicating his companion should do the same. "We will rest a few minutes."

"How do you know *it's* up ahead?" Jace asked, wondering what was waiting for them.

The old man's face split into a grin, the first one Jace had seen. His gnarled fingers pointed toward the ground near his feet. Drying muck was disturbed by large depressions in the earth. "His tracks are plentiful here, but around the bend there is a wallow. We will find him there."

Jace eyed the tracks warily. A duck hadn't made those marks. Suspicion began to coil unpleasantly in the pit of his stomach. "Just what is it we're after, Chi-ke-ka?"

"Hal-pa-te," the old man said in a low voice. "Gator."

Jace tried to keep his expression from becoming incredulous. Impossible! Easier to win a dogsled race with a team of Chihuahuas than kill an alligator with no more than a snare and a piece of pipe! If this was a test, if it was Chi-ke-ka's way of determining whether he should help him or not, Jace was ninety-nine percent sure he'd fail. Miserably. He cleared his throat. "Just how big...how big is this fellow?"

The Seminole's features regarded him impassively. At last he asked, "How tall are you?"

"Six-one."

"Then you must grow a little to match his length."

Jace's knees suddenly wouldn't support him. He slid down the tree trunk, the pine bark scraping roughly against his spine. "I had a feeling you'd say something like that."

"Are you afraid?"

"Damned right. I never went hand to hand with an alligator before."

Chi-ke-ka laughed. It had a rumbling, husky sound, as though rocks had lodged in his throat. "Yet you wish to battle a man ten times as cunning as hal-pa-te. Burkhardt will find many more ways to bite you than he who waits for us."

The moment had come. Jace spoke slowly, feeling his way past the hard, steady gaze that seemed to impale him. "I can't let that be a factor in my decision. The thought of harm hasn't kept you from seeking out your gator friend up ahead."

"No," the old man agreed, then indicated the simple weapons at his side. "But we have come prepared."

Jace could have argued that point, but he knew better. Absently, he dropped his hands to the earth, tracing along the cracked ridges of hardened mud. His mind tumbled in mental gymnastics to find words to sway Chi-ke-ka. He suspected whatever reasoning he offered, it might not be enough.

Before he could speak, the Indian said bluntly, "Night Dove pleads your cause. She cares for you."

The truth seemed the only answer. "I love her."

Chi-ke-ka's voice whipped like steel between them. "Yet you have placed her life in danger. The long darkness could have stolen her away. And your search for this man resulted in pain for my son."

Their gazes locked, wrestled. "I would change that if I could."

"You broke your word to my son. You were to keep Night Dove out of your trouble."

"I tried. But Kerry came to my camp demanding the truth. If I hadn't told her everything, she'd have gone looking for Burkhardt by herself. I couldn't chance that."

"So much trouble follows in your path. Still, Night Dove pleads for me to help you."

"She believes you can."

"The question is not whether I can," he said, "but whether I should."

"Burkhardt is running illegal guns here in the swamp."

The old man's shoulders hitched. "The white man's troubles do not interest me."

"They could be your troubles too, Chi-ke-ka. There are bound to be men from the reservation on his payroll. Good men just looking for a way to make easy money. Sooner or later they're going to end up in jail."

"The clans and I do not walk the same path any longer. I do not care what they do."

"They're still your people," Jace pressed on.

"My people are here with me."

"All right. Then consider this. The government wants to crack down on operations like Burkhardt's. You're going to see more and more cops here. Eventually, some of their attention will focus on you. You might want a peaceful life, but you're still roosting here illegally."

The black eyes, with their faintly veiled disinterest, suddenly sparked. "The swamp has many secret places. We have been forced to move before. We can again."

"The Everglades is a sacred place to you. Can you sit back and watch a man like Burkhardt destroy it?"

"Over the years I have seen many things I dislike. Seminole land drained and covered with cement. My people shunned and spat on. I left the reservation at a time when half the young men of the clans were sniffing gasoline fumes, their minds nearly broken by the white man's idea of fun." Aware that his voice had climbed in volume, Chi-ke-ka suddenly stopped talking. When he spoke again, his tone was quieter, but it had not lost its bitter edge. "I could not stop these things."

Taking a deep breath, Jace tilted his head back. Through the lacy network of branches overhead he found the sun, closing his eyes against its blinding light. It painted a warm, healing touch along his eyelids. He felt suddenly tired, knowing there was no argument to brook the Seminole's stiff resistance. Frustration ripped through him. He wanted to howl with it. *No good, Warfield. No good at all. You've blown it.* He let his head slip forward, eyeing the old man with a look of quiet desperation, grimly determined not to give up. "Chi-ke-ka," he said in a weary voice, "I need your help."

To Jace's utter dismay, the Seminole smiled.

"Then do not give me reasons that should matter to *me*. Give me reasons that matter to you."

Jace went still. Swallowing around a surge of foolish hope, he said quietly, "Burkhardt murdered my brother. He had your son beaten and tried to kill Kerry and me. There are others who have suffered. I want to see him behind bars. I want justice."

Chi-ke-ka fingered the line of bone buttons along his shirt. When he finally looked up, his eyes carried an electric sparkle. "Times have changed. In days long gone we used to call it revenge. You should not be ashamed to hate well, Warfield."

Somehow Jace remained composed though his heart went into a double-time rhythm. "I can see where Kerry gets her sharp tongue."

"She and my son are the last of my blood. The one who hurts them hurts me as well. It is time to stop this man Burkhardt."

"You know where his camp is, don't you?"

"The problem is not to find his camp," Chi-ke-ka said with a wry smile, "but what you will do with that knowledge."

"There are federal agents ready to step in and arrest him. I'll make sure your name is kept out of it."

The old man shook his head. "That is no concern to me."

"Then you'll help?"

With surprising agility, Chi-ke-ka rose to his feet. Two hundred years ago the expression in the Seminole's eyes might have frozen the blood of some unlucky settler.

"First we will release the spirit of hal-pa-te. Then we will make a bargain."

The gator at Kerry's feet was an ancient, armored creature that could evoke a tingle of fear even in death. The Seminole women clucked in delight at the amount of meat the animal would yield, and Kerry knew every inch of the monster would be put to good use for the tribe.

So why weren't Jace and her grandfather—those two intrepid hunters—here to gloat over their kill? And the other men in the camp. Why hadn't they come to admire such a prize?

Her eyes searched the area. Lilly sat in the cooking chickee, unzipping peas from their pods. The women Kerry had picked chokeberries with had already drifted away. Uneasiness sifted through her. Seminoles were a quiet people, but the silence in the village was unsettling. Something was different, wrong.

She joined Lilly and tipped a full bucket of chokeberries into a wooden bowl. The older woman offered a brief smile, then bowed her head over her chore.

"Where is everyone?" Kerry asked.

"What do you mean?"

"Grandfather and Jace to start with." She indicated the alligator. "With a catch like that, I'm surprised they aren't strutting around like peacocks."

Lilly didn't look up. "They have gone to the other side of the island with a few of the men. To fish for gar."

Hiding her disappointment, Kerry washed up and began sorting berries. Curiosity to know the outcome of Jace and Grandfather's meeting ate at her. The signs were positive—why else would Jace be with the men now?—but with Chi-ke-ka she could never be sure. With a mixture of pride and exasperation, she remembered how easily the old man had rebuffed the advice of others in the past.

She hadn't given up the idea of bringing in the police *before* a confrontation could take place. Thinking about it this morning in the woods, Kerry became convinced Mac-Gruder was the man to contact. Sheriff Crant might be in Burkhardt's pocket, but Mac had always been a straight shooter, and he'd probably know who else in the state trooper's office could be trusted. And he liked her. Kerry didn't mind the idea of playing on their friendship a bit if it would keep Jace from getting killed.

Convincing Jace would be the problem.

She bit her lip, wishing he and her grandfather would return. Why were they fishing at this time of day? Early morning was the time to catch gar. Everyone knew they never ran in the—

Kerry jumped up, chokeberries rolling off her lap to race across the dirt floor. Yes, everyone *did* know gar only ran in the morning. Her grandfather most of all. Her eyes narrowed as she regarded the huge gator. And why would Chi-ke-ka and the men be out fishing, when there was enough meat there to feed the entire tribe for a week?

The uneasiness she'd felt earlier tightened into fear. No. They wouldn't, would they? Without a backward glance,

Kerry rushed out of the chickee and went in search of an answer.

"Tell me, Lilly," Kerry demanded for the third time. "You know I'm not going to give up."

Kerry had drawn the old woman into the privacy of Chi-ke-ka's hut, determined to know the truth. Lilly had spent the past five minutes denying she knew anything, but Kerry persisted.

"The men are fishing."

Kerry shook her head. "Your boats are gone from the beach. I just went past Ocelopi's chickee. She's reciting a chant for Billie. I haven't lost so much of our language that I can't recognize a prayer for protection. Protection from what, Lilly?"

Lilly lifted her chin in stubborn denial. "Ocelopi is a foolish woman."

"She's a scared woman worried about her husband."

"You are mistaken."

Kerry strode to the wooden chest containing her grandfather's private belongings. His entire life lay in that box— the glorious years of a disappearing heritage. Lost dreams and broken promises. Grandfather's mementos were off limits. If fear hadn't lodged such an impregnable hold in her stomach, Kerry would have been amazed by the audacity of what she'd done.

She lifted the lid. "All of Grandfather's amulets and war bracelets are gone, along with his war pouch to bring good fortune. There isn't a decent weapon in camp except my shotgun."

Wide-eyed, Lilly stared at her. "You went through your grandfather's belongings?" She shook her head in disbelief. "You have forgotten how to wear your manners, Night Dove."

Out of patience, Kerry gave up waiting for Lilly to confess willingly. "They've gone after Burkhardt, haven't they, Lilly?"

"No."

"Yes. They have."

"No."

"Lilly, for years you've been a good friend. Don't destroy what we have by lying to me." She could see her words distressed the older woman. Kneeling, she took hold of Lilly's withered fingers. "You're not very good at it, you know."

Lilly's mask of stubbornness faltered. "Your grandfather did not want you involved," she replied softly.

"So you all tricked me."

At the accusation, two burning spots of color appeared on Lilly's cheeks. "You have two men who love you very much."

"So I'm left behind while Jace and the Over-the-Hill-Gang go on the warpath to get Burkhardt." She sighed. "All right. Where did they go?"

"I do not know."

"Lilly, you might as well tell me."

"Why?"

"Because if you don't, I'll never come here again."

Lilly's spine lifted. "Then we will miss your visits, but take comfort from the fact that you remain unharmed."

Kerry struggled to keep anger and frustration from coloring her voice. "I'll still go. You know I can track as well as Grandfather. It might take me a while, but I'll find them."

Lilly rose. Her eyes remained fixed on Kerry. With a peculiar little smile, she said, "You will do what you feel you must. By the time you find them, the danger will be past."

* * *

Where?

Kerry slumped on the beach and gazed across the sluggish current. A few feet away, her airboats slid slowly back and forth in the water, tugging against their anchor lines as though taunting her inability to jump aboard and give chase. She buried her face in her arms and tried to replay every conversation she'd had with Jace, as well as that one meeting with Burkhardt. Had the man said anything to give her a clue as to his whereabouts? What about those two idiots, Collins and Dawson?

So? What about them? Think, Kerry. Think!

The fact that Chi-ke-ka had left her airboats behind and taken only the dugouts meant one of two things—the engines would generate too much noise to make sneaking up on Burkhardt's camp possible, or the man's hideout was close enough to be reached by a man-powered vessel. Lilly had told her the men would return by early evening.

And Collins and Dawson. Once they carried out Burkhardt's orders, their fuel tanks wouldn't have taken them much farther.

Fuel. Something about that one word bothered her.

She rose to fish her best map from one of the airboat's storage compartments. Spreading it on the coarse grass, Kerry knelt to examine every island located within a fifty-mile radius of the Seminole camp. Some were clearly unsuitable for anything—too small, underwater all the time—but a few would make terrific hideouts. They probably had for centuries.

But an operation like Burkhardt's would need more than secrecy. After meeting the man, she couldn't imagine him being happy with a crude camp hacked out of the wilderness. He'd want a cabin, wouldn't he? And he'd said he needed planes—*refueled!*

That was it! The marina at Dobb's Landing. The only place in the area with an airstrip and storage tanks big enough to handle refueling. The very same destination she and Jace had headed for yesterday!

Kerry leaped up, crumpling the map into a ragged square and stuffing it in a back pocket of her jeans. It was possible. It made a logical choice. She hadn't been there in over a year, but the marina had been struggling to stay alive even then.

Besides, she reasoned grimly, what other ideas did she have?

The fuel tanks of her best boat were dry as a bone, but she hoped the one Chi-ke-ka had brought from Paradise Found held enough to get her there. Without saying goodbye to Lilly, Kerry grabbed her shotgun, which had been loaded, tossed the anchor into the boat and shoved off.

She was forced to approach from the leeward side of the island. If Chi-ke-ka hadn't attacked yet, she didn't want the engine to announce her presence. Sloughing through the wild and tangled undergrowth, she thought again how furious she was with the two most important men in her life. She wouldn't have to be doing this if they'd seen fit to include her. What had Jace said to make Grandfather conceive such a plan? Help in locating Burkhardt was one thing. But this attack bordered on insanity.

A spate of gunfire broke the stillness and sent a dozen white egrets to cloud the blue sky. The chatter of automatic weapons followed, then the anemic reports of rifles.

She ran.

The sounds eventually dwindled to an occasional burst, or maybe her heart pounded so loudly in her ears that she was unable to hear anything else. By the time she'd run a mile, the swamp was quiet once more. She didn't want to think what that ominous silence could mean to the people she loved.

She tore aside long fingers of kudzu vines and found herself suddenly on the edge of Dobb's Landing's cracked, weedy airstrip. A short distance away, three battered Cessnas sat on the tarmac, their cargo holds wide open and waiting. While she watched, a disheveled-looking man ran to the first of the planes, jumped inside, and appeared moments later in the cockpit window.

Bending low, Kerry ran across the pavement, coming up behind the plane. She pulled herself into the baggage compartment just as the Cessna's propellers whirred to life. The man in the cockpit was so busy flipping switches along the instrument panel he didn't hear her soft-footed approach. She nudged him on the shoulder with the end of her shotgun and he turned. His eyes widened. Kerry recognized him as one of the men who'd been with Burkhardt at Paradise Found.

"Shut it down," Kerry shouted over the noise of the engine.

The man shook his head. "You're not a killer, lady. Unless you plan on shooting me right now, you'd better get the hell off this plane. I'm getting out of here."

"I don't think so." She pumped a bullet into the center of the instrument panel.

Dials exploded in a fireworks display of burning cables and crackling pops. Stunned, the man in the cockpit swore and slammed himself back against the seat as electrical sparks showered his lap. Knowing she wouldn't get another chance, Kerry lifted the butt of her shotgun and brought it down sharply behind the man's ear. The criminal sagged forward, unconscious, as the destroyed instrument panel fizzled into uselessness. Because she couldn't lift him, she tied him to the pilot's seat with the lines of a parachute she found in the hold.

There was another burst of gunfire from the marina area. Desperate now, Kerry jumped out of the plane and moved toward the second Cessna. No more of Burkhardt's crew would attempt an escape by air.

The interior of the plane was stifling. She had to climb over crates filled with weapons so menacing-looking that they made her simple shotgun seem woefully inadequate. From the cockpit opening, she again fired into the instrument panel. Smoke curled upward as glass shattered. Not too inadequate, she thought with a grim smile.

She raced to the third aircraft. The cargo hold stood empty, crated weapons still on the pavement in front of the open doorway. Climbing aboard, Kerry hurried to the cockpit. Fishing two shells out of her jeans pocket, she shoved them into the chambers of the shotgun, then closed it with a snap. She lifted the gun to her shoulder, aiming for the place she thought would do the most damage.

"Please don't do that, Miss Culhane," a voice said behind her right ear. She felt the gun barrel jab into her ribs.

Kerry didn't know where the man had come from but she didn't have to turn around to recognize him. It would be years before she'd forget the slick, cruel inflections of Burkhardt's voice. Years. She wondered suddenly if she'd have them.

"Take your finger off the trigger and hand me the shotgun. Quickly," he directed.

There was no doubt in her mind he'd kill her if she didn't do as he said. No doubt he'd kill her anyway. Where were Jace and Grandfather? Could she hope to buy time?

"Do you have so little to live for you're willing to test my patience?" Burkhardt asked. "Perhaps so, now that your lover is dead."

Her stomach spiraled. Jace dead? No! Her breath left her lungs in a gasp of horror at the same moment that she brought the barrel of her shotgun whipping back. She didn't know why she did it or what she expected to accomplish. She just knew nothing mattered in that moment except striking out, finding a release for the sudden, devastating rage that flooded her senses. Her action caught Burkhardt off guard; the shotgun slammed against his ear in a ringing blow. Before he could react, she drove against him, sending him backward with as much force as she could muster. He banged against the plane's wall, momentarily stunned, but lucid enough to knock the shotgun out of her hand. She grabbed for his pistol, but in spite of his slight build, he had superior strength. There wasn't any hope of wrenching it from his grasp.

They struggled a few moments, stumbling around the interior of the plane like clumsy wrestlers. Burkhardt's slim fingers suddenly clutched at her throat, cutting off her air with relentless power. Inches away from hers, his face no longer looked placid and emotionless. His eyes were wild, his lips no more than a grim, determined slash. Blood trickled from a cut over his left ear.

She knew he would kill her now.

Kerry clawed at his hand, kicking out desperately to gain leverage, but connecting with nothingness. She strained upward to draw air, but there wasn't any. Through her clouding vision, she saw the glint of metal. Burkhardt's gun, coming up...up...finding her heart. She closed her eyes because she didn't want to see the bullet coming. She thought of Jace, of never seeing him again. She—

The pressure against her throat suddenly eased. Her eyes flew open as her lungs instinctively hitched for gulps of air. Through a blurred, shadowy haze she saw Jace. At his feet Burkhardt lay in a crumpled heap. She didn't know if the man was alive or dead, and in that moment she didn't care. Coughing, sputtering, she launched herself into Jace's arms.

"Are you all right?" he asked hoarsely, his eyes connecting with hers in concern.

She nodded, still dazed and so happy she could hardly find the words. "Jace!" she gasped. "I thought you were dead."

He smiled at her, a smile that quickly washed away in a tide of seriousness. "And I thought you were back at camp."

Chapter 16

Kerry sighed in relief as she put the finishing touches of a makeshift bandage around Billie Tiger's arm. Doc would have a bullet to remove, but no serious damage had been done. Emathla had tripped over a tree root and broken his ankle. Willie Cypress would probably have a headache for days from a scalp wound. But it could have been worse. None of her people had been killed or seriously injured.

None too gently, Jace had tossed the unconscious Burkhardt over his shoulder and returned him from the plane to the boarded-up bait-and-tackle shop the man had used as his headquarters. After seeing the criminal tied in a chair, Kerry had left Jace sifting through the man's attaché case while she checked on the Seminole's injuries.

Billie smiled approvingly and joined the rest of the men heading for the marina's long dock. Her grandfather seemed in complete control, shepherding a group of Burkhardt's men who had their hands locked behind their heads. Along the line of disgruntled captives, the Seminole warriors prodded and issued low, grunting commands. In spite of the residue fear and anger within her, Kerry had to smile at the sight of Joseph Ocilla nudging one of the criminals forward with the tip of his longbow—an old warrior suddenly feeling young again.

She jogged to her grandfather's side. He turned, displeasure still apparent in his features.

"Still angry with me for showing up?" she asked, determined not to be intimidated.

"You have the stubbornness of your mother."

"Who had the stubbornness of her father," Kerry countered.

The old man placed his hand lightly against the base of her throat, frowning as his tired eyes saw the bruising Burkhardt's fingers had created. "You were very foolish to fight this man alone, Night Dove."

"I didn't intend to. If it hadn't been for Jace—" She broke off with a shudder. "I'm all right, Grandfather." She changed the subject before he could voice further objection. "I'm going to see if he's had any luck with Burkhardt."

"I do not think you should go near that man," Chi-ke-ka warned. "John Coffee has already left for the doctor's place. The government men who want him will be here soon."

"It may take Doc awhile to contact the men on Jace's list."

"You are not needed in this. And your man will not want you there," he added.

"Well, it's too late for that," Kerry replied firmly.

Tucked into a nest of encroaching palmetto bushes, the ramshackle store looked forlorn and forgotten. A sudden shiver went down Kerry's spine. She knew Jace was furious with her for being here, but she didn't like the idea of the two men being alone together. Her fears were silly, she knew. The worst was over and Burkhardt was securely tied, but she couldn't help the feeling of unease she experienced as she ran up the wobbly front steps.

Sick relief cooled her nerves when she opened the door and found nothing had changed. Jace was still sifting through ledgers and leather-bound journals, occasionally glancing Burkhardt's way to make sure the man stayed put.

A telltale bruise blossomed on Burkhardt's chin, and blood had dried over his ear from the blow she'd given him with her shotgun, but other than those small signs of trouble, he looked remarkably unperturbed.

She strode to a worn, stain-speckled sofa and sat down. Jace gave her a sour look, but she cut off any objection he might have made with a determined shake of her head. "I'm staying, Jace."

As she suspected, he was too emotionally tired to indulge in a clash of wills. "Fine. But stay out of the way." He turned his attention back to a scattered pile of papers lying on top of an empty display case.

"There's enough here to put this bastard away for years," he told her. "Bank books, lists of weapons suppliers here in the States. His connections in Latin America." He offered Burkhardt a mirthless smile. "Not such a poor adversary after all, I guess."

"You don't have to do this," Burkhardt said calmly.

"Shut up."

"I can set you up for life."

Jace tossed a ledger back on the stack and picked up another one. "Sorry, not interested."

"Don't be a fool, Warfield. You're walking away from a gold mine."

"Remember me?" Jace chided. "I'm the guy who doesn't have a price."

The criminal's nostrils flared. "You damned paper heroes make me sick. So full of principles and ideals, it's a wonder you don't have a broken arm from all that flag-waving. I should have killed you myself. I'd have enjoyed it. Just the way I enjoyed killing your brother." The man's lips curled into a sneer. "Do you think he wasn't scared to die? I watched him, Warfield. He knew what was coming when we held him down and cut off his air. Eventually he didn't have a choice—he *had* to breathe. Some of the purest coke that's ever been cut went right into his brain—"

The ledger slammed onto the display case with a sound like a gunshot. Jace's features bled deathly white as the look in his eyes turned lethal. "Shut up," he growled. "Or by God, I'll kill you."

Kerry shifted uneasily. *Don't, Burkhardt. You fool...you don't realize...*

"You should have seen him afterward," Burkhardt continued to taunt. "Not very brave then. He was so stunned—"

"God damn you!"

"—he just curled up in a ball and wet himself like a baby. Such a waste of good coke—"

"You son of a bitch!"

It was a savage roar, a mixture of so much anger and pain that it brought Kerry out of her seat even as Jace leaped across the room. He yanked Burkhardt up, chair and all, and slammed him back against the pine wall so roughly that the chair splintered and dust sifted from the rafters. Using one arm like a bar across Burkhardt's throat, Jace swung the gun up, pointing the muzzle at the man's head. Kerry's stomach twisted as she guessed Jace's intentions. She ran to his side, her breath coming in gasps of sheer, unreasoning terror.

"Jace! No!"

He didn't look at her. His attention was centered solely on Burkhardt, who unbelievably, regarded him with mild surprise.

"Get out of here, Kerry!"

"No!" She clutched frantically at the arm holding the gun.

"Go ahead, Warfield," the man jeered. "Show me you've got more guts than your brother."

"Don't listen to him."

"Get out, Kerry!" Jace ordered hoarsely. "Please get out!"

"No, dammit. I won't let you do this."

Jace shook his head. "J.D. didn't deserve to die that way."

"I know, Jace."

"He's right. I'm being stupid. In a few years Burkhardt will be back on the streets. He's not going to pay the way J.D. did."

"Maybe not. But doing this won't bring Joel back."

"No. But I'll be doing everyone a favor," he said, his voice low with cold rage. He dug the gun barrel into Burkhardt's cheek, slipping off the safety. "Look into his face, Kerry. He's not sorry or worried. Do you think he feels remorse for the killing he's done? Look into his eyes. Can't you see the monster in there?"

Her gaze flickered between the two men. The dark, frightening expression on Jace's face was a bleak contrast to Burkhardt's light, unimpassioned features.

Desperation made Kerry cry out wildly, "If you do this, it's the same thing I'll see in your eyes, Jace. You'll be no better than he is. Don't let this bastard bring you down to his level."

"It doesn't matter. J.D.'s dead—"

"And you can't change that," she snapped. Fear made her tone sharp. God, she was shaking. Even her voice. She couldn't seem to draw breath, unlike Jace, whom she'd never seen so calm before. "Are you saying everything you love in life doesn't matter? Because you're about to destroy it."

"Kerry—"

"There won't be anything left, Jace. Your family. Your career. Everything you care about will be gone." She threw words at him, hoping that in some far corner of his mind the man she knew and cared so much about would be listening. Through the film of tears that rose before her eyes, she saw the sharp, white ridges of her knuckles. Her death grip on his arm was tight, as though her bones had been forced through the skin. "If you care about me, don't kill any chance we have for happiness. I want that chance. I need you." *Turn him loose, Joel. You don't need him anymore, but I do. Give him to me.*

Silence encroached, thickening the air in the small store. Long moments passed, frozen in place like statues. Kerry stared at the uncompromising fury in Jace's features. Beneath her hand she felt the fluid ripple of muscles in his arm, a slow gathering of somber forces, as though he had to physically fight for control over his emotions.

She didn't know what else to do. She felt empty, drained. "Please, Jace," she begged, her voice breaking on a sob. "Please, stop this."

After a long moment, a very long moment, Jace turned his head to look at her. There was an unfocused, dull glassiness in his gaze, and he frowned, as though aware of her presence for the first time. He blinked slowly, and while she watched, the black turmoil in his eyes lightened as his thoughts returned from the tormented outer reaches of his mind.

Relief came to her in slow degrees.

He stepped back from Burkhardt quickly, as though he couldn't bear to be close to the man. "Let's get him down to the water with the others," Jace said tonelessly. "I want him out of my sight."

Chi-ke-ka leaned close to her. "He will never learn the steps."

Kerry smiled at her grandfather and turned her attention back to the dancers. For the second time in less than a week, there was cause for celebration in the Seminole camp. The small band of renegades had certainly surprised everyone, perhaps even themselves. Glancing around the circle of men and women, Kerry saw excitement flickering in their eyes. Even Chi-ke-ka and Uncle Charlie looked pleased.

Federal agents were going to charge Burkhardt and two of his men with the murder of Joel Warfield, as well as several others. One of the men captured at the marina was only too eager to turn state's evidence in exchange for a lesser conviction. If Burkhardt somehow managed to beat the rap on one charge, it seemed likely there would be many more to take its place. Why then, Kerry wondered, didn't Jace seem more pleased?

Her gaze slid slowly to find him among the dancers. Along the line of Seminole men, Billie Tiger, his arm now encased in a sling, was trying to teach Jace the movements of The Screech Owl Dance. Her grandfather was right. Jace wasn't very good at it, but the mere fact that he'd been allowed to participate meant a certain degree of acceptance from the tribe.

Since that terrible confrontation in the bait shop yesterday, he'd been quiet and introspective. He'd hardly spoken to Kerry, and in fact, seemed to be avoiding her. Something was wrong. She'd drawn her own conclusion what that something might be, and it didn't bode well for their relationship.

"You look at him with your heart in your eyes, Night Dove." Chi-ke-ka's voice interrupted her thoughts.

"Is it that obvious?"

"No more so than when he looks at you."

She might have believed that yesterday. Today, she wasn't so sure.

"He will never be Seminole, but he is a good man," her grandfather said. "You will deal well with each other."

"I'm not so sure he wants to."

"You doubt he cares for you?"

"We're very different, Grandfather. I'm not certain we'd make a good match. We come from two separate worlds."

Chi-ke-ka shifted closer so that no one else could hear his words. "If this man speaks of marriage to you, and you agree, he will take you far away from us. That will bring sadness to our hearts. But it is time you found your place in his world."

Kerry stared at him, wide-eyed with surprise. "I don't belong in his world. You, of all people, should understand what that's like."

"Listen to me, little Night Dove, and hear what I tell you," her grandfather said softly. With one hand he made an abrupt gesture around the Seminole compound. "This is the past, an old man's dream to keep the dogs of progress at bay. For now, it is good." He shook his head slowly. "But one day we will lose this battle. The white man will force us to return to his world. We will live in his stone houses and sleep in soft beds, but in our hearts we will still be here, listening to the roar of Koo-woo-she and walking with the tall grass. These things cannot be taken from us." Placing one weathered hand along her arm, Chi-ke-ka peered down his hawk's beak nose at her. "It is the same for you, Night

Dove. You will always be Seminole, no matter where this man's path takes you. He respects your people, and who you are. He will not try to change you. You must stop acting like little Yok-che, hiding your head in your shell. There can be much joy in your life, but you must be willing to accept it.''

Kerry tried to smile at the old man. She didn't know how to tell him he could be wrong. Jace had never mentioned love, much less marriage.

He might not want to change her.

He might not want her at all.

Tangled in a web of confused emotions, Kerry sat on the narrow beach, letting sand that sparkled like ground crystal sift through her hands. Fireflies stitched through the darkness, and behind her she could hear the muffled sounds of the celebration as it continued, the soft throb of the water drum as it set an energetic pace for The Catfish Dance. She wished she could summon the enthusiasm to join her friends and family, but it eluded her. The echo of low, gentle laughter seemed almost an obscenity to her ears.

Jace was going to leave tomorrow, and she would never see him again.

He hadn't told her that, of course, but she felt it in her heart. Saw it in his eyes every time their glances happened to meet. All too clearly she could read the message in their dark brown depths.

Please try to understand.

She did, but understanding didn't make the pain easier to bear. Only pride and a disgusting lack of courage kept her from tackling the problem head-on. She didn't want to watch him fumble unhappily for the right words.

The ragged intensity of the past two weeks had created a need for two people to search for common ground. They had found solace, and perhaps even love, in each other's arms because they had both needed it so badly. But fear and uncertainty were behind them now. Reality had stepped in to take its rightful place. And the reality of it was, that no matter how she might wish it, in ways that went far beyond their outward differences, she and Jace were not suited for one another. If she had mistakenly thought they were, all she had to do was take one long look in his eyes.

She heard the crunch of footsteps on the sand and didn't have to turn her head to know who it was. All too quickly she had come to recognize the sound of his walk. One more thing about him she would struggle to forget. She didn't want to talk to him now. She wanted space and time to think things through. But she was afraid her legs wouldn't support her if she tried to run. Instead, she pulled her knees up under her chin and wrapped her arms around her calves. She bit her bottom lip, hard, hoping the hurt would distract her from anything he might have come here to say.

He sat down beside her on the sand, making certain their bodies didn't touch. Already, in the smallest ways, he was putting distance between them, she thought. He was quiet for a long moment.

"My watchdog seems to have been called off," he said at last. "Your grandfather even told me where to find you."

"Maybe he doesn't regard you as a threat any longer," she replied coldly.

"Are you angry with me for leaving you behind here yesterday?"

"Yes. But it doesn't seem that important now." *Not compared to a broken heart.* She concentrated on breathing deeply, forcing every muscle to relax.

"Chi-ke-ka and I thought it best. We didn't want you hurt."

She found that comment richly ironic. Physically, he'd kept her safe, all right. But emotionally, he didn't seem to give a damn. Nausea sat in her stomach like a lump of cold o-sof-kee. She had to fight a blasting wave of sickness that threatened to overwhelm. In a voice devoid of any inflection, she said, "How thoughtful."

He must have heard the stirring of anger in her tone, because another long silence descended. She felt the sharp, achy pain lying just beneath her eyelids and wished he'd go away. Afraid she might cry, she tried to focus her attention on the sky, the way soft moonlight threaded through the eye of a cloud.

When Jace spoke again, his voice was so low the faint breeze nearly stole it. "I know I've made a mistake in our relationship. I got carried away." He stopped for a moment, a faintly apologetic pause. "I'd like to think you can forget, maybe even forgive, but . . ."

She sat there, stunned. She had expected this moment would come, but nothing as direct and cruel as this attack on her emotions. She didn't want to believe the man she loved could be so insensitive. But he was. She swallowed down the rage that seemed in imminent danger of spilling over, unwilling to give Jace even that small satisfaction.

In a voice as cold and sharp as a rattler's strike, she said, "No. I don't think I can forget."

She sensed a sudden loosening within him, as though everything between them had hinged on that one response.

He sighed heavily. "I never meant to go so far." His voice was webbed with strain. "I want you to believe that."

Oh, please stop. Please. She labored to put brittle disinterest in her words. "Just one of those things, huh?"

"I honestly believed I had it under control. I don't blame you for hating me," he said hoarsely.

I do hate you. I do! When I stop loving you so much, I'm going to hate you even more.

Hot tears spilled down her cheeks, and she knew herself to be a coward after all. She couldn't sit here calmly any longer and listen to Jace rip to shreds what was left of her heart. She had to get away.

She turned to look at him for the first time. His features were barely discernable in the moonlight, and she hated herself for imagining she saw some of her own pain reflected in his eyes. "Damn you, Jace. I've let you off the hook. What more do you want from me?"

He looked at her in startled confusion, but unwilling to humiliate herself any more, Kerry pushed off the sand in a sudden movement and fled.

"Kerry!"

She ran through the tall trees, and she could hear him behind her. Hoping her familiarity with the camp would give her the needed advantage to outrun him, she kept going. Her heart plummeted when his hand latched around her wrist. She turned and fought to break his hold, but Jace soon had her backed against an ancient pine. Breathing hard, she lifted her chin and regarded him in mutinous silence.

He pinned her close, his eyes piercing hers through the darkness. "What did you mean just now? About letting me off the hook."

Her throat was so clogged with tears she couldn't find her voice. She wasn't sure she wanted to. She shook her head, feeling the rough pine bark scrape against her scalp. His grip on her arms tightened, and for one second in time, she was actually afraid of him.

"Dammit, tell me!" he demanded roughly. He was assessing her in a hard way, as though trying to extract silent information from her mind. "What did you mean? Why are you crying? You should be relieved."

That statement was so ridiculous, Kerry's anger easily found its way past her grief. "How can you say that to me? I love you. Don't you know what you've just thrown away? I'm probably the best thing that's ever going to happen to you, but you're too stupid to know it. You go back to Denver and find some other woman who makes you feel half as good as I can. She'll be very proper and very... blond and she'll bore you to tears inside of a year. She'll make your life miserable, and I only wish I could be there to see it!"

Jace stared at her in astonishment. Kerry looked miserable; the tears were tracking down her face freely now, glistening silver in the moonlight. His gut wrenched to know he'd been the cause of them. Later he would find a way to make up the hurt he'd caused in his inept attempt to make parting easier for her. But for now, his heart pounded with such vague hope he could feel the blood throbbing in his veins.

"Kerry, are you telling me—" his voice trembled so badly he had to stop a moment before going on "—that in spite of everything that happened yesterday, you love me?"

She looked at him as though he'd taken leave of his senses. "What about yesterday? Yes, I loved you then, and God help me, I'll love you tomorrow. Satisfied?"

He shook his head, like a man coming out of a long coma. "Don't you understand? Yesterday I came close to killing an unarmed man in cold blood. I wanted to." He looked away briefly, then met her eyes again. He lifted his hand to her cheek, a pressureless touch. "I probably would have, if you hadn't talked me out of it. I saw such a dark side of myself yesterday, Kerry. A side I was ashamed to have you witness."

The pain in his voice, in his eyes, was her undoing. Her anger began to fade, replaced by tentative hope. "But you didn't kill him,'' she said in a voice that was soft and textured. "It wasn't in you, Jace.''

"It might have been. I heard what Burkhardt was saying. I could see the way...the way J.D. died, and I couldn't think of anything but killing that bastard.''

"But you didn't,'' Kerry said again, more firmly. "*You* made the decision not to.''

"Later, I didn't want to face you. I wanted you to understand, but I was afraid. I kept seeing your face that night after you fixed dinner for me at Paradise Found. Do you remember that talk we had about your father, and what you suspect he did in Ireland? You looked so repulsed. Betrayed. I didn't want to see that in your eyes when you looked at me, so I took the coward's way out. I didn't look at you at all.''

"Oh, Jace. I thought you were trying to tell me it was over between us. I thought now that everything was settled you'd somehow decided what we'd shared had been a huge mistake.''

He dragged her to him, pressing her face against his shoulder. His hand threaded under the heavy fall of her hair, massaging the nape of her neck.

"The only mistake that's been made has been mine. I tried to keep you at arm's length.'' He shook his head violently. "But I can't. I can't. You make me feel whole inside. When I'm with you, there isn't any room for revenge or grief. I love you, Kerry Night Dove, and if you won't marry me, nothing's ever going to be right for me again.''

She lifted her gaze to his, letting her smile curve stronger, wider, as the night air cooled the last vestige of tears from her cheeks. "How can I refuse? John Wayne always gets the girl, remember?''

His chest rumbled with the sound of his laughter. "With a little time, you might be able to talk me out of my chauvinistic ways." He brushed the corner of her mouth with his lips. "Convince me, Kerry."

"You're so stubborn. It might take years."

"I'm willing to invest the time."

She pretended to give it some thought. "I don't know. I kind of like the idea of having John Wayne for a husband,. With me as your sidekick."

"The only one I'll ever want," he said, nuzzling her throat with lips and tongue until she gasped, working to find breath. When she could think again, he arched a look down at her, prepared to meet their next problem head-on. "How do you feel about living in Denver?"

She shook her head. "Too cold. How do you feel about living in Flamingo Junction?"

"Too hot. Too small. Too buggy."

Her head tilted back to find his eyes. "Where does that leave us, then? After Washington, I don't think I'll ever enjoy living in a big city."

"Actually, I had given this some thought. I have journalism assignments that will take me the next five years to complete. I wouldn't mind changing direction a little. Maybe concentrate on nature and environmental pieces. You could come with me. There's a lot of great country we could see. In between jobs, we could visit my parents in Denver and your people out here. What do you think?" His eyes begged her to give it serious consideration.

"I couldn't just tag along. I'd have to have something to do." Very softly she added, "Do you think you could teach me to take pictures? Like Joel used to do for you? You said yourself, I've got a good eye."

His hand arrived feather-light at her cheek. He was quiet a moment, and she saw emotion sparkle in his eyes. "I think," he said in a husky, tender voice, "that J.D. would be happy to know his camera and his brother were in such gentle, caring hands.''

He kissed her, a light bonding of their lips that spoke of sweet promise and sent ripples of joy chasing down her spine. The past was wiped clean; the future lay ahead of them with bright, cherishing strength. A new life. With Jace.

"We're wasting the moon," he murmured as he pressed his lips to her throat.

She lifted her head to the night breeze, letting her eyes drift toward the silver glow. "Jace?"

"Mmmm?"

"It's not flamingo tonight."

She felt his lips stretch into a smile against the wild throb at the base of her throat.

"So we'll get a head start on the next one."

*   *   *   *   *

NORA ROBERTS

Love has a language all its own, and for centuries, flowers have symbolized love's finest expression. Discover the language of flowers—and love—in this romantic collection of 48 favorite books by bestselling author Nora Roberts.

Starting in February 1992, two titles will be available each month at your favorite retail outlet.

In February, look for:

Irish Thoroughbred, Volume #1
The Law Is A Lady, Volume #2

Collect all 48 titles and become fluent in the Language of Love.

LOL192

THE LANGUAGE of LOVE

Silhouette Special Edition

is pleased to present

A GOOD MAN WALKS IN
by Ginna Gray

The story of one strong woman's comeback
and the man who was there for her, Travis McCall,
the renegade cousin to those Blaine siblings,
from Ginna Gray's bestselling trio

FOOLS RUSH IN (#416)
WHERE ANGELS FEAR (#468)
ONCE IN A LIFETIME (#661)

Rebecca Quinn sought shelter at the hideaway on Rincon
Island. Finding Travis McCall—the object of all her childhood
crushes—holed up in the same house threatened to ruin the
respite she so desperately needed. Until their first kiss...
Then Travis set out to prove to his lovely Rebecca that man
can be good and love, sublime.

You'll want to be there when Rebecca's disillusionment turns
to joy.

A GOOD MAN WALKS IN #722

Available at your favorite retail outlet this February.

® *Silhouette Romance*®

LONG, TALL TEXANS

DONAVAN
Diana Palmer

Diana Palmer's bestselling LONG, TALL TEXANS series continues with DONAVAN....

From the moment elegant Fay York walked into the bar on the wrong side of town, rugged Texan Donavan Langley knew she was trouble. But the lovely young innocent awoke a tenderness in him that he'd never known...and a desire to make her a proposal she couldn't refuse....

Don't miss DONAVAN by Diana Palmer, the ninth book in her LONG, TALL TEXANS series. Coming in January...only from Silhouette Romance.

LTT192

Take 4 bestselling love stories FREE

Plus get a FREE surprise gift!

Silhouette Special Edition

salutes

MOMENTS OF GLORY

from Lindsay McKenna

In a country torn with conflict, in a time of bitter passions, these brave men and women wage a war against all odds . . . and a timeless battle for honor, for fleeting moments of glory, for the promise of enduring love.

February: RIDE THE TIGER (#721) Survivor Dany Villard is wise to the love-'em-and-leave-'em ways of war, but wounded hero Gib Ramsey swears she's captured his heart . . . forever.

March: ONE MAN'S WAR (#727) The war raging inside brash and bold Captain Pete Mallory threatens to destroy him, until Tess Ramsey's tender love guides him toward peace.

April: OFF LIMITS (#733) Soft-spoken Marine Jim McKenzie saved Alexandra Vance's life in Vietnam; now he needs her love to save his honor. . . .

SEMG-1